Saving Lucas

Jeff McCoy

CONTENTS

DEDICATION

*This book is dedicated to all the priests and nuns
who give their all for Christ, and Father George
Pucciarelli, the priest who changed my life,
and My Mother, Susan King, who dedicated years of her life
tirelessly working with the deaf community.*

ACKNOWLEDGEMENTS

The author would like to thank Bonni Burkowitz, who serves as his agent, for the countless hours of encouragement, dedication, and hard work that she puts into all his projects.

And Senoria James, Frank Morrison, and the team at Audiobook Publishing Services for their support.

And you, the reader, for taking this adventurous trip with me!

ABOUT THE AUTHOR

Jeff McCoy has worked as a newspaper reporter for years, covering stories across the U.S. and overseas. Those mud and blood assignments had an impact on him. Watching the suffering and death of others made him realize what was important in life, and what was not.

He has experience as a stockbroker, but most of his adult life has been spent behind one camera or another, including time in the movie business. Writing scripts, short stories, and novels was something that he did to step out of his high-stress world for a few hours. It was an escape. Writing news articles came easily, but it required a heavy mental toll. Sometimes writing a newspaper article about the oppressed would cause some relief to the least, the lost, and the forgotten.

At other times, it made no difference at all.

Often, a newspaper reporter is the court of last resort. He loved it when he could shine a light into the darkness of corruption or help the working man right a wrong, but he still carries the memories of the tragedies of those lost but not forgotten.

Today, he enjoys his time writing stories in his Appalachian home.

CHAPTER 1
A NEW MISSION

Father Mark Rossi walks out of Los Angeles International Airport. It's a bright sunny day, and he slips a pair of cheap sunglasses on his face. He is young, slim, fit, and handsome. A cab pulls up, and the driver gets out. "Need a ride, Father?"

"Yes, I do. Thank you." He opens the door before the driver can get to him.

"Any luggage, Father?"

Father holds up a small bag slung across his chest. "Just this."

The driver closes the door, returns to his seat, buckles his belt, and drops the car into gear. They pull out into traffic. "Where to Father?"

"West Adams Boulevard." The driver slows down.

"West Adams?"

"Yes, sir."

The driver pulls over to the curb and looks back at the priest. "Father, you don't want to go to West Adams, do you? Have you heard that there is a one in fifteen chance you'll get mugged there? They strip cars while they're moving."

"Sir, I am going there to open the Catholic Deaf Academy. It should be almost finished."

"Where?"

"5728a, the old grade school."

"The old grade schools? That place is drug and hooker city!"

"Please, I need to go there, and then I need to report in to the bishop."

The driver is discouraged. "I'll take you there, but I ain't waiting around. You'll have to call for a cab to bring you to the bishop, and I'm telling' ya now ain't none coming."

He pulls back into traffic. Father looks out the window at the city. A million people and cars are moving. Smog lies low over the valley. As they get closer, the surroundings begin to deteriorate. Gangs on the street, hookers wave as he passes by, and drug dealers are running an open market. The driver constantly checks all his mirrors and drives at a high speed.

They arrive at the school, and Father is shocked. The two-story building is in a state of complete disrepair. The school and property occupies the entire block. Houses flank the side streets. The school is situated in the center of the lot, surrounded by open spaces on all sides. An old fence borders the property at the sidewalks, but is in disrepair. It is a large, two-story brick building with a stone foundation. The grounds are covered in dust, with a few patches of grass that have escaped the trampling of foot traffic. A pole for a basketball backstop and hoop stands bent to a side.

He sees people in the school yard. A large hole is in the fence, allowing people to walk through. They arrive at the front, and Father sees that the gate is busted off the hinges. A scantily clad woman lies on the ground. A few drug dealers walk the yard, selling.

"Father, let me take you out of here. It's not safe." He looks in the mirror and sees Father staring with his mouth open.

"This place is not almost finished."

"Father, it's finished, it's finished."

Father opens the door and hands some money through the window. "Thank you. May God bless you for bringing me here."

"I hope He doesn't hold it against me. Good luck, Father." He drives off - fast.

Father turns and walks through the broken gate, moving toward the woman on the ground. He kneels beside her, and she starts to wake. "Ma'am, are you alright?" She looks through glassy eyes and smiles. Several teeth are missing.

"Hello, Honey, are you looking for a date?" Father is taken aback.

"A date? No, I'm a priest. I'm concerned about you. Would you like me to call an ambulance?" She starts laughing.

"Here? You're gonna call me an ambulance, and they are going to come here?" She laughs harder. "You're sweet."

"GET AWAY! Get away from her!" Father turns and sees two black men rushing toward him. He stands, and they lightly shove him back. "Ya have to pay, man!"

"Pay?" he asks.

One of them runs out of the yard and up the street. He goes to a broken-down dope house. A man is selling from a card table. Some customers are standing by, and a few boys are at the ready to run drugs. The man at the table sees him running. "Jamal! 5-o?"

"Nah, well maybe. A man dressed up is in our yard. Where Luggs?" The man points to the house, and Jamal runs inside. "Luggs!" A big well well-dressed Black man walks into the room. He is very muscular with a scar on his jawline.

"Jamal, what do you need?"

"Luggs, a man in the yard messing with our property. He is white and clean. It just seems out of place, ya know what I'm sayin'?"

Luggs quickly marches out the door and starts down the street. He gets to the school with Jamal and a couple of other people in step with him. As he walks along the fence, he can see into the yard. Father is standing there talking to a couple of people. The woman is sitting on the ground. He marches to the gate and goes in. "Hey! What you doin' in my place?" he asks Father.

"Your place?"

One of the men standing there steps up. "Luggs, this fool says he owns the place!"

"No, I don't own it; the Catholic Church owns it. I'm here to -"

"Shut up! He's a cop, possibly a federal agent. Ain't nobody brave enough to come up in here like this unless he has a big band of brothers! Search him!" Luggs orders.

"Actually, I have a big band of angels protecting me," Father replies.

"Whatever," Luggs says as they hand him Father's wallet. They continue to search for him. Luggs opens the wallet and pulls out cash.

"Twenty-four dollars. Are you kidding me?' He pulls his license out. "Mark Rossi....says from Maryland."

One of the searchers holds up a rosary. "He has this necklace too," he says. Father takes it back.

"That is a blessed rosary. I don't think you want that."

Luggs drops the wallet to the ground. Father picks it up. "What are you doing here?" Luggs asks.

"I'm opening the Catholic Deaf Academy."

"Say what?"

A police car pulls up. The cop taps the siren. People scatter. The men who searched Father, along with Luggs, stand their ground. Two police officers walk up.

"What's going on here today?" one asks.

"Luggs, what are you doing out in the sunshine?" the other asks.

"That's Mr. Luggs to you," he answers.

"Posing as a priest to meet some of Luggs' woman roaches?" the cop asks Father.

"No officer. I am a priest and I'm here to open the Catholic Deaf Academy. We're gonna-"

"You got some ID?" the cop asks. Father pulls his wallet out again and hands his license over. "I'll be right back," the cop says to his partner. He walks back to the car.

"Catholic Deaf Academy?" the other cop asks Father. "Here?"

"Yes, sir. I thought it was further along than this, but we have some donors who are going to help us. Mr. Luggs was just saying he wanted to give twenty-four dollars to it." Father looks back at the lungs, reaches over, and retrieves his money from Luggs' hand. Luggs is not happy.

"Is that right, Luggs?" the cop asks.

"Yeah, something like that."

"You see, officer, I came from Maryland to-"

"That explains why you would come out here without bodyguards," the cop says.

"Well, sir, I am going to head up this school. We'll bring deaf children here from across the country. We'll offer classes for the hearing so they can learn to communicate with our brothers and sisters who are deaf. It's going to be great! I'm so excited!"

The other cop walks back. "No wants or warrants," he says to the other cop as he hands the license back to Father.

The cop looks around. "Luggs, you got somewhere to be?"

"Yeah, I was just leaving." He turns and walks away with his men following.

The cop looks back at Father. "Mister, I'm not sure, but this building may be condemned. I do know that there are more whores and dope dealers in there than cockroaches. The best thing you can do is go back to Maryland. I mean it, I'm not against the deaf or the church, but you won't live long here." Father looks to the other cop for some reassurance.

"He's right. The city is not going to allow you to open this school back up, and as far as having children here...well, you have never been on a mission field, anywhere on this earth, as deadly as this place. Parents are not going to allow you to have their children here. Sorry."

"Are you telling me I have to leave?"

"No, sir, you're not breaking the law. We're just giving you some good advice."

The other cop looks to Father. "Consider it a public service announcement. Be careful." They walk back to their car and drive off. Father walks into the building.

It is a mess. Several small windows are broken, trash is scattered everywhere, and graffiti covers the walls. He walks down the hall and into a classroom. Two people run out of the building. The chalkboard is broken, a PA speaker hangs by a wire, and a ceiling fan is missing its blades. He walks into another room. A makeshift bed is there, and more trash and graffiti fill the rest of the room. He exits that room and sees a set of wide stairs. He goes up to the next floor. It's more of the same. He walks over to a window and looks outside, and sees a drug deal taking place. He goes to the next room, and it has several pigeons on the windowsill. He then moves to a bathroom. A man and a woman are in a stall. They step out. The man is angry. "Wait your turn, mister!" The woman is covered in tattoos and has sores on her face. She looks at him and smiles. He steps out into the hallway. "Lord, oh Lord," he says as he crosses himself. He continues his inspection and finds the fire bar on an exit door has been busted off and hangs on the door, touching the floor. He tries to shut it, but it will not shut because it is off its top hinge. He works with it and sees there is no way to secure it. He moves back downstairs and goes to a window. The sun is setting. He finds a janitor's closet. It is a little cleaner, and the door can be closed. He moves a few items out and goes back in, sits down on the floor. "The Lord is my strength and my shield," he says out loud to himself.

CHAPTER 2
BAD NEWS

Hours later Father Rossi is happy that a new day has begun. Gunshots, people screaming, people laughing, and someone crying were all he heard throughout the night. He opens the door, slings his travel bag, and slowly walks out of the closet. He goes into a classroom and looks outside. The yard is full of people, most of them passed out. He inspects the entire place. He steps around the people, knowing there is no need to move them out until he can secure the doors and windows. Every room is a mess. A few classrooms have broken desks in them. Trash is everywhere. He walks into a room, opens a closet, and sees a small sleeping bag. There are a few comic books by the bag. He is puzzled. He puts everything back like he found it.

Father Mark arrives at the Catholic Diocese of Los Angeles headquarters on Wilshire Boulevard after a long walk and a short cab ride. The building is high, and he stands there a moment, enjoying the view as he wipes the sweat from his forehead. He enters and goes to Archbishop Kennedy's outer office. It is well kept with two large sofas, a coffee table, and several chairs. Bridgette, the secretary, greets him. "Good morning, Father. How may I help you?"

"I am Father Mark Rossi. I have a 10:30 appointment today with Bishop Kennedy." She seems confused and searches her appointment calendar on her computer.

"Father Rossi. That name strikes a bell, but I do not see you on the schedule for today."

"I don't understand. I'm from Baltimore and I -"

"Oh, yes, Father! I'm sorry. I do remember. But your appointment was canceled. Didn't you get the letter?"

"No ma'am. What letter?" She looks at him for a moment.

"Father, would you have a seat please, and I'll be back momentarily."

"Sure."

She walks into the inner offices, and he takes a seat. He looks around, then stands to look out the window. Los Angeles is busy. Traffic moves through the city. He sees several people window shopping.

"Father, Bishop Kennedy will see you today. Give me a few minutes to round up his secretary, Father Muller, and also Father Roberts."

"Thank you."

She sits down and calls another office. "Janie, is Father Roberts down there?.... Could you please send him up? Bishop Kennedy would like to see him right away.... Thank you, oh, have you seen Father Muller today?... Okay, thank you. If you see him, can you send-" A priest walks in. "Never mind, he just walked in....Thank you." She hangs up the phone. Father Muller walks to her desk and grabs a few envelopes from the mail. He is grey-haired, in good shape, with a military type appearance. "Father Muller, may I introduce Father Rossi? Father Rossi, this is Father Muller, personal secretary to Bishop Kennedy."

Father Muller turns around with a puzzled look on his face and shakes hands with Father Mark. "Good morning, Father Muller." Father Muller is still puzzled.

"Good morning. Are you Father Rossi from Maryland?"

"Yes, sir."

The elevator doors open, and Father Roberts walks in. He is slightly overweight with a round face that seems to have a small permanent smile attached. He has a disarming demeanor. "Father Roberts, this is Father Rossi," Father Muller says.

Father Mark reaches for his hand. "Good morning, sir."

Father Roberts also has a puzzled look on his face. "Good morning to you, Father."

Bishop Kennedy sits inside his office, signing a few papers. He is well-groomed, serious, and seems to weigh the world on him. He quickly places his signed papers in a folder as the three priests, led by the secretary, walk in. He stands. She says, "Your Excellency, may I present Father Mark Rossi, Father Rossi, His Excellency, Bishop Kennedy." They shake hands.

"Good morning, Your Excellency."

"Good morning, Father. Please be seated." The priests wait until the bishop sits down, then they all sit. Father Roberts sits at the side of the large desk, Father Muller sits near the front corner. Father Mark sits directly across from Bishop Kennedy. The secretary walks out. "Father Rossi, I'm sorry you made the trip out here. We sent a letter last week explaining the turn of events here. It's most embarrassing, and we find ourselves in a quandary."

"I don't understand, sir," Father Mark replies.

Father Roberts leans forward. "Father, we have raised over eight hundred thousand dollars for the building repairs. Father Simms and Deacon Markley were in charge of that operation. They reported each week the progress that was being made. We thought everything was fine."

Father Muller clears his throat. "Then we get a call from the general contractor. He tells us that we must get started, or we will see a large increase in the budget due to the delays. We asked him why was he behind schedule. He tells us that we have not allowed him to start. Imagine our surprise. It was a shock. We immediately drove to the location. All the material and money were gone. So was Father Simms and Markley."

Father Mark is stunned. He doesn't know what to say. "I, ah,.. I..."

Kennedy speaks up. "Our words exactly. Almost a million dollars – poof – gone."

Father Mark looks to Roberts. "What about the progress reports?" he asks.

"Fake, made up. Even the receipts," Roberts replies. Father Mark sinks back in his chair.

Kennedy presses and intercom button. "Rose, could you bring some coffee and refreshments in, please?"

"Yes, sir," she replies.

"Father Rossi, take a moment to let this sink in. We had to. We explained this in the letter and asked that you tell no one except your bishop, at least until the investigation is complete," Kennedy says.

"Do we know what happened to the priest and deacon?"

"No," Muller answers.

"Maybe there is an explanation for this, maybe the money or materials are somewhere, and we can start again," Father Mark offers. Roberts shakes his head no.

Kennedy says, "Son, believe me, how we wish that was the case. We haven't told our parishioners, donors, or supporters yet. This is going to cost us future support. We have broken their trust, an issue that I promised would never happen in this diocese again. The sexual perversion lawsuits and now this..." The room falls silent. Father Mark stares ahead; his throat and lips are dry. He tries to clear his throat. He stares at the floor.

"We will, of course, cover all your travel expenses here and back. Just turn last night's hotel bill to Rose," Roberts says.

"I don't have a hotel bill. I stayed in the school last night," Father Mark says, still looking at the floor.

"What? In the school?" Muller asks.

"Yes, Father." The men look at each other in disbelief.

"That was dangerous. We can't even get LAPD to patrol the place regularly," Muller says.

Rose comes in with a tray of beverages and donuts. She sets it on the desk. "Thank you, Rose," Kennedy says.

"My pleasure, Your Excellency." She walks across the room and unlocks the bar, then pulls the base out. Father Mark looks over and sees a well-stocked bar. Roberts pours a cup of coffee and puts it in front of Kennedy.

"Thank you." He then looks to Muller.

"No, thank you."

He looks to Father Mark. "Father, can I offer you a cup of coffee, water, soda, or would you prefer something stronger?"

"Just water, please."

Father Mark looks up to the bishop. "Sir, wait, maybe there is a way to stay the course."

Kennedy leans back in his chair. "I'm open to suggestions, but we cannot raise that money again. We cannot ask the poor parishioners again. We just can't. What do you have in mind?"

Father Mark takes a deep breath. "Sir, we have to do it for the deaf and those who live and work with them. Your Excellency, if you took all the deaf people in the world and placed them in one spot, they would be the third-largest country on earth! Over ninety percent do not know the Gospel of Jesus Christ, and you know why? Lack of communication. There are a few churches that have a deaf ministry, God bless them for their work, but the deaf don't go to church in most places because of – lack of communication. We can change that. We can! I have an entire program for teaching the deaf and a program to help people learn sign language to communicate with their loved ones, neighbors, and co-workers. There are many here in Los Angeles. We will not only start a mission here, but we will use it to launch many missions in the USA and across the globe eventually. Families will send their children here; they would walk here if they had to, just to give their children a chance to make it in this world, to be taught the Catholic faith. Sir, I have met with parents -"

Kennedy raises his hand. "Your compassion is admirable, Father. You remind me of when I was a parish priest. I had a parish one time that was so poor that other churches had to help us pay the electric bill, but I loved it there. I loved them, just like you love the deaf. But you have seen the building. Father Roberts and Father Muller went there for me and took pictures. It looks to me like a strong wind could blow it over."

"Yes, Your Excellency, it's in very bad shape, but please don't send me back. Let me pray about this, let us pray about this, let me find a way to keep it going."

Muller asks, "Father, wouldn't it be easier to start over somewhere else, somewhere that you can start at even instead of in the hole for a mil? This building could end up in lawsuits. We don't know what this Simms and Markley have done, or what contracts they entered into."

"Father Muller, that is sound advice, and I thank you for it, but no, sir, I firmly believe God has a plan for this place." He looks back at Kennedy. "Sir, let me come back in a week and present a plan." The three men are surprised.

"A week, Father? We have a group of lawyers on this, and they, nor we, have come up with even the slightest idea," Kennedy says. He leans back again, thinking. Muller and Roberts watch him. "Alright, one week. But here are the terms. One, you can't stay there overnight, at least until the place is secured, which can't happen in a week. We do not need to have a priest killed here. We have retreats, a hostale, or you can have a hotel room if you want. Two, you cannot talk to the press or address any congregation until we announce the investigation, and three, you can't spend a dime on the building until we have a plan in place – AND that plan may be to sell it. Do you accept these terms?"

Father Mark smiles. "Yes, sir, thank you, Your Excellency!"

"Father Roberts, will you please be sure to secure a room for him?" the bishop asks.

"Yes, sir. I know we have space at the retreat and that's just a few miles away."

The bishop stands, and the priest rises with him. He shakes Father Mark's hand. "I'll pray Father Rossi. I'll pray that we are given a solution to this problem."

"As will I, Your Excellency."

They exit the office, and Father Roberts has Rose make a call for the room. He then escorts Father Mark to the parking deck. They get in a small car and pull out into traffic. "Father Rossi, I'm taking you out to eat, then we'll go to where you will be staying and make sure you have everything you need."

"Well, thank you, but I don't want to be a burden-"

"No burden, besides, I want to learn more about the deaf and your mission."

They drive through the traffic and pull into a small restaurant parking lot. They park and go inside, where they are quickly seated. "I like to eat here. The food is fantastic," Roberts says.

A waitress walks over to the table and sets some menus down. "Hello Father, how are you today?"

"Fine, just fine. This is Father Rossi from Baltimore. Father, this is Cheryl." He stands and shakes her hand. "I was just telling him how great your food is," Roberts adds.

"It's nice to meet you, Cheryl," Father Mark says.

"Welcome to L.A."

"Thank you." He sits back down.

She pulls out her order pad. "What can I get you gentlemen to drink?"

"I want a steak, a large water, and a shot of whiskey," Roberts says.

Father Mark picks up the menu and scans it quickly. "Father, you should try their hamburger. Oh, it's out of this world," Roberts says.

"Okay, one hamburger and water, please," he replies.

"Salad with that, Father?" she asks.

"Yes, please, Italian dressing," he answers.

She collects the menus. "Be right up," she says. She walks off, and Father Mark looks around. It is a place where a working man would bring his family. "So, this is your preferred restaurant?"

"Yes, it is, but if you would rather try somewhere else, I'll cancel our order and we can go, we have every type of restaurant here in L.A."

"No, no, this is perfect."

The waitress comes back and places their drinks on the table. "Thank you," Father Roberts says as she hustles away. They bow their heads in prayer. "So Father Rossi, tell me how you got into the deaf ministry."

Father Mark leans back in his chair after taking a drink of his water. "Well, my mother was a single mom and a deaf interpreter, and I was her only child. Where she went, I went. We went to hospitals, the courts, doctor visits, church, lawyer offices, you name it, she was there for the deaf."

"So, you had a passion for the deaf from an early age," Roberts says.

"Well, not exactly. Don't get me wrong, I have always loved them, but I was trying to figure out how to get outside to play baseball for the first couple of years, but it eventually sunk in, and I started being a part of what was really a ministry, her ministry. She was so happy when I became a priest. I told her I was going to find a way to start the Catholic Deaf Academy. We talked and talked about it. She helped me write the proposal."

"I'm sure she is still proud of you." Father Mark is silent for a moment.

"Yes, in heaven. She passed away last year."

Roberts sits back. "I'm sorry."

"Don't be, she lived a great life and really built a strong foundation for me. How about you? How did you get here?"

Roberts laughs. "My father was a lawyer, a good one. He died when I was fifteen."

"Oh, I'm sorry. That's a bad time for a boy to lose his father."

"It was, but he was a devout Catholic and a real inspiration to me. He was a criminal defense lawyer and dealt with some tough criminals, but he always had a great amount of peace. I wanted that peace, so I became a priest and have never regretted it. I was assigned to an Indian mission in Arizona. I loved it there, but they closed that mission after the whole boarding school fiasco. You know we are getting blamed now for converting Indian children to Christianity two hundred years ago. I really feel bad for the churches in Canada; some of them were burned to the ground." There is a moment of silence as he man considers the situation.

"Well, I can tell you how this all ends," Father Mark says. "God wins."

The waitress returns with a salad and their meals. "That was fast," Roberts says.

"We aim to please," she answers before quickly moving away. They talk as they finish their meals. Father Roberts pays the bill, and they go to the car. It is a short drive, and traffic is light as they continue talking. They seem to hit it off well together, and there is a mutual respect.

They arrive at Mary's Sacred Heart Retreat. It's a building set back from the street with a lawn covered in manicured grass, bushes, and trees. The men walk inside, register, and Father Mark is given a few papers. "Well, I'll be heading back. I'm sure you'll like it here. Call me if you need anything." He reaches into his pocket and pulls out a business card, writes his cell number on it, and hands it to Father Mark.

"Thank you for your hospitality and kindness today."

"You're most welcome, Father Rossi."

"Can I ask you something before you leave?"

"Sure."

"How can I get to the school in the morning? Are we far, or can I walk?"

"No, Father, it's too far to walk. I'll send someone for you in the morning who can drive you there. What time do you want to start?"

"Six-thirty?"

"Six-thirty? How about eight?"

"Okay. I really appreciate all that you're doing for me. Please keep the school in your prayers tonight."

"I will." He turns and walks out.

CHAPTER 3
ASSESSING THE DAMAGE

The next morning finds Father Mark sitting on a small bench at seven-thirty. He has already spent an hour in prayer in the small chapel and patiently waits for his ride with his travel bag slung over his shoulder. The smog is already heavy, but the sun shines through. He smiles and enjoys the day. The same car that he rode last night makes its way to him. He stands and opens the door and is surprised to see Father Roberts behind the wheel. "Well, what a pleasant surprise. I wasn't expecting you, Father." He gets in. Father Roberts pulls out.

"Good morning, Father. I was planning on sending someone for you, but I changed my mind and thought I should come here and learn more about your mission, help in anyway I can, and stay there with you because it's really not safe."

"I'm glad you made that decision. I want to try to find out what is needed. I thought I would make a list and then we could maybe get a look at what the contractor wrote in his original proposal."

"Good idea."

They drive through the traffic and make their way to the school. Somehow, if it's even possible, it looks worse than yesterday. Dealers are selling drugs. People sit on the steps smoking crack. Some are passed out in the yard. Father Roberts is totally shocked. He pulls through the broken gate. "It wasn't this bad when I was here with Father Muller to take pictures. That was just six days ago!" He pulls up to the school, parking close to the front door. They both get out. Some people start leaving the property. Father Mark pulls a pad and pen from his bag. Roberts retrieves a pad from his briefcase. He then puts a bar on the steering wheel to deter theft and locks the car. They go to the gate.

"I think we need to reinforce this gate," Father Mark says.

"They'll just cut another man-sized hole in the fence," Roberts says. They walk the fence, noting every place that needs to be repaired. Finally, they make it back to the front door and walk in. Father Roberts tries to latch it. "It won't lock in place, Father."

"I noticed that when I first got here," Father Mark says as he continues to write in his pad. Roberts continues to work on it. He tries to shut it, but it will not latch. He inspects the latch closely and finds duct tape jammed inside the openings, blocking the latch from going into place. He digs the tape out and tries again. The bottom latch is the problem now, and he does the same thing for it as he did on the side latch. The door shuts with a thud and latches. "Well, how about that?" he says. Father Mark turns around and sees the result.

"Well, that is a good sign. Maybe with you here, we can finish this place today!" They both laugh and move into the building, filling their pads with work that needs to be done. Several hours pass.

"Lots of broken windows, Father Roberts."

"Yes, there are." He sets his pad down, stretches tall, and rubs his back. "Father Mark, let's go to lunch.

Father Mark looks at his watch. "Wow! Thirty minutes after noon. Time is flying!"

"And we still haven't made it to the second floor yet," Roberts replies.

"Yes, let's take a lunch break."

"I know a great hot dog stand on the beach, and I want to take you to it."

They make their way back to the front doors. When they exit, they are horrified at the sight of their car. It is covered with graffiti. The tires are painted pink, the trunk has a face of a man in fear, and the roof is painted with the words 'FIVE-o Pol Pol'. Both men are discouraged. "Oh no, oh no," Roberts says.

"Don't worry, Father, I'll take responsibility for any cost."

"No, it's not that. This is just going to be another black eye for this project. Why do they do this? This is serious damage!"

"Perhaps we should call the police?" Father Mark suggests.

"No, they will not help." He walks to the car, and they get in and pull out onto the street. They drive for a while and arrive at the beach. There is a permanent hot dog stand there, and the priests make their way to it, order some hot dogs and drinks, and take a seat at an outdoor table. They bow their heads in prayer.

"I'm sorry about the car," Father Mark says as they eat.

"It's not your fault, Father." They look out at the ocean. People are walking on the beach, a few are swimming, and boats sail near the horizon. "Does it look like this in Baltimore?"

"No, we have the Inner Harbor, and it has many boats there, but it's different. It's colder in the winter there than it is here. I used to go to Ocean City for a vacation. It's a grand place. People are laid back. I guess because most of them are on vacation."

"Yeah, I know what you mean. People here aren't on vacation, but they are laid back too - except for the inner city. The gangs there, well, you can see their handiwork," he says as he points to the car. "I like coming here. I like to relax, get a couple of dogs and a soda, and take a break. I don't get to do it as often as I would like, but I'm thankful for the time I have here." They both finish their hot dogs and enjoy the ocean breeze.

"So, have you thought of anything, Father Rossi? A new plan?"

"No, I just know God has a plan, and His plan is perfect. I will wait on the Lord."

"I agree, I just hope He will tell you by the end of the week."

"I do have some donors back East and a grant writer. Nowhere close to what is needed, but I thought maybe I could contact them after the bishop lifts my gag order." Father Roberts laughs.

"I think he just wants to have as much damage control as possible."

"Oh, I agree. I see his point." They make their way back to the car and start on the journey back.

"Are your donors in your past church?"

"Yes, some, but I have donors throughout the deaf community. They are poor, but they will support a deaf ministry. I even have some in central West Virginia. There is a large number of deaf people in Appalachia. They are even poorer, but they are faithful donors. I have a few who want to come here to start their own deaf ministry. We'll call on them when the time is right, but like I say, they're poor."

"But faithful. God rewards that," Father Roberts replies.

CHAPTER 4
LOOKING FOR THE GAME PLAN

Bishop Kennedy stands at the large floor-to-ceiling window in his office overlooking L.A. The smog has settled in, and the world moves by at a fast pace. Rose calls in on the intercom. "Your Excellency, Father Muller is here."

"Send him in, please," he replies without breaking his gaze out the window. The door opens, and the bishop turns to see Muller coming in with a report in hand. He turns his gaze back out of the window. "How bad is it?" he asks.

"Well, sir, it's a thick report but...."

"How bad?"

"Some churches have suffered a sixty-percent drop in donations. I think it's just these sexual lawsuits that have produced a real fatigue in giving."

"Um..." the bishop exclaims. "Lawsuits, lawsuits. I think Satan has a foothold in our beloved church. What makes a man be attracted to a little child if not Satan?"

Father Muller stands at the desk and places the report in the center. "I agree." The bishop walks over and takes his seat after motioning for Muller to sit in the seat across from his desk. He looks at the report but doesn't pick it up. There is a long pause. Muller adjusts his collar and fidgets with the cross on his lapel.

"Any word on the school investigation?"

"No, sir."

The bishop shakes his head, discouraged and at a loss. "We need to plan a press release. This problem is not going to go away."

"Sir, the timing could not be worse. The people will really stop supporting the church."

"That's why we'd better get ahead of it. Suppose the police make an arrest, and that hits the papers. It would look like we are withholding bad news. Then they really won't trust us," the bishop responds. "I'm not saying today, but let's get a press release together and I'll draft a letter to the faithful. Let's be transparent and get ahead of this. We must preserve the little trust we have." Father Muller looks down and starts to say something, but stops.

Rose comes across the intercom. "Your Excellency, a reporter from the L.A. Times is on the phone. He is asking about a yacht purchase that was made by Father Simms. He wants to know if that is a purchase by the Catholic Church or Father Simms and if it will be sold to help with the last lawsuit settlement." The two men look at each other, shocked.

"Get his number and tell him we will call him today. And get the investigators that we have over here as soon as possible," the bishop says.

"Yes, sir."

He looks to Muller. "Too late."

Back at the school, the priests continue their work. They split up and spend the next few hours filling pages with problems. Father Mark is looking at an outlet that has been pulled out of the wall as Father Roberts walks and flops down in a student's chair.

"Graffiti everywhere. Prostitutes running a business full-time, drug dealers selling dope. It's going to take a whole lot of Holy Water in the dedication, like a fire truck load."

Father Mark laughs. "Yes, it is."

"In one of the closets, I found a small child-size sleeping bag, comics, and candy wrappers," Roberts reports. Father Mark turns to him, then walks over and takes a seat.

"I saw that too. There is no way a child could be living here, is there?"

"I would think not, but in this place, anything is possible." They both are silent in thought for a moment.

"We need to come in the middle of the night," Father Mark says.

Roberts exhales hard. "In the middle of the night? It's not safe to be here in the middle of the day. I hate to see what the walking dead are doing here at night."

At the Diocese headquarters, several lawyers, priests, and investigators meet in the press office. Everyone is talking, no one agrees. Father Muller sits in front of a laptop, listening and taking notes. Michael Bergman, the lead lawyer, a tall man in his early fifties in a custom suit, stands and holds his hands up to get everyone's attention.

"Listen, please. We must keep this meeting short. We are running out of time." He looks down at his pad. "We are not aware of private purchases made by our priests, staff, or any employees. We refer any questions about any purchase directly to the purchaser. Now that is what we should say."

Janet Baker, Press Secretary, a woman in her sixties with years of experience working in the press, shakes her head no. "They will see right through that."

A priest shouts out, "But it's true!"

"Doesn't matter," she replies. Everyone starts voicing their opinions. It gets loud.

"Hold it! Hold it!" Bishop Kennedy says. Everyone gets quiet. He leans forward in the chair, puts his face in his hands, then brushes his hair back. "Look, we need to be transparent. Here is what I recommend as a draft." Baker and others start to write. "When I stepped into this office twenty-six months ago, I promised that we would be open and honest about what is happening in your church. I have done - no - I have kept that promise. The news has not always been good. We know that our parishioners want, and should demand, to know what we do with funds, how we handle priests or anyone on staff who breaks the sacred trust, or jeopardizes the well-being or safety of our families. I can honestly say today is the first time we have heard - no wait. We are currently seeking – no- we are hoping to get answers from Father Simms as soon as possible, as to how and if a purchase of that size was made. Father Simms, along with Deacon Markley, is currently listed as a missing person by the Los Angeles Police Department. Thank you."

Bergman rolls his eyes. "That will open us up to a lot of questions, maybe even a lawsuit. The courts will have a reason. I do not recommend that release."

Baker looks to Kennedy. "Your Excellency, I agree it will leave more questions than answers to the press corps. They will dig in on a statement like that."

Bishop Kennedy stands. Father Muller quickly stands, and then everyone else. "Courts, lawsuits, the press corps. I have to answer the parishioners. I am their shepherd. Knock the rough edges off of it and let's get it out there." He walks out with Muller right behind him.

The sun has set as Father Roberts pulls up to the retreat. Father Mark steps out, turns to the open window of the car, and says, "Thank you, Father Roberts. I not only appreciate all you have done at the school, but also for believing in this project. God has a plan. Your help has meant so much to me."

"No problem, Father. I'll be here in the morning after Mass. See you then." He drives off.

Father Mark goes inside to his room, washes his face and hands, and goes to the empty chapel. He kneels at the front, crosses himself, and starts praying.

CHAPTER 5
LUCAS

The next morning, Father Mark is back in the chapel.
He finishes his prayers and steps through the door. A woman is walking towards him. "Father Rossi, there is an urgent call for you at the desk."

He picks up his pace. "What is it about?"

"I don't know, but it's from Father Roberts. He said it's very important."

They make their way to the front desk. Father Mark picks up the phone. "Hello."

"Father Rossi, have you seen today's newspaper?"

"No."

"I'm on my way, don't talk to the press, not yet."

"What's this about?"

"The school is in the news. I'll see you in about ten minutes."

It is a long ten minutes as Father Mark watches out the window. Finally, Roberts pulls up in the graffiti-covered car and parks. Father Mark walks outside. "Good morning," he says.

Father Roberts has a very worried look on his face. He is sweating. He holds up a newspaper, then hands it to Father Mark. "Morning. Look on page eight." Father Mark opens the paper to that page. He sees a picture of the school with a headline that reads, 'Over A Mil and Counting'. Father Roberts leans back against the car and folds his arms.

"This is bad. This is what Bishop Kennedy did not want to see. The phones are ringing off the hook at the office. Parishioners, donors, and a couple of reporters have the lines lit up." Father Mark reads over the article, folds the paper, and hands it back to Father Roberts.

"Have you had breakfast yet?" he asks.

Father Roberts stands there dumbfounded. "Breakfast?" He holds his thumb close to his finger. "The bishop and everyone there are about this close to shutting this down! We're in trouble!"

"God has a plan," Father Mark says as he goes to the passenger side of the car and opens the door. "Let's go to breakfast."

Reluctantly, Father Roberts gets in and drives to a restaurant. He is nervous and fidgets with the menu, his collar, the silverware, and anything else he can touch. Father Mark seems calm and takes his time reading the menu. A waitress walks over. "Can I get your drink orders?"

"Yes, orange juice for me," Father Mark says.

She looks to Roberts. "Coffee."

She walks away and quickly returns with the drinks. "Do you know what ya want?" she asks. Father Mark hands the menu to her.

"Yes, a number five please." She takes the menu, tucks it under her arm as Father Roberts hands his to her.

"Nothing for me, coffee will be fine." She takes it and walks off without another word.

"You must eat." "Father Rossi, what are you going to do if this project gets closed down?"

"God has a plan. Last night, I think he shared some of it with me. We are going to be alright."

He starts explaining the plan, and Father Roberts slaps the table lightly with a big smile. He turns to the waitress. "Ma'am, can we get that to go?"

Across town, Bishop Kennedy and Father Muller sit in his office with a few people, Bergman and Baker included, who are sitting at the large conference table. Different ideas are being proposed on how to shut down the property and deal with the press. Baker holds a legal pad in her hand and scoots back from the table. "Have we even audited the project? Are we sure that we know of all the monies involved?" she asks.

"Or any liabilities that may be coming?" Bergman asks.

Robert Stillman, an accountant, looks up from his notes. "Then there is the closing idea. Even if we sold it, it would be a loss, a complete loss. I'm not sure, but we may be responsible for fees that were waived by the city and county at the time of purchase if we sold it."

Everyone starts talking. Kennedy places his face in his hands again and lets them go on.

Rose steps in and motions for Father Muller, who stands and walks out with her. The doors open, and Fathers Muller, Roberts, and Rossi walk in. Everyone stops talking and looks up at them. Roberts is grinning ear to ear.

"Your Excellency, I apologize for barging in like this, but Father Rossi has a proposal."

"That's quite right. We'll open to any ideas at this point."

Father Roberts motions with his hand as if he had just introduced someone on stage. "Father Rossi, the floor is yours," he says.

Father Mark is nervous now. He looks down and sees everyone staring at him. He clears his throat. "Um...I think, well, I know I can raise some money from back East....and I believe we could get a crew from there, that has experience in construction, that could at least get the place presentable. Also, I know several deaf people who would be willing to come out working one and two-week shifts as volunteers."

Everyone looks to Kennedy. "Father Rossi, we are almost a million in the hole. That sounds like a plan that the Knights of Columbus could do here. How does that get us out of today's mess?"

Father Roberts grins. Father Mark clears his throat again. "Well, sir, you see, ah,... It's a mission, an approved mission from this diocese. It could be sold for one dollar, and the new buyer assumes the debt."

"That's insane!" Bergman says as he tosses his pad on the table. "Who would be dumb enough to buy it?" Father Mark slowly raises his hand.

"You can raise that much money?" the bishop asks.

"I don't know, but I know God is with us. He has a plan."

"Wait, wait, wait a minute," Stillman says. "If we wrote off the debt, sold it for a buck, and the school was finished, it would look good for us. It would look like we did get it done."

"I don't want to be deceitful," Kennedy says.

Baker speaks up, "Actually, we could still disclose the whole thing. It looks like, even though we were cheated, we still did what we said we would do!"

Father Roberts stands. "We all saw the picture in the paper this morning. The next picture will show progress, new paint, the doors and fence repaired, windows replaced, and lights installed!"

"How?" Kennedy asks.

"Sir, I can get some people out here in a few days. In a week, we can at least have the place secured," Father Mark says.

Baker leans back again as if she has seen a vision. She holds her hand up as if she is reading a headline. "Catholic Church Boldly Goes Into Dangerous Area, Reclaims Neighborhood."

Everyone is silent and looks to Kennedy. He thinks a moment. "I like it. I like it. We could turn this whole thing around." Everyone nods in agreement.

Rose watches as everyone exits and moves into her lobby area. Fathers Mark and Roberts exit first with Father Mark explaining to Father Roberts, "I need a laptop, phone, bank account, secretary for a day, a letter of endorsement from Bishop Kennedy, some bunk beds, water, food, a report from the contractor, a-"

"Hold on. You're going too fast," Roberts says. He turns to Sarah. "Sarah, any chance we could get Patty today?"

"I think so. You could have the office at the end of the hall. It's empty, and yes, I'll pull the contractor reports."

Within the hour, the little office at the end of the hall looks like a war room. A large blueprint is tacked to the wall, a copy machine has been moved in, and coffee is brewing on a file cabinet. Reports and files are on the desk and floor. Father Mark works the phone. The work continues for the day and into the evening. Several empty pizza boxes litter the flat spaces. The crowd thins out as the sun sets until only Patty, Fathers Mark, and Roberts remain. She flips on the light as it gets dark outside.

Father Roberts rubs his eyes. "Father, you slave driver, let's call it a day."

Father Mark leans back in his chair. "Will we have someone at the airport to pick up these people as they arrive?"

"Yes, that's what Sarah did, she organized a list of local volunteers for drivers," Father Roberts says.

"God Bless her," Father Mark replies as he brushes his hair back. We have drivers for everyone," Patty says as she holds up a paper.

"Good job! Okay, let's call it a day. But Father, I think we should make a surprise visit to the school to check on our guest who lives in the closet."

Father Roberts is horrified by the idea. "That's dangerous."

"Yes, imagine how dangerous for a little child."

"Maybe I should write out my funeral now."

Father Mark laughs. "God will protect us."

They make the trip in silence. The little car pulls into the schoolyard. Jamal runs into the drug house and tells Luggs. They grab some pistols and start over to the school. A police car stops a van in front of the school. The police put all their lights on the van. The police get out behind their doors. "Driver! Put both hands out of your window," one says through the PA. Luggs and company turn back for the house. "Use one hand and open your door from the outside!" the cop says to the van driver. He does so. "Step out slowly." The driver steps out with his hands raised and turns to look back at the police, but can't see them for the bright lights. A helicopter arrives overhead and shines its lights down on the scene. Even the school is lit up like daylight. "Turn around," the cop says to the van driver, still using the PA. He does so. "Walk backwards." He does. "Stop, now open the rear doors on the van!" The drivers do so. The lights shine inside, and they can see that there is a passenger. "Driver, take two steps back, lay down with your hands extended out from your side." He does so. "Passenger! Put both hands out of the window and open your door from the outside!" The passenger does so. "Step out!"

Father Mark taps on Father Robert's shoulder. "Come on, now is our chance." They walk inside and quickly move to the closet. They jerk the door open and find a young eight-year-old black boy with blond curly hair. He tries to run, but they grab him. Light shines in from the outside.

"Stop, we're not here to hurt you," Father Mark says. The boy struggles with a look of pure fear on his face.

"Stop, stop," Father Roberts says.

The boy grunts and tries to speak. "Oh Lord, I think.... can't be," Father Mark says.

"What?" Roberts asks.

Father Mark starts signing. The boy immediately calms down and replies in sign language. "Yep, he's deaf," Father says to Roberts. Father Mark signs and says, "Who are you? I'm Father Mark. This is Father Roberts." The boy looks at him and stalls. Father Marks signs and says. "It's okay. We will not hurt you. We will help you."

Over the next ten minutes, they learn that he is a runaway foster child and his name is Lucas. He signs to Father Mark, who leans back.

Father Roberts says, "What? What is it?"

Father Mark stands and looks at him. "He has lived here for the last six months. How can that be? Someone from foster care or the foster parents must be looking all over for him!" Father Mark bends down again and starts signing. A long conversation goes on, then Father Mark covers his mouth in shock and stands upright.

"What?" Father Roberts asks.

"His foster parents sold him, he says. That can't be."

"Oh yes, it can, Father Rossi. It's a sad fact, but so common."

"Well...I mean...where is child protective services?"

"Father, they have new cases every day. They can't keep up with the workload, and cases get lost or forgotten."

"Lost or forgotten? This is a child we're talking about!"

Father Mark paces the floor. "Let's get those police officers before they leave. Maybe they can help. Both men look out of the window to see how the police are coming along with their traffic stop. The van driver and passenger are lying on the ground in handcuffs. The police are pulling guns and drugs from the van. The priests turn around, and Lucas is gone. They search everywhere. The helicopter flies off. "Come on, Father Rossi, the police are going to leave. Let's go. He's long gone. We'll be back, and we will find him again."

CHAPTER 6
HELP COMES FROM THE EAST COAST

Two days later, Fathers Roberts and Rossi are in one of the classrooms. Lucas has been nowhere to be found, but they did see that he took the food that they left in his sleeping bag. Each trip to the school results in a quick search.

They have hung a blueprint on the wall, and Father Mark has a clipboard in his hands. "Alright, a generator will be delivered soon. We have to use a local licensed electrician to do the wiring that is needed."

"We have that," Father Roberts says.

"Good, need-" The men see Luggs and several gang members walk into the classroom. "Good morning, Luggs," Father Mark says.

"Don't good morning me! I ain't yo friend. You're in my hood, my building! I'm here for the rent!" The priests look at each other.

"Well, you see-" Father Roberts starts to say.

"Shut up! I ain't even talkin' to you! I'll deal with the boss!"

Father Mark smiles, "Well, Luggs, the boss is our Lord and Savior Jesus Christ."

"SHUT UP! Just give me my rent!" He throws a student desk into the window. Glass comes crashing down. The room quickly fills with the volunteers. Father Mark gets concerned and raises his hands.

"Hold on, everyone. Let's not let this get out of hand." He looks back at Luggs. "Luggs, we own the building. Let's be fair. I know deep down you want to do the right thing." More volunteers roll into the room. Two big rednecks, brothers Scott and Jake from back East, come in and stand between Luggs and Father Mark. Luggs looks at them.

"Boy, you don't want to mess with me. I am the god of this place. I can make you disappear." The boys start to step closer. Father Mark gets in front of them.

"Hold on now. We will not have any violence here!"

Luggs looks at him, puzzled. "What planet did you come from?" Father Roberts is silently praying the Rosary. Luggs sees that and turns to walk out. "Tomorrow. Have my rent tomorrow," he says as he walks out with his entourage in close step.

Father Roberts sits down, spent. "Whew. This could get very bad."

Scott laughs. "Father, the bigger they are the harder they fall."

"Hold on. We must show Christ-like love."

"Even to him?" Jake asks.

"Even to him."

Everyone goes back to work. Father Roberts looks over to him after everyone has left the room. "Father, this is going to be a problem. These gangs will kill you for walking in front of them." Father Mark smiles. "I mean it. I'm not joking. These gangs would kill their own mother." He looks at Father Mark, who is very calm. "I know, I know. God has a plan," Roberts says. Father Marks smiles even more.

Outside volunteers replace and fix a section of the fence. Others mount security lights to the walls of the school. An electrician pulls into the yard with his van. He rolls the window down but doesn't get out. Father Roberts greets him. "Good morning!"

"Father, this is a bad neighborhood. Are you sure you want me to fix up your electric?"

"Yes, sir."

"Father, the truck that has your generator will be here within an hour. You know they are gonna steal it as soon as we leave today, right?"

"I hope not," he replies. The driver gets out, and two men from the back step out of the van from the back door. They start loading tools into their belts. Other volunteers come out and shake hands with the electricians. They move inside and take a tour of the damage.

Outside, a volunteer pulls in with six people in the front and back seats. He sees the graffitied car with the pink tires that Fathers Mark and Roberts have been driving. He exhales hard. The driver shouts out to a volunteer who is carrying fence posts. "Sir, is Father Rossi here?"

"Yes, he is."

"I have some guests who flew in from Maryland. They're deaf. I need some help trying to understand them."

The man runs inside. One of the deaf men grabs an envelope and writes, 'This place?' The driver is sweating. He swallows hard. "Yes," he says, shaking his head. The deaf crew gets out of the car as if they have no concerns about the neighborhood. Father Mark comes running out. He hugs some of them. Their hands are flying as they communicate. They laugh and are happy to see each other. Father Roberts walks out. He is amazed at how well they manage to communicate. He can't understand what they are saying; it seems their hands are moving one hundred miles an hour. A woman in the group hands Father Mark an envelope with cash inside. She signs 'From us'. One of the men points to the trunk of the car. The driver unlocks it. They pull a big box of tools out and ask Father Mark where they should start.

Across the street, Luggs watches from the yard in front of the house. Minion, a young black teen man, walks over to him. "Hey, they're gettin' more people there by the minute." Luggs just sits there, steaming. Jamal sees that his boss is getting beyond mad.

"Hey, they ain't gonna last." He reaches over and retrieves a newspaper. "They've lost a bunch of money on the joint." Luggs looks at him, confused. Jamal hands him the folded paper. Luggs opens it and smiles.

"These cats are rich."

"We'll go there tonight and get your rent. I've been watchin'. They got tools, materials, and I bet they'll leave a car or two there," Jamal says.

Luggs is still looking at the paper, smiling. "Yeah, yeah, that's what we're gonna do."

Inside, the volunteers work in almost every room. Windows are being replaced, pipes are being installed, and cleaning, a lot of cleaning is being done. A trash pile forms outside. The work continues for hours. Father Mark is rushing from one problem to the next. He is called into a utility room. The electrician is there with a disappointed, concerned look on his face.

"Your panel box has been ripped out. Ripped out without disconnecting anything. We'll have to trace every line now." He shakes his head. "And we're not going to be able to connect the generator directly. This is going to take time." Father looks at the damage. Even the wall is broken open from where the vandals and thieves ripped the box out. The electrician looks at him. "I don't even know how they did that. I can guarantee you the electricity was not live when they did this. We would have some dead bodies in here if it were."

Father Mark is silent for a moment. "How long?" he asks almost in a whisper.

The electrician exhales hard. "I don't know. I don't know what is behind this rat's nest of a mess."

"Can the generator work as a standalone unit?"

The electrician nods his head. "Yes, Father, it can. We're gonna need extra wiring, but yes, I can do that." Father Mark pats him on the shoulder.

"Good man. Thank you. I know you will do your best. Thank you."

He walks out into the hall and is met by Father Roberts. "Good, I've been looking for you."

"I just found out we have a few bigger problems with the electricity," Father Mark says.

"That's not all," Roberts replies. They walk into the "headquarters" classroom.

Father Mark pours some coffee. "Like a cup?" he asks.

Father Roberts shakes his head no. "I just found out our permits may have expired. I got Patty looking into it. Also, I'm very concerned about this guy they call Luggs. There is a large congregation across the street now. I have taken the liberty of calling a security company. They wouldn't take the job here for any amount of money."

Father Mark sits down. "These gangs are a real problem," he says.

"Father, you don't know the half of it. These guys are killers, cold-blooded killers, and we have them for neighbors."

"Those big boys that flew out here, well, I think they discourage these gangs just by their appearance."

"Well, I called the Knights of Columbus. They are coming out to make some suggestions for us. I also called the police to ask for additional patrols. I don't think they took the call too seriously."

Father Mark reaches over to a desk and retrieves a paper. "Our volunteers are turning in lists of needed materials."

"We have to have security here or it will walk off," Father Roberts says.

"God will provide," Father Mark replies.

They walk outside. A volunteer hands each of them a cold bottle of water from a cooler. "Thank you, sir," Father Roberts says. Father Mark signs 'thank you'. The man smiles and signs 'you're welcome.' Both men open their bottles and drink them.

"It's gonna take a little time for me to realize we have deaf helpers. They must be making quite a sacrifice to be here."

"Father, they live in some pretty rough conditions. Even the strongest are not hired because employers don't know how to talk to them, and sometimes there are safety issues that have to be considered, so they work at any low-paying job they can find. Yes, they are making a big sacrifice to be here, but they will do it without complaint." As they stand there, the generator arrives. Volunteers come out to the truck. The work continues until late afternoon.

Father Mark is in a bathroom, scrubbing down the walls with several volunteers. The lights come on. They stand amazed. People throughout the building start applauding. Father Mark looks up at the ceiling. "Thank you, Father!" He walks out and goes to the generator. Father Roberts is there with sweat dripping off his head as he leans over, pulling plastic away from it. His face is red and slightly sunburned. "Easy, Father, or these guys are going to offer you a full-time job!" Everyone laughs.

"That's one that I would be happy to decline," he says as he wipes his forehead.

The work continues. Luggs watches them closely from his yard. He drinks a cold beer while they sweat and toil at cleaning the place out. Trash piles high until another truck arrives with a large dump trailer. Everyone comes out and puts the trash in the trailer. It is loaded within minutes. The driver and a passenger drive off. Luggs laughs. "Yeah, you take that trash away, but leave all the big tools there. He sees Father Mark signing to the deaf workers. He is amazed at how fast their hands move. "Hey, Minion!" Minion runs over to him. "Weren't yo cousin deaf?"

"Deaf and dumb! She sits in front of that TV at my uncle's house all day watching it. Can't hear it, but she loves watching it."

"She's still at your uncle's?" Luggs asks.

"Yeah, she does the cookin' and watchin' and sleeping."

"Hey, where does she go to school?"

"Riverside. The California School for the Deaf, but she quit."

"I bet I need to go see her. She was really fillin' out the last time I saw her. What's her name?"

"Carla. No problem. I'll bring her down next time I come over here."

He smiles and turns his attention back to the school. "They look like a bunch of ants over there!" Luggs says.

"Yeah," Minion answers.

"Well, we'll keep 'em busy-busy replacing all the stuff we steal!" Luggs says. Everyone laughs.

As the night drags on, the workers continue to light up the place and clean. Luggs continues to drink. By three a.m. Luggs is on the ground sleeping, and the Knights of St. John Paul are singing as they work. The school is now lit up like daytime, but only as long as the generator runs.

CHAPTER 7
ANOTHER SETBACK

In the morning, the priests, deaf, and all daytime volunteers are back. Fathers Roberts and Mark have inspected where Lucas sleeps and see that he has managed to sneak in and out again. The canned food is missing, and they hope that he got it. The Knights of St. John Paul have a large military "water Buffalo" tank in the yard. People are filling buckets with water to clean the school. Father Roberts walks over to one of the Knights. He taps the water buffalo.

"This is great. I wish we could get one big enough for the showers."

"Oh, well, Father, I think Bill Mackey is working on the plumbing today, but he has to be at work by noon. But we have him until then."

"You guys are doing a great job."

The work continues, and the place is starting to shape up and not look like it's sitting in a war zone. Gunshots can be heard from time to time. Father Mark has the deaf on three different jobs and rotates helping them so he is available to interpret instructions and needs. It's hard work, but everyone has a positive attitude. A new set of doors arrives to replace the side doors. The men start replacing them. The electrician is hard at work with his crew and a few volunteers. A new breaker box has been installed, and what seems like miles of cut cable is being replaced. Windows are still being replaced, and some are being temporarily boarded up. The trash trailer arrives and is reloaded.

Jake and Scott come down from the roof covered in dirt and sweat. Father Roberts goes into the "headquarters" office and starts writing in a pad. Father Mark walks in as Scott and Jake enter through the other door.

"Father Mark, that roof is gonna need a lot of help," Scott says as he gets a cold bottle of water out of a cooler and throws it to his brother. He pulls another out and opens it.

"What? Oh no," Roberts says.

"Yep," Jake says. Scott drinks the whole bottle down and says, "The whole roof will have to be covered, tarred, but first, about half of the plywood will have to be replaced."

"What? Half?" Father Roberts asks.

Scott gets another bottle out and opens it. "Yeah, half at least."

Roberts looks to Father Mark. "Add it to the list," he says as he gets a bottle out of the cooler, opens it, and walks to the window. Father Roberts exhales hard and starts writing.

"This is adding up," he says.

He finishes writing and looks up in time to see Father Mark running out of the room. He drops his pad and chases after him. "What's wrong?" he shouts as he tries to catch up, but Father Mark is already out the door. Father Roberts gets outside and sees that Father Mark is on a slow walk. He looks past him and sees a deaf man signing to Lucas, who is standing on the outside of the fence. Both priests walk slowly towards him. Lucas sees them and takes off in a run. Father Mark bolts back to the gate and takes off after him. He runs like he is in the Olympics, and Father Roberts cannot catch up. He is not in shape for such a run. He stops and tries to get his breath. He sees that he is now a full block away from the school and the safety of the volunteers. He makes the decision to go forward to Father Mark. After a minute of walking and checking for gangs, he sees Father Mark signing to Lucas. They are signing something, but Father Roberts has no clue what. He watches as Lucas bolts away again. Father Mark starts to go after him.

Father Roberts shouts, "Let him go! He'll be back!" Father Mark stops running and watches Lucas disappear. He then turns around, brushing his hair back, and starts walking to Father Roberts.

A low rider car does a U-turn in the street. Several gang members are inside. The priests look at each other, and Father Mark picks up his pace for a retreat back to school. As soon as he reaches Father Roberts, the car speeds up and pulls onto the sidewalk. Both men freeze.

"Holmes, where ya going?" the passenger asks. The car bounces up and down with the air shocks. It backs out, and the priests take two steps, and the car flies back on the sidewalk, blocking them again.

"You lost, Holmes?" the passenger asks. Father Mark swallows hard and uses his finger to open his collar. Father Roberts pulls out his Rosary and discreetly and silently starts praying. The driver looks towards the school and sees the volunteers coming in a slow walk. He slaps the passenger on the arm.

"Let's go." He drops it in reverse, backs up, and slowly drives past the volunteers. They look back and see the crowd surrounding the priests.

The car cruises around the block, taking a slow drive past the school to see what is being done. Father Mark watches them as they slow down to about two miles an hour, checking out the tools and materials. They look back and see the crowd getting closer and a police car coming up behind them. They turn and disappear. Father Roberts is soaked with sweat. Father Mark pulls his handkerchief out and wipes the sweat from his forehead.

"Thank you all for coming out to us. I wasn't sure what their plan was."

They turn to start through the gate. Father Roberts tugs Father Mark's sleeve as people file back to work.

"That was close. You can't go out like that. They could have shot us dead. We didn't even have anything to get behind." Father Mark nods his head in agreement. The police car pulls up and stops. Two policemen get out. One is a sergeant.

He asks, "Who's in charge here?"

Father Mark steps closer. "I am Father Mark, this is Father Roberts. We're in charge."

"Okay, we have been getting complaints all day from the neighbors about the noise from a generator." Both priests stand there stunned. The sergeant looks over to see the generator. "You're going to have to shut it off."

"Officer, that generator keeps the lights on, which keeps us from being robbed," Father Mark says. Father Roberts looks across the street and sees Luggs standing there with a big smile on his face.

Scott is standing on the inside of the fence listening. "Of all the noise from gunfire, and you're worried about the generator?" he asks.

The sergeant frowns and steps to the fence. "I ain't got one complaint over gunfire, but I have several over the generator. If you hear gunfire and it's close, call us. Until then, turn off the generator." He looks back at the priests. "I mean it. Shut it down."

He walks back to the car. Both cops get inside and drive off. Father Mark looks to Roberts, who has his head hung low and his shoulders drooped. He knows his friend is shook.

The volunteers look to the priests. "You heard the man, shut it down," Father Roberts says.

"We will try to secure everything in one room," Father Mark says, almost in a whisper.

The workers start gathering tools and materials. A team starts adding padlocks to the new storage room. The volunteers work silently. One of the deaf men looks in a classroom and sees Father Mark sitting in a student's seat, just staring into space. He walks on after a moment.

By the end of the day, the place is locked up in many places. Father Mark is trying his best to put on a good face, but the people can see he is hurt. Scott walks up to him as people gather around for the van ride home. "Father, Jake, and I will stay here tonight."

Father Roberts walks over as Father Mark is deep in thought. "I don't know Scotty," Father Mark says.

"It'll be alright," Scott says.

Father Roberts looks at them. "I don't think that is a good idea," he says.

"No, Father, it'll be alright. We'll stay inside, use flashlights in different rooms, make it look like there are more of us than there are."

"What could you do if they come in?" Father Roberts asks. "You can't arrest them, shoot them, they will just kill you and your brother."

"Really, we'll be okay." He looks to Father Mark.

"Call me the minute there is any trouble. Don't engage them, call the police, then me," Father Mark says.

Scott smiles, makes a fist in the airing pulls it down. "Yes!" He turns to get his brother.

"This is a mistake,' Father Roberts says.

Later that night, Father Mark tosses and turns in his bed. He readjusts the pillow, the sheets, and he gets up and paces, only to return to bed and start the whole ritual all over again. Finally, out of pure exhaustion, he nods off to sleep. After a while, he hears something pounding, a steady drone of noise. He tries to wake up.

"Father, Father Rossi!" He hears his name and wakes. He looks around, trying to figure out where he is and who is calling his name. "Father Rossi!"

"Yes."

"Father, open the door. You have an emergency call!" He wakes up and jumps out of bed. He pulls his pants on and opens the door. Sister Maria is standing there in a robe.

"What's wrong, Sister?"

"Come to the desk. You have an emergency call!"

They almost run down the hall to the front desk area. He grabs the phone off the desk. "Hello!" The nun watches him for a reaction. His face becomes tense. His eyes dart side to side. "Hide! Hide and call the police again! I'm on my way!" He hangs up. "Sister, can you please call a cab while I get dressed?"

"Yes, Father. Where do-" she looks back, but he is already gone back to his room.

He gets dressed and runs outside as a cab pulls in. The driver has his window down. "Where to?"

"West Adams," Father says as he reaches for the back-door handle. The cab speeds off without him. "Wait!" The driver floors it and bounces into the street. Father Mark turns to run back inside to call another cab and almost knocks Sister Maria down. "I'm sorry, Sister." He steps past her and goes inside with her behind him.

"Father, there is not a cab company that will take you there at this time of night." Father looks at his watch, 4:23 a.m. He paces. "Father, I will drive you if you will sign out the car."

"No, Sister, way too dangerous. Can I drive it?"

"Not unless you're on the list."

"Oh Lord, I need a ride!" She goes down the hall to her room and quickly returns, dressed in her habit. She holds up a set of car keys.

"Let's go, Father." He shakes his head no, but she goes out the door, around the corner, and returns with an old VW Beetle. She throws the passenger door open. "Get in, Father." He jumps in, and she flies out of the retreat and into the city night.

"Sister, it's too dangerous there. They are shooting up the place. Two men are inside, hiding, I hope. I should have listened to Father Roberts! Slow down a little!" Father Mark holds a hand grip on the ceiling. She is passing cars and driving over the speed limit.

She starts singing. "On a hill far away, stood an old rugged cross." The car goes airborne and hits with a thud.

"The emblem of suffering and shame!" Father Mark sings. "Watch those cars up ahead!"

"And I love that old cross!" Sister sings.

At the school, Scott and Jake are watching the mayhem from the roof. Some gang members are trying to load the generator. All the supplies are being loaded and hauled off. Several more shots are fired at the school. Jake and Scott can hear windows breaking. "Jake, this ain't good. I wish we had our pistols!"

"Call the cops again!" Jake says. Almost everything that is not nailed down has been loaded and hauled away. The boys look over and see the VW car driving fast. One of the gang members who is just walking out of the busted gate sees them and aims his pistol.

"NO! NO!" Scott yells. The man turns and sees them, then turns his attention back to the car. Sister Maria and Father Mark both see him at the same time.

"LOOK OUT!" Father yells as a bullet comes through the windshield between them. Both duck as the car crashes through the fence and stops with a thud when it hits the school. The engine dies, and the night is silent.

Father gets out and rushes to the driver's door. Sister opens it. "Sister, are you alright? Are you hurt?"

"No, Father." She coughs and brushes some glass out of her hair.

"Inside! Quick!" he orders. They get inside, and Father runs to the closet where Lucas sleeps. He jerks the door open and finds he is gone. He turns back and, in the dark, makes his way back to the front as Jake and Scott come running down the steps. He moves into a classroom with Sister Maria.

"Father! Are you alright?" Jake asks.

"Yes, we're in the first classroom!" Jake runs to them. Scott runs past and steps out past the broken front door. He returns in a moment.

"They're all gone. Sorry, Father."

"Thank God you boys are alright!" He hugs them both. They shine their flashlights on the wall. Several bullet holes are there. Glass is scattered across the floor. So much of the hard work is wasted. Jake steps closer to the shot-out window.

"Hey, a police car just drove by!"

"Maybe they're getting ready to come in. Let's go let 'em in," Scott says. They walk out. Father takes Sister's hand.

"Shall we pray?" They both kneel down and cross themselves. Jake and Scott come right back because the police didn't stop. They look at each other, then kneel down in prayer.

The sun rises, and they move outside. Father leads the way, inspecting the damage. He finds the generator missing, wires cut, windows broken, and graffiti everywhere. The cameras are shot to pieces. He makes his way to the broken main gate. Even the posts are broken down, and the chain and padlock is gone. He looks over to Luggs' place and sees him laughing and dancing with the chain and lock over his head. Father stares a moment, then starts marching over to him. Scott and Jake rush in front of him.

"No Father, no."

"YOU'RE LAUGHING NOW, BUT YOU WON'T BE LAUGHING SOMEDAY, LUGGS! HELL IS HOT." The boys struggles to hold him back.

"Oh yeah! A little righteous anger there! You're on my property. Pay your rent!" The boys hunch down and shove Father Mark back to the gate. He stops resisting. The boys stand tall.

"Father, I never thought I would say this, but remember, Christ loves him too." Father Mark is embarrassed.

"I'm sorry. You're right. I just see all of our hard work shot to pieces. Let's get back inside with Sister Maria." A police car pulls up. Inside is a female cop and a male cop. They get out and survey the damage.

"Whew!" the man says.

CHAPTER 8
OUT OF THE ASHES

Patty stands beside Father Mark in a conference room at the Diocese headquarters. She nervously paces. Father Mark just stares at the wall. Father Roberts comes in.

"Thank God no one was hurt!" He sits down beside Father Mark.

"You were right. I should-"

"Hey, let's work on what the next step is. I'm here for you. I know God is with you," he laughs. "Sister Maria just got her driver's licence last month!" As sad as Father Mark is, he lets that sink in for a moment, then he laughs out loud.

The door opens, and Michael Bergman walks in. He flops his briefcase on the table, opens it, retrieves a legal pad, and pulls a pen from his shirt pocket. He sits down, looks at the priests, takes a deep breath, and says, "Okay, where do we start? Maybe we should start with everything that was stolen last night, no, maybe the two crashed cars, no, how about almost getting a nun killed, or the volunteers, or let's see, we could talk about how we will ever explain this to the parishioners!"

"It was a mistake to leave them there, and I'll take full responsibility for that," Father Mark says.

Bergman writes something on his pad. "Father, with all due respect, I'm going to work hard to send you back to Baltimore!"

"But the school! We -"

"I hope that building burns to the ground!" It's killing us!"

"Mr. Bergman!" Father Roberts says. The door opens, and Bishop Kennedy and Father Muller walk in. Everyone stands. The bishop motions for them to sit and takes a seat at the head of the table.

"Big night last night," he says.

"Your Excellency, I... ah..."

"Hold on, Father," The bishop says. "I know you have put your heart into this, but I do think we need to shut it down. St. Michael must have been riding with you last night. I could be on the phone notifying next of kin for you, Sister Maria, and your volunteers. No, that's it, we're done. We'll take the beating, make up the losses, and move on."

"Sir, please, let us work this out. There is a little deaf boy who lives there, and he really needs someone. I can-" Father Mark says before a knock is heard on the door.

"Come in!" the bishop says. Sarah steps in.

"Your Excellency, a reporter from the LA Times is here. He is very insistent."

"What?" the bishop asks.

Bergman stands. "I'll set him straight and bounce him out of here!"

Father Muller grabs his sleeve and stops him.

"No!" the bishop says. He looks back at Sarah. "Tell him to go through the press office." She turns and walks out.

The bishop looks back at Father Mark. "I'm sorry. Turn the info over to Mr. Bergman about the little boy. We'll do what we can. I know you are trying to build your mission, but perhaps this is not the place. Father, when you do find a place, let us know, we want to contribute and we want to pray for you and the people you serve." Everyone stands. "God bless you," the bishop says as he shakes hands with Father Mark, who stands there speechless.

"But...Sir..." He nods his head in surrender. "Thank you, Your Excellency." They all walk out into the hall.

As they make their way, the reporter pushes past Sarah. "Good morning, Bishop Kennedy. I'm Tom Bowers with the L.A. Times. I was -"

"I know who you are. You have written so much against us."

"Well, Bishop, if I have been wrong in anything that I have written about the sexual predator lawsuits, just let me know. I'll gladly run a retraction."

"You need to go through the press office!" Bergman says.

"Who is in charge of the school?" Bergman starts to push against him. The bishop stops him.

"Father Mark Rossi. We'll have a press release ready in two hours."

"Are you Father Rossi?" Bowers asks Roberts. Father Roberts points to Father Mark. "You are?"

"Yes," Father Mark answers.

"You are a very determined man. Maybe the church could use some more men like you." Father Mark doesn't know what to say. He looks to Bergman and the bishop.

"Ah.. well...This is an important mission. We just want to build a place where we serve one of the most underserved communities in the world. The deaf are at a real disadvantage. We want to share the good news of Christ with them, we want to help them, we want to teach the hearing not only how to communicate with them but also go out into the world and build their own missions!" He looks to Bishop Kennedy, who nods at him. "Ah...you see the deaf live in a world that we take for granted. They need more people to cross that line, to make a stand and say I will stand with you, I will help you, and I will do that in the name of Christ my Savior!"

Bowers is writing fast in his reporter's notebook. "You know that's a bad neighborhood. Not too many businesses survive there," Bowers says.

"With God nothing is impossible," Father Mark says. Bowers asks a few more questions about future staffing, current volunteers, and goals for the school. Father Mark answers them vaguely while always gauging Bishop Kennedy and Bergman.

"Alright, that's enough questions," Bergman says as he takes Bowers by the arm to escort him out.

Bowers shakes him loose and extends her hand to Father Mark. "Thank you, Father, for taking the time to answer my questions." He looks to the bishop. "Your Excellency, I want to thank you for allowing me this interview." He walks around Bergman and goes out the door.

The drive back to the retreat is done in silence. Father Roberts is at a loss. He wanted to see the school work out. He doesn't know what to say. He drives through the L.A. traffic. Father Mark stares at the floor. Finally, he speaks up. "It ... it just doesn't seem right. I feel that this is not the will of God. I will pray at the chapel and seek God's will. I will be obedient to the bishop, though. I will pack my bags."

"I'll be here to pick you up in the morning and take you to the airport," is about all Father Roberts can say. They get to the retreat and shake hands.

"Be of good cheer, brother," Father Mark says before turning and walking inside. Father Roberts watches him until he is out of sight, then slowly places the car in gear and drifts into the traffic.

Father Mark goes to his room, then quickly leaves for the chapel. He sees the nuns are inside singing a song, so he retreats back to his small room. He kneels down beside his bunk and prays and prays. Hours pass and he gets up, showers and crawls into bed for a restless night's sleep.

He is up before dawn and goes to the chapel to pray. After a while, he hears the door open and sees Sister Maria starting to come in. She sees Father and steps back out into the hallway. Father crosses himself, stands, and leaves the chapel to catch Sister Maria. "Sister, I am finished with my prayers. Please you go ahead inside."

She walks back and stops in front of him. "Father, I heard what happened. I'm sorry. I'm sure God could have used you here. You have revived my faith in our missions. I will miss you."

He looks down at her and takes her hand. "Sister, I will miss you. You are the most adventurous sister I have ever met." She laughs.

"Not really, Father. I live a very quiet life."

"I find that hard to believe. A nun who has been under fire and still remained fearless!" She laughs, nods her head, looks away, then back at him.

"Father may God bless you wherever you end up." He hugs her and walks outside to wait for his ride.

He checks his watch as the sun comes up. The smog lies low over the city, but the sun is bright. He looks up at the sky. "Lord, I will go where you send me. May Your will be done!" He crosses himself as Father Roberts comes into the driveway, almost sideways in the pink wheeled car. Father Mark jumps up. The car skids to an abrupt stop. Father Roberts hits his head on the windshield but jumps out quickly.

"God has a plan! We, you, ah, the bishop."

Father Mark holds his hand up to the stop position. "Slow down."

Father Roberts takes a deep breath. "Have you seen today's paper?"

"No." He runs back to the car and tries to reach through the passenger window, but it is not rolled down enough. He pulls his hand back and tries the door handle. It is locked. He runs around the front of the car so close that he bumps his knee.

"Ow!" he says with a laugh. Father Mark raises his eyebrows. Finally, Father Roberts gets the driver's door open and retrieves the newspaper. He runs back to Father Mark. "LOOK! Right here, front page!" He taps the article many times. Father Mark takes it from him. 'Priest Makes A Bold Stand' the headline reads.

He starts reading the article. 'Father Mark Rossi, a priest from Baltimore, Md., is just what the ailing church needs. He's bold, humble, and is like a bulldog that has bit into the postman's britches. He has taken over a school building to build the Catholic Deaf Academy. A school building that is controlled by gangs. Threats, intimidation, and lack of funding and manpower did not discourage this man of God. The embattled Bishop Anthony Kennedy, busy settling lawsuits and battling dropping church attendance, has had the foresight to push ahead on Faith, the fuel that long ago drove the Catholic Church.'

Father Roberts grabs the paper back like a little child with a birthday gift. "Look here," he says, as he thumbs through the paper to page eight. He folds it over. "Look right here!" He points to the story and begins reading it. "'Rossi with the assistance of Father Andrew Roberts' – that's me! - 'have boldly claimed the real estate in West Adams.'" He hands the paper back to Father Mark, who tries to resume reading. Father Roberts grabs the paper from him again. "Come on! You can read in the car. We've been summoned to the office!" He starts back around the car and bumps his leg again.

"The office? Bishop Kennedy's office?"

"No, the one on the moon. Of course, Bishop Kennedy's office. Their phones are ringing off the hook! People are pledging support! They are all behind you! They want to help! Come on, we have a school to build!" Father Mark is stunned.

Father Mark holds on tight to the handle above the passenger window as Father Roberts weaves through traffic. "I see you and Sister Maria attended the same driver's ed course." "Hold on!" Father Roberts says.

At the office, Rose is answering phones. Janie and Sarah have been brought in to answer the phones that have been added to the desk. It is busy. Father Roberts waves to Sarah, then Rose. They do not notice him. He starts to walk into the bishop's office when Rose sees him and motions for them to come in.

Father Muller is sitting in front of the Bishop. They both stand when they see Father Mark walk in. "The Lord works in mysterious ways!" The bishop says, and he motions for them to take a seat. They all sit down and remain silent for a few seconds, unsure of where to begin. Bishop Kennedy touches his fingertips together.

"I take it the public has liked the article?" Father Mark says.

The bishop leans forward. "Father, we are now taking pledges from other states! This article is making some ground. I guess they are reading it online. I don't know." He reaches over to a stack of phone message slips. He flips through them. "Two Catholic papers want an interview with you. A local TV show wants an interview with you, also."

"But isn't that something that the press office should handle?"

"No, Father, these are the ones asking for you. The press office is handling the others." Father Mark leans back in his chair and exhales. Father Muller stands and walks to the bar and retrieves a cold bottle of water. "Needless to say, the project is back on." Father Mark smiles. "You will have some help, and we will need to put a firm completion date up."

"We can do that!" Father Roberts says.

"We're going to open a new bank account, we're going to hire an outside C.P.A. firm, we're going to hire a security firm to be there at night, and we are going to report to the public through social media using video footage of the progress," Muller adds.

"Wow! That all sounds good to me. This is better than getting on an airplane today!" Father Mark says.

CHAPTER 9
THE PLIGHT OF LUCAS

The next few days pass by in a blur. Father Mark deals with schedule problems because so many people have volunteered to help or make material donations. The deaf need his attention for instruction on what they are to do next. So many people have stepped forward that a complete roster has been created. When that filled up, people were turned away, at least temporarily. A small staff has been assigned to his project from the church. Father Mark takes time each day to seek Lucas to no avail. On the third day, he is looking at a repair on the window outside the school. He feels a tug on his pants and turns to see Lucas standing there with a big smile. He is holding a paper and pointing at the newspaper article. He signs, 'This you?'.

Father smiles and takes the paper, underlining his name, hands it back, and signs, 'This me'.

Lucas stomps his feet, shakes his head, and smiles from ear to ear. He struts around in a circle, stops, points at Father's name, then repeats the whole ritual.

Father kneels down in front of him. 'I can help you,' he signs.

Lucas gets serious. 'You super hero, help me?' he signs.

'Yes,' Father replies. Lucas looks at him, then starts strutting around again. Father Roberts walks over and sees them. He is sweating, but he is happy to see Father Mark and Lucas together. He watches Lucas sign.

"I'm glad you found him," Father Roberts says.

Father Mark stands and laughs with joy. "He found me."

"What's he saying?" Father Mark laughs again.

"He says I'm a superhero."

Father Roberts smiles. "I have to agree." Father Mark kneels down again and opens his arms. Lucas looks at him for a minute. He hesitates. "Maybe he's just not ready yet," Father Roberts says. Father Mark starts to stand, and Lucas rushes to him, hugging him close. "What do I know about this?" Father Roberts says as he walks away with a smile on his face.

Later that day, after a meal is served on site for the workers, the priests sit on the steps outside in the shade of the setting sun. They wave as some of the volunteers leave. Father signs 'thank you' to the deaf volunteers. The priests sit there drinking a soda.

"You know, we are mandatory reporters. We have to tell LAPD or the Los Angeles County Department of Children and Family Services," Father Roberts says.

"They are the ones that 'lost' him," Father Mark says as he holds up air quotes.

"Father, you are a rock star right now. The spotlight is on you. Believe me, a lot of people are here for you, but some out there would love to see you fall and fall hard, flat on your face. Something like this is just the thing that could really backfire."

"Yeah, but he is trusting me now. If I betray that trust and if he goes back into the hell that he just crawled out of, how will he ever trust someone again – especially a priest?"

Father Roberts looks out over the city. "I don't know," he says in almost a whisper.

Father Mark finishes his soda. "We don't tell anyone just yet." He gets up and walks away.

That evening, Father Mark takes Lucas to a small room. He shows him a set of keys. He hands it to Lucas. He holds the other up, then places it in his pocket. He steps inside the room with Lucas and closes the door. He locks the door by turning the button on the doorknob. He shakes the handle, showing it is locked. He unlocks and opens the door, stepping back out in the hall with Lucas behind him. He shuts the door and locks it. He points to the locked door and signs 'Open it'. Lucas steps up, unlocks, then opens the door and looks back at Father Mark. He smiles. 'This is your room for the next few days. Guards will be downstairs. You are safe here. Lucas looks at him, then the room, then back to him, and hugs Father close.

"Father Mark!" someone yells from downstairs.

"I'm coming!"

"The security guards are here!" He pats Lucas on the head and walks downstairs to fill out paperwork, meet with security for a briefing, arrange tomorrow's schedule, and attend to the many details that have been overlooked today. He doesn't even feel tired.

The next day, Father Mark is busy and has postponed a short meeting with Father Roberts, claiming he will take the meeting when he catches up on the work. Father Roberts sees through that but plays along. By afternoon, he is looking for his opportunity to force a face-to-face, private meeting. A contractor sits with Father Mark in the temporary work office.

Several people are sitting on a bench in the hall waiting for their meeting. Father Roberts walks in and sees the line. He engages in small talk with them, praising them for their work. The contractor walks out, and Father Roberts goes to the head of the line. "I'm sorry. I have to take this meeting. I promise I'll be out in five minutes," he says to the man who is next in line. Father steps through the door and closes it behind him.

"Father, I am going to get to you. I know you want to talk about Lucas," Father Mark says.

Father Roberts stands at the door. "Angel's Flight for Runaway and Homeless Youth. They are part of Catholic Charities. They would like to talk to you. Father, this will be fine. They will ensure that Lucas doesn't get lost in the shuffle. Sister Mary Anne promised. You have a meeting scheduled for tomorrow at 9:00 a.m. I'm sorry. I know you'll be mad at me, but believe me, I'm only looking out for you...and Lucas." He turns and steps out.

At the end of the day, as the employees and volunteers are leaving, Father Mark sees Father Roberts packing away the tools. He walks over to him. "Father, I'm not mad at you. That wouldn't be very Christ-like now, would it? I just feel that Lucas has been betrayed by the system." He walks over, gets two bottles of water from a cooler, and hands one to Father Roberts. "It's really hard for me to understand how a child, the most vulnerable in our society, can be treated like a number on a page."

"Thank you," Father Roberts says after taking a big drink of the water. He sits down on a ladder. "Father Rossi, you have to know that we are placing him into the hands of a nun who has a lot of experience with this. She will do her best to ensure that he is going to be okay. I know it's hard, but we couldn't put him into better hands."

The next morning, Father Mark is sitting in an office across the desk from Sister Mary Anne Miller. "Sister, it's that, well, I just established trust with him. I don't want him to feel betrayed. Maybe we should wait a couple of days."

"Father, I understand your concern, but leaving him on the street is far too risky. I can tell you horror stories about what I have seen of children that we get off the street. I promise you it will keep you awake at night. The damage that could be done on the street is far greater than what could happen to us. We are well-equipped for a case like this. We will evaluate him, stabilize him, and then find a home for him through an adoption agency with which we work. You can be a part of the process."

"I would like that."

"Where is he now?"

"I'm not sure." She looks at him over the top of her glasses. "Honest Sister. He leaves before dawn. He'll be back later today."

"Very well. I will personally follow you there; besides, I want to see this new school that you are building. I'm sure we will be working together a whole lot in the future."

When they arrive, Sister is shocked at the amount of work underway at one time. Father Roberts walks over to greet them. After exchanging pleasantries, Sister walks around looking at the place. "You don't look so good, Father," Father Roberts says.

"I could use a drink."

“I didn't know you did drink.”

“I don't, but today would be a good day to start.”

Father Roberts laughs and slaps him on the back. “I'll go with you to talk to Lucas.” They make their way inside and up the stairs to find Lucas in a classroom, looking at a textbook on sign language. He smiles widely when he sees the priests coming in.

Father signs 'Did you eat yet?' Lucas nods his head yes. “This isn't easy,” Father says as he sits on a five-gallon bucket. Father Roberts watches the two of them in a conversation. Lucas gets a panicked look on his face and shakes his head no. The conversation continues. Father Mark grabs him and hugs him close. 'I love you,' he signs after releasing him. Lucas looks back at him and signs it back. Sister Mary Anne walks in. Father Roberts can't look. He turns and walks out, goes down the steps, and wipes a tear.

After several minutes, he watches as Sister places him in her car. They drive out of sight. Father Roberts goes back inside and finds Father Mark with tear-soaked eyes sitting on the bucket. He wipes his face and stands. “I think that was the hardest thing I've ever done.”

“It will be fine. You'll see him soon.”

“Tomorrow she said.”

“That's good, that's good!”

CHAPTER 10
GONE AGAIN

The next day, Luggs is sitting at a large table in the drug house. Uniformed policeman J.P. Stalker walks in with a small book bag. He sits it in front of Luggs. "I can't just keep bringing it here. We gotta find another way," he says. Luggs pulls the bag over and opens it. Cocaine is inside. He takes a deep breath and exhales hard, reaching into a drawer and pulling out a stack of cash, then slides it over to the cop.

"What can you do about that priest over there?"

The cop looks at him for a moment. "You serious? That priest is a hero, a rallying cry."

"A rallying cry for cleaning up the neighborhood. That could be bad for our business."

"Look, Luggs, we can't do nothing, I mean nothing about him. He's a darling to the media. A big spotlight shines down on him right now. If I were to write a parking ticket, the people would have a fit, and my Captain would have my badge. No way. Now on the other hand...if you saw fit to shoot him...well," the cop says with a shrug.

"You know you make a lot of money from me, and you do little to earn it."

"Luggs, you got pure grade powder in that bag. Some problems you have to work out for yourself." He turns and walks out.

Several gang members enter and take seats wherever they find them. Someone turns on a video game. "Turn it off!" Luggs orders. The game goes off, and several people leave. Jamal sits at the table. "We need to kill a priest," Luggs says while deep in thought.

"No problem, we can kill whoever you want dead!" Jamal says. Bullets suddenly fly through the windows and walls. Both men hit the floor. A car speeds away as Jamal and Luggs run outside and return fire on the speeding car. "That's Mo-Mo for sure," Jamal says.

"Mo-Mo be dead too!" Luggs says.

The volunteers, except the deaf, at the school are lying on the ground watching the whole thing. Luggs looks over at them and points his pistol in their direction. The deaf volunteers then get down on the ground. Luggs turns and goes back inside with Jamal behind him. The workers get up and go back to work.

Father Mark is sitting at a drafting table and rubbing his eyes. Father Roberts enters and takes a seat. "We need to move the deaf volunteers inside. That was close," Father Mark says.

"Yep. I agree. The roofing contractor will be here today. Which team do you want to work with them?"

"I think they are fully staffed; if not, send Scott's team."

Father Robert's phone rings. "Hello, ...oh hello Sister....Yes, he is, he's right beside me, hold on please." He hands the phone to Father Mark.

"Hello, Sister, how is he doing?...WHAT! When?... Oh no....Ok, keep me informed.... I wouldn't know....He did...Ok, thank you...Pray and I'll pray too....He must feel all alone now....Goodbye, Sister." He hands the phone back to Father Roberts.

"What happened?"

"He's gone, missing, they don't know how, but he somehow escaped the premises last night at some point."

Father Roberts exhales hard. "What'd we do now?"

"Pray, that's the only thing we can do."

As the day goes on, Father Mark becomes much slower. His mind is deep in thought. Father Roberts tries to keep him busy to keep his mind off of Lucas. "I need you to sign some papers for the church, showing that we need those new windows."

"Hummm?"

"The windows, we need to"-

"Oh yes, of course." And so, the day drags on. Father Mark makes several calls to Sister Mary Ann. Each time she promises that he will be the first to know when they find him.

He works his way back to the room where Lucas was staying. He stands there in silence. Scott comes in covered with sweat. "Good news, Father, the roof will not need as much work as we originally thought! How 'bout that?"

"That's good news," Father says in a low voice.

"Father, that boy will be back."

"How can you be so sure?"

"Well, remember the mountains of Appalachia? An animal that is injured will head for safe places. A place that they know."

"Scotty, I appreciate your help, but Lucas is not an injured deer. He is a street-smart kid who grew up in this city."

"I know, but mark my words, he'll be back."

"I think he will stay away. He probably feels that I betrayed him."

Scott steps closer. "No, Father. No way. People can feel the love you have for them. That boy will be back within 48 hours – back here."

"I pray you are right."

Gunfire is heard on the street. Both men rush out of the building. By the time they get outside, the drive-by shooting is over. They see some workers pointing down the block. One of them says, "Down there. Two cars are shooting at each other."

"This is crazy. How can these people live like this?" Scott asks. A police car flies by with lights and sirens on. They watch it as it disappears around a corner. Father looks over and sees Luggs with a mad look on his face.

CHAPTER 11
LUGGS HAS AN ASSOCIATE RETURN

Luggs walks into his house and sits in a plush chair. A woman is passed out on the sofa, and two more walk out of a bedroom, kneel at the coffee table, and start shooting up. Jason Braxter, a young white man, walks in. Luggs stands up and walks to him.

"Well, look who's home!"

"Yeah, I'm back," Braxter says as Luggs hugs him.

"How was the 'California Institution for Men'? Anything changed since my time there?" Luggs asks with a smile.

"Nothin', same 'ol stinkin' place."

Luggs pulls some cocaine out of his pocket. "Got something for ya!"

Braxter looks at it. "Maybe later. I need a woman now."

Luggs grabs the girls at the coffee table. He rips the buttons off the shirt of one of them. "Hey, don't rip it! You can touch, just don't rip it!" She stands there with her bare breasts exposed. The other girl pulls her t-shirt and bra up, exposing hers.

"Naw, man, not some crack whore," Braxter says.

"We ain't whores!" The girl in the t-shirt shouts as she pulls her shirt down.

"That's right? I bet you just came out of one of those bedrooms in the back," Braxter says.

"Shut up! You...meanie!" the other girl says.

"And such a way with words," Braxter says as he turns away.

"Look, my man Brax!" Luggs says as he pulls a wad of cash out. "You need a nice hotel on the West Side, one of them fine call girls. That'll cheer ya up!" He pulls off several hundred dollars and stuffs it in Braxter's shirt pocket.

Braxter smiles. "Yeah, that's a plan. Got to go to my probation officer first."

"Ah, skip him. Go tomorrow."

"No man. It's Spitzer."

"What? Spitzer? How did you get him?"

"Bad luck of the draw."

"Yeah, man. He's a pain," Luggs says. He thinks a moment. "Jamal! Jamal!" Jamal comes running in.

"Yeah, Luggs?" "Look who's home." Jamal looks at Braxter.

"Hey! Seems like just yesterday you were sent up!" Jamal slaps Braxter on the back.

"Maybe to you. Four years, two months, three weeks, and one day. No, not yesterday."

Luggs takes some tension out of the air, saying, "Take Brax downtown, to his P.O., then to some nice hotel. He's gonna meet the woman of his dreams!"

"Yeah, at least for a few hours she'll be the woman of my dreams." They laugh.

Luggs looks to Braxton. "I'll see you tomorrow. We got lots of business to catch up with, especially the new neighbors."

Jamal made the trip and pulled up to the P.O.'s office. "I'll wait for you over there," he says, pointing to an empty parking spot.

"Thanks. I don't know how long I'll be."

"Awhile, they love to read you the riot act and give you all the rules on your first visit." Braxter gets out of the car and walks inside the building.

The probation officer's waiting room looks like it has been lived in without a maid. The place is dirty with some broken-down furniture from the last century. A few fluorescent lights shine off the green walls, making the place look even more depressing than it is. A black man, dressed well and muscular, sits swatting at a fly with a rolled-up newspaper. Braxter looks around at the desk where a secretary should be sitting. "She left an hour ago," the man says.

"An hour? How long have you been here?"

"Over two hours!"

"Spitzer must be busy today," Braxter says. "That prick busy?"

Braxter looks through the sliding glass window to see if Spitzer heard him. "Shhh! This dude locks up people more often than the LAPD."

"I've dealt with this jerk before. He may think he's God, but he ain't." The man stands and walks over to Braxter. "Cole, Billy Cole." He extends his hand. Braxter shakes it.

"Braxter. Everyone calls me Brax. Just got out this morning."

"Yeah? I've been out a year. A whole year and this jerk just loves dragging me over the coals." Cole slaps the fly and kills it. "I should charge him for pest extermination!" Braxter laughs. Cole returns to his seat. "I really hate that guy."

Braxter looks him over. He looks tough but has no scars. He might be in his late thirties, no more for sure. He is very confident, even cocky. He seems fearless. Braxter is impressed.

"A year, huh?" Braxter asks.

"Yeah, a whole year and still showing up twice a week."

"You must have had some serious charges and time."

"Assult and battery. That's it. I'm a dope dealer by trade, but they got me on assult and battery."

"I did time for possession with intent. They framed me," Braxter says.

"Not me. I'm guilty. Caught an eighteen-month prison sentence and did eleven in county."

"For assult?"

"Yeah, you know how it goes in this business, some people want to push their luck."

A few minutes pass by, and the door flies open. Spitzer, a tall man, steps out. He is wearing glasses, has grey wavy hair, a loose tie, and a short-sleeved shirt that does not fit him well. He is also wearing a nine-millimeter pistol on his belt.

"Oh, Cole. I hope I didn't keep you waiting," he says. Cole stands and walks towards him.

"You did."

Spitzer puts his hand up and stops him. "I have a criminal before you." He looks to Braxter.

"That's okay. I can wait my turn," Braxter says.

"GET IN THERE!" Spitzer shouts. Braxter jumps up and goes into the inner office.

CHAPTER 12
A NEW PLAN FOR LUCAS

The days turn into a week and then another. Father Mark is getting work done, but he doesn't have that high step he had before. No word about Lucas has worn him out. He begins to doubt his own mission. Father Roberts sees this and becomes concerned. Some of the volunteers have rotated back east, including Jake and Scott. They left with promises to continue to pray and support the mission. Some said they would return when they built up enough vacation time again. The work continues. Father Mark is being pulled out of it from time to time for interviews.

On this day, he returns to the work site after a radio interview. Workers applaud when he steps out of the pink tire car. He gives a quick wave and goes into the building, embarrassed. "Father, we listened to your show. Great job!" Father Roberts says.

"Thank you." He starts to go up the steps.

"Father, the electrician wants to see you outside about the new motion detector lights," Roberts says as Father Mark turns around.

"Is something wrong?"

"No, they put them behind bulletproof glass, and they want to show you."

"Wow. Okay, let's look."

They walk outside and start around the building when Father Mark sees Lucas. He is stunned. Lucas looks at him with a slight, sheepish smile. The priests stand there a second. Father Mark starts to step forward slowly. A car revs its engine and flies down the street for a drive-by shooting. Everyone hits the ground except Father Mark and Lucas, who has his back to the street.

Father Mark screams out " —NO!" and charges after Lucas. That scares Lucas, but in a fraction of a second, Father has scooped him up in his arms and shields him from the shooting by turning his back to the speeding car. Bullets fly around Father Mark in the ground, kicking up dust. Suddenly, the world is silent. Everyone looks to Father Mark as he stands there, clutching Lucas tightly with his eyes shut. The people stand up and come over to him. Father Roberts takes Lucas and places him on the ground. Father Mark looks down at his robe. He pulls it to each side and sees bullet holes. He looks at Lucas, who is standing there unharmed, then he pats himself to see if he is hit.

"Miracle of miracles!" Father Roberts says. Father Mark looks back down at his robe, then back at the bullet holes in the ground. He turns slowly at first, then grabs Lucas and hugs him close. They both start laughing. He hugs him again. 'Happy to see you, 'he signs to Lucas. 'I missed you! 'he adds.

Everyone goes back to work except Father Roberts, who stands and looks at the bullet holes in the ground. He places himself in the exact spot where Father Mark was standing. He looks back, then to the ground again. He is amazed. "Miracle of miracles."

Father Mark goes inside to the office, sits Lucas in a chair and kneels in front of him. Lucas explains where he has been.

Father Roberts stands at the doorway and still has a surprised look on his face. Father Mark gets up. "He was afraid they were going to send him back to the home he had been in. Poor kid." Father signs something to him.

"That was a real miracle, Father. Those bullets curved around you," Father Roberts says.

"He says he wants to stay here. He wants me to look after him. He wants to go to school here," Father Mark says as he looks down at Lucas.

"I wouldn't believe it if I hadn't witnessed it," Father Roberts says.

Father Mark signs something to Lucas, then looks to Father Roberts. "Let's go to lunch."

After lunch, they go back to see Sister Mary Ann at her office, but without Lucas. She looks disappointed. "So you just let him go?" she asks.

"Sister, this child has had a rough life. He doesn't trust anyone in the world."

"But to think that we would send him back to a home where he says he was abused, well, that's just crazy! We would never do that!"

"You know that, I know that, but he is a child, a deaf child. Put yourself in his shoes. This is a prime example of why we need the Catholic Deaf Academy. We all assume that they know what we know, but when you're deaf, you miss a lot. He doesn't understand all the rules or the rights that he has. Now I'm afraid it will get even harder to help him," Father Mark says. Father Roberts loosens his collar slightly and feels very uncomfortable. Sister takes a deep breath and exhales hard. Father Mark speaks up. "I have an idea. He stays with me, at least until the school opens."

Sister looks at him for a moment. Father Roberts wrings his hands. "That will be a tough sale. The state will never agree to it."

Father Mark leans forward. "Sister, you know the ropes. You can make it happen."

"Father, you give me more credit than I deserve. It will be a hard sale. The state will say"-

"They will always say something. Remember, a child's life is in the balance. Sister, it's not just helping him, it's grounding him in the faith. It's for eternity. If a family gets him and let's say they don't even believe in God, they never go to church or accept the sacraments. Where does that leave this little boy who has been kicked around since he was born? I mean"-

"Okay, Father, I will try. No promises."

Both priests stand. Father Mark extends his hand. She stands and shakes it. "Thank you, Sister," Father Mark says. Father Roberts is now sweating. He shakes her hand nervously and almost runs out the door. When he gets to the hall, he hears her call to him.

"Father Roberts!" He looks at Father Mark with terror on his face.

"Yes, Sister?"

"Come in here, please." He slowly goes back to the office. "You know the church will never allow Father Rossi to keep this child. I pray you may be able to get him to understand this. I'm sure you have informed our bishop of these latest developments."

"Uh, well, Sister, uh, actually I haven't been back to the office yet, yeah, I haven't made it back there yet." He adjusts his collar again.

She looks at him for a moment. "He is your friend. Try to keep him from getting hurt. This is a brutal business. Many a good man and woman have left this field broken."

"Yes, ma'am, yes, you're right. I, uh, you're right. I'll do my best."

"Very well, Father." He looks at her for a moment while still wringing his hands. "You may go now, Father," she says. He turns and exits quickly.

CHAPTER 13
GOOD NEWS FOR FATHER ROSSI

Sister Mary Ann sits across a table from Mr. Jack Nicks, Ms. Janie Milton, and Ms. Terry Arquette at the California Department of Social Services. Jack Nicks tosses a folder on the table. "We've been at this for forty-five minutes! You just don't get it! No, no, no is the answer! You do not impress me with your robe and cross and Christ."

Sister is taken aback. The other ladies look at Nicks with a stunned look on their faces. "I mean it. We're supposed to cater to you? Just because you have some fancy church doesn't mean anything to me. You, your priest, your God, none of it impresses me! Personally, I would rather see the kid go to a crack whore!"

Terry leans forward. "JACK! I think that's enough!" Janie is stunned and looks at Sister, who hasn't moved. She sits there like a rock, staring at him. Janie speaks up. "Sister, I'm sorry. Please don't take offence to -"

"Mr. Nicks, you may mock me and our priests, but God will not be mocked, but that's a different lesson, one that you will learn in time." She stands and leans over slightly, placing both hands on the table. "Do not think that you intimidate me. That Catholic Church that you hate-"

Janie speaks, "He didn't say-"

Sister holds her hand up to stop her without taking her eyes off Nick. "That you hate has done a wonderful job placing children into good homes, safe homes. I think we should hold a press conference tomorrow and show our success rates. Get your numbers together, and we'll get ours. Let's let the world see what this church and our Christ has done compared to your results. Good day, Mr. Nicks!" She looks over at the women. "Sorry, ladies. See you at the press conference tomorrow."

Sister walks out and goes to her car. She drives back to her office deep in thought. When she arrives, Sister Annie holds up a message. "Sister Mary, CDSS called. They want a meeting with you, in person, today." She looks at the note. "A Miss Janie Milton was the one who called. She said she would even meet you after hours if that was better for you."

Sister Mary stands there a moment. "Call her back, please. Tell her I am here and look forward to meeting with her."

At the school, Father Mark is signing with Lucas. They both laugh. Father Roberts walks in, covered in sawdust. They both laugh again. "Very funny. A whole bucket of sawdust got knocked over four feet above me on the scaffolding." Lucas laughs harder and points at him. "I'm glad I can entertain you two," Father Roberts says.

Father Mark pulls a chair out. "Have a seat, take a break." Father Roberts sits down and continues to try to remove the sawdust on his back. Father Mark stands up and does it for him.

"What a mess you are making," he says jokingly.

"You should fire me."

"What? Then what would we do for entertainment?" Lucas signs something.

"What did he say?"

Father Mark laughs. "He asks if you eat sawdust!" Father Mark signs to Lucas, then looks at Father Roberts. "I told him only for breakfast." They all laugh.

Father Roberts stands and walks to a clipboard that is hanging on a nail. He writes something in a report. "I think we should head back now, call it a day."

"I'm staying here with Lucas tonight."

Father Roberts looks back at him. "Are you sure?"

"Yeah, security is here, but he'll feel better with me being here too."

Janie Milton is escorted into Sister Mary Ann's office. "Thank you, Sister, for meeting with me."

"Please have a seat," Sister says, pointing to the chair in front of her desk. Janie sits down but is nervous.

"Sister, first of all, I want to apologize. I also have a signed letter here from Mr. Nicks that he wrote and signed apologizing." She hands the letter to Sister. "He said he will come here and apologize in person today if you want."

Sister doesn't open the letter; she just puts it in her top desk drawer. "That won't be necessary."

Janie sighs in relief. "Sister, he was out of line...but, we...we decided that it, in this case, it would be alright for Father Rossi to have temporary custody. Now-"

"That is wonderful news, Janie!" Sister says as she leans back, smiling.

"Sister Mary, ah, I... I don't want to turn this into a big deal, but we have just a few conditions."

"And they are?"

"Father Rossi would still have to pass a background check."

"Of course. Absolutely!"

"And...we still have some protocol to follow, so here's how we recommend moving forward. One, Father Rossi passes the background check, and agrees that, for now, it is only temporary custody. Two, that we transfer Lucas to your agency, and you be the one who places him with Father Rossi. Three, Lucas will be given complete mental and physical examinations, and four, we all agree and work hard to find a stable home for Lucas."

She searches Sister's face for any clue. Sister Mary Ann leans forward. "Yes, I agree to those terms."

Father Mark is pitching a baseball back and forth with Lucas. They don't have baseball gloves, so the pitches are easy. Father Roberts comes flying up to the gate, jumps out of the car, and starts running towards them. "I've been trying to call you! Sister has been trying to call, also!" he shouts.

Father Mark reaches into his pocket to find he doesn't have his phone. "I left my phone upstairs. Sorry. What's wrong?"

"Wrong?" Father Roberts says as he steps close. "Brother, I have great news for you! You will get at least temporary custody of this young man here!"

"What? I.. Are you...how...who told you?"

"Sister worked it out for you, I guess. She called me because she couldn't reach you."

Father Mark grabs and hugs Lucus close. "PRAISE GOD ALMIGHTY!" He starts signing to Lucus. Lucas is confused, then a smile crosses his face. He hugs Father Mark. "I'd better call Sister now!" he says as he lowers Lucus and takes off running for the school.

Father Roberts sits down to catch his breath. He finger spells h-a-p-p-y? to Lucus, who smiles and nods his head. He starts signing to Father Roberts. "Whoa, slow down. I have a lot to learn before I can sign that fast." "WHOPPIE!" he hears from upstairs in the school. Father Roberts points to the window, "He-" he then fingerspells h-a-p-p-y.

CHAPTER 14
NEW PRESS INTERVIEWS AND CARLA
IS UNHAPPY

Press secretary Janet Baker walks into Bishop Kennedy's office as he stands. She is well-dressed and organized. "Good morning, Your Excellency. Thank you for meeting with me this morning."

"I believe this meeting could be beneficial for both of us. Please be seated."

They both take a seat, and she unzips her notebook. "Father Rossi is hot in the press right now," she says.

"He is indeed."

"Sir, I have requests here from a major national morning TV show. I also have one from a late-night show. Those are the ones I would like to discuss with you. There are several radio stations, podcasts, the Catholic Press, more than a few newspapers, and regional TV stations that also want an interview, but these two national shows will put him in front of millions of people – each show will."

The Bishop leans back. "Well, he has done very well with the others. You know he's had five reporters show up at the school?"

"Yes, sir, I'm aware. I agree that he has done well with the others, and I think he will do well with these as well. I just wanted to draft a few talking points for him." She pulls a page from her notebook and hands it to him as he sits forward on the edge of his seat. He starts reading over it.

"Wait a moment. I see you have me listed as a leader. 'Under the leadership of Bishop Daniel Kennedy, he has excelled-' wait, drop all of that." He sets the paper in his lap and leans back again. "Father Rossi, well, honestly, he has done all the hard work on this. Let's keep the credit with him, our Blessed Mother, and Christ."

"Sir, we will be in front of millions. This office has been in the national press many times, but this is even bigger than that!"

"I can't take credit for the work that he has done." He pulls a pen from the side table and starts scratching out lines. "Miss Baker, you are an excellent press secretary, and I would never want to tell you how to do your job, but we do need to make these changes."

At Lugg's house, Minion walks in to see the room filled with TV game systems and radios. Several of the dealers are sorting things out. "It's true! I heard every game station was here," Minion says. He reaches over and pulls a game system over to him. "Yeah, this is the one! Where is the cord for this?"

"Minion, don't touch it!" Luggs says as he enters the room with a girl on his arm and a drink in his hand. "You think I'm runnin' a store just for you?" he asks.

"No, ah no. I just thought I take this one and you spot me until I get paid again."

"Minion, I ain't no bank," Luggs says as he removes the game system from Minion's hands and puts it back. Minion is embarrassed and looks around at everyone staring at him.

"Ah, well,....yeah."

Luggs turns and faces him. "UNLESS... you get that pretty cousin of yours over here. What's her name again?"

"Carla. Yeah, I can do that. I can have her here next week. Yeah..." He reaches over and takes the game system. "Then I can have this game system?" Luggs takes it back.

"When she is here and agrees to the terms." Minion stares at the game system.

"How 'bout I go get her now?"

Father Mark is hard at work at the school. Several volunteers are also very busy, and the place is shaping up very well. Lucus is wearing a toy tool belt and working beside Father Mark. Janet Baker pulls in with a big man driving. She slowly gets out of the car and looks around, then across the street. She sees drug dealing and prostitution along the block. She quickly makes her way to Father Mark. "Excuse me, Father."

Father Mark turns around. "Oh, hello, Miss Baker. I didn't know you were coming today." He brushes his hands on a work apron, then removes it and shakes her hand.

"I just want to see if I could have a moment with you. I have a few things that we need to go over."

"Sure." He signs to Lucas, who removes his tool belt. "Let's go inside." Baker, Lucas, and Father Mark go to the school and into an office. "Please have a seat," he says as he points to a plush chair. She sits down, then he sits across from her. Lucas sits in a child-sized chair beside Father Mark.

"I see he is adjusting well to being with you," she says with a smile.

"He is. We're a two-man crew. Would you care for coffee or tea, or water?"

"No, thank you."

She opens a small folder case. She removes two files and hands them to Father Mark. "We have received many requests for interviews. The press loves your story. Bishop Kennedy agrees that this could be a great opportunity for the church and your school."

Father Mark looks through the file. "What? These are big national shows."

"Not all of them, but, yes, you could be in front of millions of people. What an opportunity!"

Father Mark sits back. "Miss Baker, I just want to run a school for the deaf. It's just a little, humble mission. I believe God has given me this desire so that many poor and deaf families may be helped. I don't-"

"Father, yes, I understand, but maybe God also gave you this mission to not only do that but also help the church at the same time." Gunshots are suddenly heard, and Baker drops to her knees. Father Mark opens the file again. He doesn't notice the gunfire.

"It would take me away from-" he looks up and sees Baker getting back in her seat. "Oh, I'm sorry. That happens a few times a week, sometimes a few times a day, but I am sure we'll get this neighborhood cleaned up soon."

Baker is stressed and not at all at ease. "Father, I could start scheduling you as early as next week."

Father exhales hard. "I'm not good at this type of thing."

"Oh, I disagree. Look how well you have done with the press so far!" He hesitates. "Look, I'll go with you if you want," she says. She can see that he is uncomfortable. "Why don't you show me around the school?" she asks.

Father Mark jumps up as if he is exiting a hot seat. "Sure! Great idea!"

They spend the next hour going through the building and eventually make their way to the back door. "Father, do you realize you have had an answer to each of my questions? That is how easy it will be with the press. They are going to ask you questions that you already have the answers to!"

The door opens, and Father Roberts steps in with a large screwdriver. "Hello, Mrs. Baker, Father, Lucas!"

"Good morning," Father Mark says. Father Roberts signs 'good morning' to Lucas, who signs back to him with a smile. As they stand there, they hear a woman shouting.

They step outside and go to the side of the building to discover Carla screaming at Luggs on the drug house's front lawn. She steps forward and hits his chest. He laughs. She steps back up and pounds his chest several times. He continues to laugh. Her shirt is ripped, her hair is a mess, and she is missing one shoe. Minion stands behind them with a game system. She grunts at Luggs and struggles to say words. She then turns and runs down the street. "Now come back soon! Minion is gonna need some games for his new system!" He laughs and walks back inside.

"That house is a place of pain and ruin," Father Roberts says.

"What's going on?" Baker asks.

"Girls go there every day and give their bodies for dope. It's sad," Father Roberts says.

"You're kidding?"

"No, I'm serious."

"To strangers? To men they don't even know?"

"Every day," Father Roberts adds before he walks away.

CHAPTER 15
MORE INTERVIEWS

Janet Baker glides her Mercedes 550 onto the 101.

"You did great last night on the radio show. Just do that again." He shakes his head. Father Mark looks at an open file.

"Can you hold my phone while I'm on the air? A landscape contractor is calling today. He's hard to book, and we need him."

"Sure, don't worry about the day at school. Just do your best."

They arrive at the Hall and Skylar television studio. Once inside, the crew begins wiring him up. They place him at the large circular desk, and he sits alone. The people who will be part of the live audience begin to file in. Cameramen and lighting personnel adjust, but the two hosts are not there. He checks his watch, then looks to the side and sees Baker. She mouths the word 'relax'. He takes a deep breath. Shelly Skylar and Tonya Hall walk out and sit on each side of Father Mark. Hall extends her hand. "Good morning, Father. I'm sorry we didn't get to meet earlier." He shakes hands with her.

"I understand you can be very busy before the show." He looks to Skylar and offers his hand. She looks at her papers and continues to make notes. The lights dim.

"Quiet!" someone in the dark shouts.

A buzzer sounds. "Four, three, two and..." someone says as he points a finger at the hosts.

Hall looks at the closest camera. "Good morning, world! I'm Tonya Hall."

"And I'm Shelly Skylar."

Hall looks at a different camera. "Today, we have Father Mark Rossi, a man who has a dream of building a mission here in L.A. for the deaf. He has been in the news recently as a man who is accomplishing the impossible! Welcome, Father Rossi!"

"Thank you, I'm uh, glad to be here," Father says.

"Father, I would like to ask why the deaf? Is there a need for that type of mission, especially here in California?" Hall asks.

"There is a desperate need for a mission of this type and not only here but around the world." As he explains the mission, Baker stands to the side smiling. She watches as Father Mark relaxes and represents his mission, the church, and his religion well.

"Sir, isn't it true that the church lost the last money that was raised for this? Skylar asks.

"Well, I wouldn't say 'lost', there is an investigation into-"

"And the location. West Adams is a pretty rough neighborhood to bring children into. I would think the church would be more concerned about children after their recent problems with lawsuits and lack of protection for these helpless ones."

Father is stunned. He looks to see Baker, but the lights are too bright. "I uh, I think a mission has to be placed where there is the most need. The Catholic Church sends missionaries into the most remote and dangerous-"

"Yes, but these children will go to a school and live there, in an area that is overrun by gangs, drugs, and prostitution! For the millions that the church is raising, I think another, safer location could be found. Maybe all the money raised should go into the mission and not go missing with a couple of priests!" Skylar adds.

Father Mark looks to Hall, who is uncomfortable with the line of questioning. "Just a second -" Father injects.

"We'll be right back after these brief messages," Skylar says.

Someone shouts, "And cut!"

"Jeeze, Shelly, what are you doing? He's not on trial here!"

Baker starts to walk over, but Father Mark waves her away and looks to Hall. "It's okay, Miss Hall. I understand her concern, and she has the right to ask these questions."

"Don't try to butter me up, Father," Skyler says.

"Shelly, we should at least let him get his story out."

"Those kids will end up like others that the church has abused!" The lights dim.

"Quiet on the set - four, three, two, and-"

"And we're back. Our guest today is Father Mark Rossi. He is building a deaf academy in Los Angeles for deaf children, as well as for parents, teachers, employers, and social workers who work within the deaf community. Father, how much more work before the school is finished?"

"We are ahead of schedule as of now, and we will have the first students take their seats in the Fall. But please give me a moment to address something here. I want to say that the Catholic church has had problems in the past. We are still addressing some issues at this time. However, the Catholic Church provides a place for deaf children to learn and live, in some cases, through scholarship programs, allowing many children to attend for free. Parents who cannot afford to send their children to school will be happy to know that they can send them for free! The Catholic Church has made a commitment, under the leadership of Bishop Kennedy, to stay the course, even though money was stolen, even though building supplies have been stolen, even though we have been threatened, shot at, and have struggled with some of the bad apples in that neighborhood, the Catholic Church has stayed the course. We have not abandoned the deaf community. We have not abandoned the good people who live in that community, the hard-working men and women who have watched their neighborhood, like so many others in the U.S., completely transformed into a battlefield. When so many others gave up and said there was no hope, the Catholic Church shone a bright beacon onto that crime-ridden street and said, 'We will make a stand.' We will do the right thing, we will stand for those that can't stand for themselves!"

The audience applauds.

Skylar looks at the audience, then back to Father. She leans back with a smirk on her face and restacks her papers together, tapping them on the desk.

In the car on the way back to school, Baker says, "I never saw a save like that. What a great job you did representing the school and the church!"

"I don't know. I'm really not qualified for this. It could all go bad in a single interview. That's a big weight to carry."

"Father, you just have to be yourself. You have a real thing deep in your heart, the Holy Spirit. Let him do the heavy lifting."

They drive back and arrive at the school. As they exit the car, many of the volunteers, along with Father Roberts and Lucas, greet them. Lucas starts signing quickly, and Father Mark responds. Lucas signs again, and Father Mark laughs. "What's so funny?" Baker asks.

"He says even Father Roberts thinks I'm a superhero now." He looks over at Father Roberts, who starts laughing as well.

CHAPTER 16
BILLY COLE AND BRAXTER MEET AGAIN, FATHER ROSSI MEETS THE NEIGHBORS

Braxter walks into Spitzer's office. Cole is sitting there again. A secretary sits at her desk typing on a computer. "Braxter?" she asks.

"Yeah, that's me," Braxter answers.

"Have a seat." He sits down, and she walks into the back office. Braxter looks at Cole and smiles, then scans the room where two people wait on plastic chairs. They resemble those from 'The Night of the Living Dead,' and Braxter isn't sure if they are men or women. He looks back at Cole.

"You should have seen the people who just left! Spitzer should charge admission to come into this house of horrors," Cole says. One of the people stares at him.

"Are you talking about me?" he asks, standing. Cole gets to his feet quickly. When the man sees his height and build, he slumps back into his plastic chair. Cole sits down.

"Never a dull moment with you around, huh?" Brax asks.

Cole stares at him with a blank look, then lowers his eyebrows into deep thought. "Braxter -" "Braxter, yeah! Sorry, I couldn't place your name."

"No big deal. How long ya been waiting this time?"

Cole looks at his watch. "Hour forty-five so far."

Braxter laughs. "He really loves you."

"Yep, he sure does."

The secretary walks back into the waiting room. "Floating Gum Ball, Mr. Spitzer will see you now." The two stand and quickly walk past Cole.

"Floating Gum Ball?" he asks.

Brax laughs. "It's a crazy world, but to each his own."

"Yeah? Well, he'd better keep 'his own' on the other side of this room or I'll catch another assault and battery charge!"

"People can be anything they want these days," Brax says as he shakes his head in disbelief.

"And they say we don't fit into society!" Cole says.

Cole looks around the office. "I think I killed all the flies."

"Looks like it," Brax replies.

"Next week, I should bring in some Ajax and scrub this place down."

"I wouldn't help him any," Brax says.

"Yeah, but I'm here a lot. Sort of a home away from home, if you know what I mean." Brax laughs.

Cole looks to the secretary. "You're new here."

"Just started two days ago."

Cole walks to her. "I'm Billy Cole. A dangerous outlaw, known throughout the land. What's your name?" he asks as he leans on her desk.

She looks at him for a moment, then, while still gazing into his eyes, reaches for the drawer and pulls out a manual. She looks down at it and opens it to the table of contents, scans the page, then opens to page twenty-three. "No fraternization. No social contact with inmates, detainees, or those on probation." She looks back up at him. "I know who you are, Mr. Cole. You're on my schedule." She points to her appointment book. Have a seat." Cole looks to Braxter, who whistles while making a motion with his hands of a plane crashing.

"Crash and burn."

Cole returns to his seat. "That hurt."

Floating Gum Ball and his partner walk into the waiting room and go straight out the door. Cole watches them leave. The phone buzzes, and the secretary answers it. "Yes, sir." She hangs up. "Mr. Spitzer will see you now, Mr. Cole."

Cole starts for the office door, then looks back at her. "Doris? It's Doris, isn't it?"

"No." He shakes his head and walks into Spitzer's office.

"I think he likes to do things the hard way," Brax says.

"I believe you are right."

At the school, Father Mark is outside looking at blocks that have been delivered. Father Roberts stands with his ever-present clipboard. "They're all there," he says.

"I'm sure. I'm just wondering why we need this many," Father Mark says.

An elderly man and woman walk across the street and into the courtyard of the school. They are huddled together and move quickly. Both priests see them. "Hello, Fathers," the man says as he extends his hand. "I am Richard Thompson, and this is my wife, Mildred." The priests shake hands with them.

"I am Father Roberts, and this is Father Rossi."

"I know. I have been reading about you guys and this school. Saw you on television, Father Mark." Father Mark smiles. "I wanted to come over and meet you men and tell you we are happy you are here. This used to be a great neighborhood," Mr. Thompson says.

"Really great neighborhood! I taught school here," Mrs. Thompson says.

"Really?" Father Mark asks.

"Yes, really."

"Now the neighborhood is shot all to He- ah,.. pieces," Mr. Thompson says. "To tell you the truth, we didn't expect you guys to last even this long," he adds.

Father Mark reaches into a cooler and pulls out a cold-water bottle, and offers it to Mrs. Thompson. "No, thank you."

He offers it to Mr. Thompson. "No thanks."

Father Mark twists the cap off and takes a big drink. "What happened here, to the neighborhood?" Father Mark asks.

"Drugs. Drugs and then the gangs moved in. We haven't left our house for fifteen years except to go to the grocery store. We used to have that delivered until the delivery drivers refused to come here anymore," Mr. Thompson says.

Father Mark takes another drink. "Let me show you around."

The four of them tour the school inside and out. They stop on the second floor and can see the progress that has been made. "You have done so much for this place. Its old glory is returning!" Mrs. Thompson says.

"Thank you. It's been an uphill battle, but the good Lord and His Blessed Mother have provided," Father Mark says.

"What grade did you teach here, Mrs. Thompson?" Father Roberts asks.

"All of them at one point or another. We had a great school and excellent teachers. When I retired, things began to slip. Actually, three years before I retired, I began to notice problems. We just lost the kids. They didn't want to learn, and that makes for a difficult student."

"I can imagine," Father Roberts says.

"Our Danny boy attended here. He was a good boy," Mr. Thompson says. Mrs. Thompson looks away with a tear in her eye. After a long pause, Mr. Thompson says, "I worked in the aerospace industry. Forty years, then retired and came home to street violence, gangs, and drugs. It's been a mess. Right next door to my house, Mr. Palmer was shot to death while sitting in his dining room having lunch. Mrs. Palmer moved shortly after that." He points in the other direction where Luggs lives. "That blue house over there belonged to Wes Snyder. Great man. He was shot while taking his trash out one day, but lived. He moved his whole family to Washington state after that. But back in its day, this neighborhood shone. There used to be a corner grocer at the end of the block. You could walk to it day or night. Mr. Caster and his wife ran it. It was set on fire one night and burned to the ground. They were both inside with their little granddaughter." He thinks for a long moment. "Yes, this place has seen better days. Maybe you boys will get things turned around."

Father Roberts looks to him. "That is our plan, sir. Let's bring the whole neighborhood back to what it once was!"

Mrs. Thompson walks to a window. "You are making progress. Don't stop, please don't stop."

Lucas walks in. Father stoops over and picks him up. He signs something to Lucas. "Mr. and Mrs. Thompson, this is Lucas. He was living on the streets, but we are making a home for him now. He has been such an inspiration for me!" Father Mark says. They shake his hand.

"I have seen you, little man. You took some trash out of my trash can a few times," Mr. Thompson says. Father Mark signs to Lucas. Lucas signs back.

"He says he is sorry."

"Oh no, don't be. I'm not mad, I was just so worried about you." Father Mark signs to Lucas.

"He won't have to eat out of garbage cans anymore," Father Roberts says.

"Yes, you are making wonderful progress here, gentlemen," Mrs. Thompson says.

CHAPTER 17
A NEW PROBLEM BREWING

Tag Collins sits in her office on Hoover Street in Los Angeles. As president of Abortion Alliance for America, she is always busy. She is wearing dress slacks and a sleeveless white dress shirt, and has a U.S.N. tattoo on her right arm. She is about eighty pounds overweight and wears a constant frown. Shelly Tally opens the door and peeks her head in. "Are you ready? They just arrived," she says.

"Yeah, move them to the conference room." The door goes shut. Collins retrieves a folder from her file drawer and exits.

She arrives at the conference room first, but only by seconds. Tally and two other women walk in. One is short and overweight. She holds an unlit cigar in her hand. The other is six feet tall, with long black hair, shining blue eyes, and a million-dollar smile. Tally steps up and brings her along. Tag Collins, I would like to introduce you to Jo Susan Little, a top model and advocate for our cause.

Collins shakes her hand. "Please be seated," she says as they all sit down. "You have done so much for abortion and abortion rights in our country. I want to thank you," Collins says.

"Thank you, and so have you!" Little responds.

"And so have so many others. It seems we make great progress and then we get kicked in the teeth, blind-sided by someone that we least expected." Collins opens the file and retrieves several photos from various news clippings of Father Mark. "This is Father Mark Rossi -"

"I saw him on TV just a few days ago. He has a school or something," Little says.

"Yes, and he is getting very big. I'm worried," Collins says.

"Worried? I thought it was a deaf school. Isn't it?" Little asks.

"Yes, a deaf school, but you know how these Catholics are! All of those Christians...they just want to take everything from us! We cannot allow him to build a world stage. Believe me, he will use it to talk about the 'sins of abortion'. We are going to stop him before he can't be stopped! Besides, all the attention he is getting will always be bad for us, even in a deferred way. People are stupid. They vote for, spend money on, whatever they saw last. Every day he is out there on the radio, TV, the newspapers, is a day that the people are not paying attention to our cause, and you know there is no cause bigger, more important, with more on the line than ours."

Little looks around at the other women. They seem to be sitting on the edge of their chairs, waiting for the next words of wisdom from Collins.

"How? How are you going to stop him?" Little asks.

"You."

"Me?"

"Yes, you." Collins leans back in her chair, takes a deep breath, as Little scans the other women again. "You see, I have a plan to trip him up. Those hypocrites preach one thing, but they all do something different. When he gets to see you in person, well, his heart will melt. I'm sure it happens with all men that meet you. They are such dogs. Predictable, pathetic, and he will come running."

Collins shoves the file to her. She pulls out a picture of Father Mark.

"Can you do that?" Tally asks.

"He is a handsome man. I worked with male models who didn't look as hot as him. Yeah, I'll do it!"

Collins sits up straight and leans in. "Good. We will now have a support team available for you. A very expensive fundraising dinner is planned for next week. Black tie affair. We got two tickets. You are going, and you will claim that your date was called out of the country for business. Because of that, you will not be able to contribute yet, but you will be alone to move in on him discreetly. Your job is to meet him, talk him into bed -"

"Wait a minute! I'm not a call girl!"

"No, no, you're not. We're not saying you are. You just have to get him into a hotel room, get his shirt off, and the hotel staff will take some pictures and release them to the press. You will at first deny any affair, but as the pictures gain traction, you will confirm it with all the naughty details! Little hesitates. "I have set aside twenty thousand dollars for this. Most of that will go in your pocket," Collins says.

"We want you to take your time. Don't rush it and scare him," Tally says. Little still hesitates.

"I want you to take ten grands with you tonight. Put that under your mattress. That's an advance for you," Collins adds.

"Okay, I'll do it. I'll meet him at the dinner, but what will be my excuse to meet him again?"

"That's where you will cast your web. You'll know then, based on how he acts, what your next step should be. This is going to be easy for you, just work your magic!" Collins says.

"It may not be that easy. You know he has taken an oath," Little says.

Collins laughs. "Are you kidding me? I don't care what oath he took; when he sees you, he will want you. Hell, I want you, everyone wants you! He won't stand a chance against your looks and charm!" Collins exclaims.

"You are already making the press from time to time. If you go out to eat, there is a chance the press will see you, so we want you to keep the first few meetings with Rossi private," Tally says.

"I would think that it would work better to be seen with him," Little says.

"No, they will rein him in immediately, and we will be playing catch-up. Better to play it out. That's why we are saying take your time, do it right, and let's get him good," Tally says.

"You know, on every march we have those Catholics show up with their pro-life signs. Then you have those guys playing bagpipes, little children holding hands with their beautiful, wholesome mothers. It's sickening. I want to slap them so hard. For the rest of the world, we don't live in their little bubble world. We fight for the underdog, the poor women who can't afford snotty kids. Those who can't be saddled down for nine months to carry a child. Abortion is the answer to so many problems. They don't see it that way."

"If I didn't have an abortion, I would not have had my career," Little adds.

"That's right. All the successful women have had abortions and moved right on with their careers! Look at the women who are running big companies today - most have had abortions," Tally says.

"So I spent some time with him, then made a date to meet at a hotel. How will the staff know to get pictures?"

"You'll go to a pre-determined hotel. We will have the room covered with audio and video. We will then hand that off to a staff member, who will release it to the press," Collins says.

"You got a guy that will do that?"

Collins looks at her a moment. "In almost every hotel, honey."

Little looks at the picture of Father Mark again. "He doesn't stand a chance against you guys, does he?"

CHAPTER 18
BRAX TALKS TO COLE ABOUT A JOB, CARLA FINDS HELP

Brax walks out of the P.O.'s office and sees Cole looking down the street. "Waiting for your ride?"

Cole looks back and sees him. "Yeah, I think she drove off and left me. Maybe she heard me flirting with the secretary."

"I didn't see her up there," Brax says.

"She's crazy. Always keeping tabs on me. Oh well, time for the next one. I'm gonna go get a beer." He starts to walk across the street to a bar.

"I'll join ya!" Brax says. Cole waves him over.

The bar is cool and dark inside. It takes a moment for their eyes to adjust. They see a booth and walk over to it. Cole motions for the barmaid. "Two beers! Whatever is on tap." They sit down.

"You do want a beer, right?" Cole asks.

"Yeah. That will be fine. Don't you think it's a little risky to drink this close to Spitzer's office?"

"Man, I don't worry about him." The beers arrive, and Cole slaps down a fifty-dollar bill. "Keep 'em coming," Cole says. She picks it up and retreats back behind the bar.

"Are ya workin'?" Brax asks.

"Here and there. Just took a job to go to Vegas and collect some money. It paid well."

"Are you allowed to leave the state? I'm not."

"Spitzer again. You worry about him too much."

"Don't you?" "If he goes to Vegas to gamble and if he happens to be in the same back alley that I was in, and if he happens to see me in my mask and if he recognizes me, well then, I guess I'm busted. Gotta make the doe, you know."

Brax sips his beer. "I wish I could be that carefree about it. I just don't want to go back. I hated being behind bars."

"Oh, it's no picnic, and I guess no one but really hard cases likes it, but I ain't gonna live in fear of nothing or nobody. I may not always be free, but at least I'll know I lived by my own code."

"Are you working now?"

"Are you writing a book?"

"No, sorry. I just thought maybe you should meet my boss. He's a good guy. Took care of me when I was locked up because he knew I kept my mouth shut. That's why I like working for him. Screw him over and you'll be dead by morning. Do your job, keep your mouth shut, and the job has lots of perks and the 'doe'."

"Yeah? Put a word in for me."

"I will. Can't make any promises, but I will tell him about you."

"Great!"

They drink several rounds, talking like old friends. Cole checks his watch. I gotta go."

Brax gathers up some of his change and stuffs it in his pocket. Cole does the same. "You need a ride?" Brax asks.

"Yeah, but I don't want to put ya out. I'll grab a cab."

"You sure. It's no problem. I mean, it's the least I can do since you bought most of the beer. Where do ya live?"

"Beverley Inn on Beverly Boulevard."

"I don't know that joint. You'll have to show me." They get up and walk out.

It's a short distance, but a traffic accident delays them for several minutes. Finally, they arrive at the Inn. Brax pulls up and stops near the office. "Thanks for the ride."

"Hey, no problem. I'll talk to my boss. He has a job for me, and maybe you can ride along with me. It's out of the county."

Cole opens the door, gets out, then closes the door and looks through the open window. "Let me know. I'm always ready to go." He taps the car roof and walks away. Brax pulls out into the traffic and drives to Lugg's house.

Inside, Jamal is counting money, and Minion is playing video games. "Where's the boss?" Brax asks.

Jamal keeps counting and motions with his head to the hallway. "Back bedroom. He has company." Brax takes a seat opposite Jamal. After a moment, he goes to the refrigerator, grabs a beer, and then returns to his seat. Luggs comes out of the bedroom.

"Brax, my man! I need you to make a short trip for me."

"Sure thing. When?"

"Now."

"Okay, ah, I also want to tell you about this dude that I keep meeting in Spitzer's office."

Luggs gets a small case with cash in it. "Alright, what about him?" Brax spends the next twenty minutes telling Luggs about Billy Cole. Luggs asks a few questions and is satisfied with the answers. "Alright, put him to work, but keep him at a distance to start until he proves how righteous he is."

"You got it, Luggs. I'll put him in with me and see how well he does."

"Don't give him too much info and be cautious if he starts asking questions."

"He'll be fine. You just watch. Besides, I can use the help."

Brax collects the cash and makes a trip to the Port of Los Angeles to deliver it. The thirty-mile trip passes quickly as evening loses the last of the daylight. Brax spends more time thinking about how to get a woman for the night than on security. He sees blue lights flashing behind him on the 110. He pulls over and sees he has the money case in plain sight. He slaps it on the floor and pushes it under the seat with his foot. It becomes stuck with part of it still exposed. The policeman walks up to the car.

"You know how fast you were going?"

"No, sir."

"Driver's license and registration." Brax pulls his licence out, opens the glove box, and retrieves the registration. He hands them over. The cop walks back to his car with them. Brax kicks the case, but it will not budge. He kicks it again, and it pops open. Cash spills out. He slowly slides some of it under the seat with his foot while constantly looking in the rearview mirror for the cop. He accidentally gets some of the money stuck on his shoe. He starts to wipe his feet when he sees the policeman approaching.

"Here's a ticket for speeding. Sign this; it is not an admission of guilt, and you have the right to contest the citation. Information is on the back to do that." Brax quickly signs it.

The cop's radio on his shoulder comes alive. "Attention all units in the sector 42 area. BOLO, white Dodge Charger, involved in a gas station robbery, last seen heading south on the 110, south of Harbor City, Wilmington. Consider armed and dangerous." At that moment, the charger speeds past Brax and the police car. The officer grabs the clipboard, rips a sheet from it, tosses the sheet into the car, and runs back to his vehicle while speaking into his microphone. He floors the accelerator in his car and passes Brax.

"Yes, sir, and you have a good day also, officer!"

He reaches down, retrieves the money, puts it back in the case, and pulls out into the evening traffic.

The next morning, Luggs is sitting on the porch. A few of his lieutenants sit with him. Luggs sees the Thompsons carrying a cake and walking to the school. "Look at that. Those old people haven't come out of their tomb for years now, they be walking a cake to the preacher. What's the neighborhood coming to?"

Jamal looks over and watches as they enter the school building. "So? Ain't like they be competing with us." Luggs gives him a disapproving look.

"Jamal, you are dumb. You need to see the big picture sometimes. They be there walking the street, then more neighbors start coming out, then they all start rebuilding their homes and yards. Meanwhile, we sit here like a sore thumb, and our buyers stop coming around."

Jamal looks back at the school, then back to Luggs. "Over a cake?" Luggs shakes his head, shoots down the rest of his energy drink, gets up, and walks inside.

A car pulls up to the curb, and Minion gets out of the back. Carla is fighting two men inside. Minion runs in the house and comes out with Luggs. From the porch, he sees the men trying to drag Carla out of the back seat.

Across the street, Father Mark sees her struggle. He starts walking quickly to the front gate. A volunteer steps up with him, "Father, this ain't none of our concern. You shouldn't go. I'll call the police and let -" Father doesn't take his eyes off the scene.

"You do that." He continues walking across the street. The volunteer stops and dials his phone.

Luggs sees him coming and starts down off the porch. "WHOA! WHOA! WHOA! You stay off my property!" Carla is now being held off the ground. One man has his arms under hers, and the other is holding her feet. She is kicking and trying to scream, but the first man covers her mouth. She sees Father now beside her. He looks and sees pure fear in her wide eyes.

"NOT TODAY, LUGGS!" he shouts. Luggs uses both hands to shove Father back into the street, where he falls. Father Mark gets back on his feet and grabs Carla's wrist. He shoves one of the men holding her, and he falls. Carla scrambles free and gets to her feet, quickly moving behind Father Mark. Luggs pulls a 9mm pistol out and aims it at Father's head.

"You are about to cash your own ticket! I HAVE HAD IT WITH YOU!" Father steps back, never taking his eyes off the pistol as he gently pushes Carla back towards the street. Luggs cocks the hammer back.

"FIVE-O!" Jamal shouts as a police car cruises up with the lights on. Luggs hands the pistol to Jamal, who hands it off to another man who quickly goes into the house.

Father Mark keeps walking backwards, with Carla holding his robe tightly. The two policemen get out. "What's going on here?" He asks.

"This man is trespassing on my property! I want him arrested!" The cop looks at Father Mark.

"This woman was being attacked. I came to help her. Ask her!" The cop looks at her. She grunts, trying to explain. Father Mark is stunned. "Wait! Are you...?" He starts signing. She signs back. "She's a deaf officer! She was being-"

"Okay. This needs to go to social services. I don't speak deaf or sign language."

"Wait, officer, I do!" Father Mark says. The cop looks to Luggs.

"Social services, Father, that's where she needs to-"

"But I can-"

"If she wants to go with you, then she can. If not, I'll call social services." Father signs to her. She signs back.

"She wants to go with me."

"Good." Father takes Carla by the arm and starts back across the street. The cop looks at Luggs, then walks back to his car. His partner is already in the driver's seat. They drive off.

Luggs walks inside and smashes the coffee table. "He's a dead man walkin' - DEAD!"

"Am I still gonna get my game?" Minion asks.

Father Mark has Carla in a classroom. A nun, Father Roberts, and two volunteers watch as Father Mark and Carla sign to each other. Father Mark stops and stares at her for a moment. He stands, turns, and faces the volunteers. "Sister, I need you to go with me to the hospital. I fear she may be in need of medical aid. She says Luggs assaulted and raped her the last time she was there, and this time he was going to do the same thing. The group stands in silence.

"I'll go with you," Father Roberts says.

"No, I need you to keep the place running, Father."

They go out to the pink-wheeled car, and Father Mark drives, while Sister sits in the back with Carla, holding her hand. They arrive at the General Medical Center and, after a long wait, move back into an examination room. A female nurse walks in.

"I'm Brandy, an R.N. here at General. Father, I think I can take her from her."

"Yes, ma'am, but she is deaf. I can interpret if you need me. Let me tell her I am going to the waiting room and who you are." He signs to Carla. She gets a panicked look on her face and shakes her head no. They sign some more.

Brandy sees that she is afraid. Finally, Father stands and signs something. "Okay, she is going to be okay with this. We'll be in the lobby if you need us."

He and his sister walk out. He paces as his sister sits in a chair and silently prays the rosary. She finally stands and escorts Father to a chair. They both sit. "Pray, Father. Worry will get you nowhere."

"You're right, Sister." He bows his head and prays silently. A minute later, Brandy walks out. Sister elbows Father. He looks up and sees the nurse. They both stand.

"She has been assaulted. We have contacted law enforcement."

"Oh, that's great! Get them involved and maybe get some justice for this young woman!" Father says.

"Can you stay until they get here? I'm sure you can provide some details that they will need," Brandy says.

"Yes, I can."

Two LAPD uniformed policemen, Sgt. Jenkins and Officer Taylor arrive a half hour later. Brandy motions for Father to return to the back. Jenkins reads the medical report that Brandy hands him. "She's deaf?"

"Yes, but there is -"

"No DNA evidence from the attacker?"

"No. It didn't happen today."

He looks up at her with raised eyebrows. "It's a she-said, he said story?"

"I can interpret for you if need be."

"Who are you?" "I'm Father Mark Rossi. I have a school next door to where the attacker lives."

"Did you see it, the attack?"

"No, I was-" Jenkins hands the papers back to Brandy.

"No witness, no DNA, she's deaf, I don't think there is much that can be done."

"What? This young woman has been raped!" Father says.

"Look, the D.A. will not touch this case with a ten-foot pole. What'd ya want me to do? Write a stack of reports that will not even be read and then have to find a deaf interpreter, fill out more paperwork, waste a lot of time for a case that will never see the inside of a courtroom!"

Father is stunned. He looks to the nurse for some support. She looks away. "This woman has been raped!"

"Says you. Nothing else supports her story."

"She has bruises. It was enough for the hospital to call you!" Father says.

Jenkins looks to Brandy. "You don't have a case here. Don't call us on something old, especially if there is no evidence!" He looks to his partner. "Come on." They start walking out.

"Who is your supervisor?" Father asks as they are walking away. Jenkins turns and rushes back to Father Mark. He pulls out a notebook and starts writing. He rips the sheet out and slaps it in Father's hand.

"Call him! What do you think goes on in that section of L.A.? Do you think people are sitting around praying with the Angels, like in church? NO! People get killed, people get maimed, people get raped. Get something solid, and I will personally make sure that someone shows up and makes an arrest!" He storms off.

On the drive back, Father Mark doesn't say a word. The three arrive at the school and exit the car. "Sister, let's see if we can do anything for her right now. Can you call Sister Mary Ann and get her up to speed?"

"Yes, Father." She turns and walks into the school.

Father looks to Carla and signs 'go with her. It will be okay. He then walks into his office. He leans over his desk and stares at the wall.

Father Roberts walks in. "That was close today. Too close! We need to be careful if we-"

Father Mark spins around. "I know! I know! I was the one looking down the barrel of a pistol!"

Father Roberts sets his clipboard down. "I was-"

"I'm sorry, Father. I'm just a little over the top. I have a lot on my plate. We have run into problems that I never imagined while dreaming of this school."

"Hey, it's okay. You are under a lot of stress. Can I get you a coffee?"

Lucas walks in, signing. Father Mark signs back and smiles. "I seemed to have even worried the little man." Father Mark picks him up and hugs him.

They all walk over to some chairs and take a seat. Father Roberts walks out. Father Mark signs to Lucas. A few minutes later, Father Roberts returns with bottled water, coffee cups, and a thermos of coffee. "What shall it be for you?" he asks. Father Mark grabs a coffee cup. Father Roberts pours some coffee from the thermos into it. He then takes a bottle of water and hands it to Lucus, then gets one for himself and sits down.

"Thank you. Taste fresh."

"It's only an hour old," Father Roberts says. Lucus signs 'thank you'. Father Roberts signs, 'You're welcome.' They drink up. "Father Rossi, that was a close one today. God's angels are watching over you. I think you need a few days off. You have been working so hard, we're all tired, so I know you're exhausted! Take a break."

Father Mark takes a big sip of his coffee. "I can't. I have these interviews, meetings, hiring, and mail... the mail is stacked high in the other room. I need to answer these letters. Then there's the finance meetings, the -"

"Yes, all of that, but you have to stop burning the candle at both ends, or you will burn out. Then where would we be?"

CHAPTER 19
FATHER ROBERTS WORKS ON
A NEW PLAN

Billy Cole is sitting in the passenger seat of Braxter's car.

They are on the 405, turning East on 2. "When we get there, I will be ready. I've got two pistols. A nine-millimeter and this," Cole says as he pulls a .380 out of an ankle holster.

"What is that James Bond shit there?" Brax asks.

"A three eighty. Clip fed. I can reload both of these fast if I had to."

"No kiddin'?"

"No, really."

"Well, we ain't gonna need to do fast reloads. We're not even gonna need a gun tonight."

"What? A drug deal with no guns?"

"That's right. They ain't gonna have one." Cole stares at him in disbelief. "Man, it's Hollywood! You know who Trace Abbott is. We're going to his crib."

Cole looks out the window, then back at Brax. "Who's Trace Abbott?"

"What? Get out of here! You know! The star of the TV series, 'Dealin'! He plays our lives on TV.

"No kiddin'?"

"Yeah, man, and I'm his main supplier. Now, look, when we get there, don't tell him you're an actor or a screenwriter or a director. That drives him nuts. As a matter of fact, don't say anything. This is a good contact for us. We'll be supplying all of Hollywood before you know it!" Cole looks out the window. "I can't believe you never saw his show. Everyone in America watches his show, maybe the whole world!"

Cole looks back at Brax. "How can we supply all of Hollywood? We'd have to haul it up in by the truckloads."

Brax pulls his sunglasses down and gives him a suspicious look. "Let Luggs do the thinkin'. We do the rest."

"Okay, man. Okay, cool."

Jo Little stands in front of a mirror in a store in Beverly Hills. She is turning side to side, showing off her perfect figure in a designer dress. A saleswoman stands beside her. "You look beautiful!"

"Thank you. I will take this one and the shoes too," Little says.

"Of course." The saleswoman snaps her fingers, and an associate comes over to gather the shoes, boxes, and other dresses. "I wish you would model for us. We do a show here twice a year. Our clients love it!" the saleswoman says.

"Call my agent. I'd be happy to do that."

"Great! Leave me with their contact info."

"Certainly."

The woman stands back and admires Little. "Men are going to love you in this."

Little unzips the side. "I only need one man to love me in this."

She steps back into the dressing room and emerges wearing her jeans. She goes to the counter and retrieves her packages. A sales clerk hands the last bag to her. "It's on your account, Miss Little."

"Thank you," she responds as she heads for the door.

Once outside, she hails a cab and gets in the back. "Good afternoon. Where would you like to go?" the male driver asks.

"I need to get a new pair of sunglasses. Any place you can suggest?"

"Oh, for you, Miss Little, absolutely."

He pulls into traffic. His radio is on, and a Father Rossi interview is heard. After a few moments, she asks, "Have you heard about this guy?"

"Yeah, I think he's great! I'm not Catholic, but for someone to make a stand like that....well, it's something we all wish we could do."

"But what about abortion?"

The driver looks in the rearview mirror. "Abortion?"

"Yeah, he is against a woman's right to terminate a pregnancy!"

"Oh."

"People like him and his church hate women. They think their place is in the kitchen, barefoot and pregnant!"

"Oh."

"I hope they shut him down."

The driver squirms in his seat. He stops the cab in front of the Saks Fifth Avenue Store. "Saks okay?" he asks.

She pulls some cash out of her purse and hands it to him. "Yes." She waits for her change.

"Oh, yes, some change," he says, counting out the change and handing it to her. She hands a dollar to him and gets out without another word. He watches her walk away. "Well, that view is my tip, I guess."

Father Roberts walks into Bishop Kennedy's office as Kennedy is closing a file. He stands and greets Father Roberts. "Good afternoon. Please be seated."

"Good afternoon, Your Excellency." They both sit down.

"How are things on the frontier, Father?" Kennedy laughs.

"Well, we are reinforcing the fort all the time."

"Good."

"Thank you for taking the time to meet with me."

"Oh, I'm glad to do it. I have been wanting an up-to-date report for some days now," the bishop says. "So how are things? How is Lucas?"

"Well, we are doing well. I really believe we will be ahead of schedule and slightly over budget. Lucas is doing great. I can't tell you how hard everyone is working - especially Father Rossi."

"I'm sure he is. There is a lot going on there."

Father Roberts clears his throat. "Yes, sir, there is. I think we need to distribute some of Father Rossi's workload among several people. I say this, not to deny the great work that he is doing, but to take some stress off of him. He hasn't had a single day off."

"What? He isn't scheduled to work every day!"

"No, sir, he isn't, but he is always there, tying up loose ends, making decisions, helping out every day. I think he and Lucas should go fishing or something."

Bishop Kennedy gets up and walks to the large window. He looks out over the city in deep thought. "You're absolutely right. I want you to design an organizational chart."

"Me?"

The bishop turns around. "Yes, you. You will be the second-in-command."

"Me?"

"Yes, you have been there since he started. Maybe a post or position for security, construction, school admin, you know what I mean."

"Ah,..yes sir,..ah we, I mean, well, yes sir, and then have it pending his approval and of course, yours also."

Bishop Kennedy walks back to his desk and sits down. "Very well. Make it happen, Father!"

Father Roberts spends the evening, night, and half of the next day writing out a proposal. After presenting it to the bishop, it was decided that two positions would be filled immediately: Father Roberts as Admin Manager, second in command, and a private secretary for Father Rossi. All other positions would be reviewed by Father Mark and the accounting staff.

Father Roberts made the trip to the school with Sister Clair sitting in the passenger seat. She had just arrived in L.A. a week prior, having come from a school in Maine. She thought she was coming to L.A. to be part of a new ministry focused on Bible study and education. That program was behind schedule, so the bishop moved her over to a new job. She was also highly trained for the task, and that was the clincher for Bishop Kennedy. She is tall with pale blue eyes and blond hair.

"Now this assignment may be a little tougher than you are used to," Father Roberts warned.

"Is Father Rossi hard to work for?"

"Oh no. Just the opposite. It's just the location has had some issues - including gunfire." He looks over at her, and she turns her head to face the windshield. She watches the town slip by in silence.

"It's okay. You know God knows what is best. He has a plan."

Father Roberts chuckles to himself. "Oh, you're going to get along just fine with Father Mark!"

They pull into the schoolyard and park beside some construction materials. They both get out, and Sister Clair looks around at her new assignment. Father Mark sees them and walks over with Lucas right beside him. They are both wearing hard hats.

"Father Mark, I would like for you to meet Sister Clair," Father Roberts says.

Father Mark wipes his palms on his cassock. "Hello. It's a pleasure to meet you."

"Hello Father," she replies.

"Are you here for a tour?" he asks. Father Roberts steps over and puts his arm around him, and starts walking to the front door. He reaches back, and his sister hands him a folder. "Let's have a talk," Father Roberts says.

They walk inside the office, and Father Mark pours some coffee into his cup. "Can I get you a coffee, Father?" he asks.

"No, thank you." Father Mark turns and sees Father Roberts sitting at the table. He joins him.

"Now let me say something. We all know what a good job you are doing." Father Mark spills a small amount of coffee on his cassock. He sets his coffee cup down and quickly wipes up the spill. "You have been the man with the vision, the man–"

"It has been a team effort inspired by God," Father Mark says.

"Yes, sir, you're right. But I asked for some help for you – not to take anything away from you except the burden that you carry every day." Father Mark has a puzzled look on his face.

Father Roberts takes a deep breath and continues. "We think it would be best to put a staff under you. Each person is responsible for their department and all reporting to you." Father Roberts wrings his hands.

"That's great. Can we afford it?"

Father Roberts exhales a sigh of relief. "Yes, Father. Yes, we can. I'm so glad you are not upset. I didn't want you to think that I or anyone was trying to upstage you!"

"What? No, Father, I appreciate all the help we can get. You have been working extremely hard for a long time now. We do need the help."

Father Roberts opens the folder and shows Father Mark his organizational chart. Lucas walks in and sits down. They take notes and engage in a lengthy discussion. An agreement is reached.

At Trace Abbott's house in the Hollywood Hills, a party is underway. Cole and Brax stand just inside the mansion. Before them is a sunken living room that is larger than any house Cole ever lived in. Waiters walk around serving glasses of champagne to anyone who wants one. Cole sees three men huddled in a corner, reading a script. The ceiling is twenty feet over their heads. A stairway, which is at least twelve feet wide, winds around a circular elevator. A butler goes to the double door, which stands two stories high, and allows more guests in.

Trace Abbott walks down the steps with two people close behind. He is wearing an outfit that resembles a woman's attire. He holds his hands out and takes Brax into a hug. He whispers, "I need more than I ordered, my friend." He then leans back and looks for a clue on Brax's face. Brax breaks into a smile.

"No problem! For you, anything Trace. You know I love you."

Trace smiles and looks around the room. "You're my main man, Brax!" He looks to one of the men who followed him down the steps. "Johnny, get Brax whatever he needs."

Cole watches as Johnny steps up, and Trace goes over to the new guests. "Let's take a walk," Johnny says, and they both step outside. Cole steps out with them, and Johnny stops and turns around. "Who are you?"

Brax steps up. "He's with me, Johnny. Be cool, it's all alright."

Johnny looks at Cole for a minute. "You wait here."

"No. It doesn't work that way."

Johnny is not happy that his order has been challenged. "I said wait here or-"

"Boys, boys. Billy, wait here a sec, huh?" Brax says as he takes Johnny's elbow and leads him to the car. Cole watches at a distance as Brax opens the trunk and they make an exchange. Johnny walks off and goes into the back of the property. Cole walks over and gets in the car, where Brax is already waiting behind the steering wheel. They pull out.

"That was a risk," Cole says.

"Nah, this is Hollywood. They ain't gonna rob us, especially with a hundred guests milling around."

"You put too much faith in people, man." They drive out of the Hollywood Hills.

"There is a place in Hollywood that I want to stop at and get a cheeseburger. You want one?" Brax asks.

"A cheeseburger?"

"Yeah."

"Alright." They get to the In-N-Out Burger restaurant. The line at the drive-through is long. Brax picks a parking spot and parks. They walk inside, place their order, pay, and then leave with a bag of burgers.

When they get back out, they see a Ferrari parked near them in the lane. "You'all gotta move that junker. That's my spot," a young black man says. He is wearing many gold chains and standing beside his car. A young woman gets out of the Ferrari.

"No, that's public parking for customers," Brax says as he walks to the car.

"No, it's my parking spot! You know who I am?"

"No," Brax answers. The man looks away with a huff, then back at Brax.

"I, Money Mo, the rap singer. I know you've heard of me! You do have a radio, don't ya?"

"I don't listen to rap. Look, we're leavin' now so you can have your spot."

Brax and Cole walk towards the car. Money Mo grabs Brax's arm and spins him around to face him. "Not until you say you're sorry."

"What?"

Cole walks a little closer and takes Brax's other arm, pulling him towards the car. "Let's go," Cole says. They turn, and Money Mo shoves Cole hard in the back. Cole pushes back off his car and spins around. In a flash, he brings his foot high and kicks Money Mo under the chin, sending him back on top of the Ferrari. Money Mo lands with a thud. He reaches for a pistol tucked inside his belt. Cole closes the distance between them and grabs Money Mo's wrist with one hand and the pistol with the other. He twists Money Mo's hand back towards his head and quickly disarms him. He takes the pistol and strikes Money Mo in the jaw.

Money Mo falls to the ground and spits out two of his teeth. Brax looks to the young woman. "You need to pick better boyfriends."

She stands there stunned. "What? You know who this is? It's Money Mo! How many, what kind, radio, how many...."

"Easy, sister. You're gonna strip a gear," Cole says as he gets in the car.

"How many songs you got on the radio?" she shouts as they back up. Cole starts ejecting the bullets out the window from the clip into the parking lot, then he tosses the clip out as they pull onto the street.

"I ain't never seen someone move so fast. MAN! You were like a Kung Fu master!" Brax says.

"Oh brother."

"I mean it. Chop, wop, smack," Brax says as he drives, taking his hands off the wheel to demonstrate. Cole rolls his eyes.

After a couple of blocks, he sees a mailbox on the street corner. "Stop here." Brax stops. Cole gets out and puts the empty pistol in the mailbox. He gets back in the car and they drive off. "All these entertainers are packin' these days," Cole says.

CHAPTER 20
CARLA

Father Mark and Sister Clair are walking down the hall at the retreat, heading for Sister Mary Ann's office. Sister Clair holds her notebook up to her chest and follows closely. As they pass another office, Father sees Sister Mary Ann and stops quickly. Sister Clair runs into him. "Sorry, Father."

"That's alright."

They step to the doorway. "Sister Mary Ann, you wanted to see me?"

"Yes, Father." Sister Mary Ann hands a file to Sister Maria.

"Hello, Sister. How are things with the stunt driver's association?" Father asks. Sister Maria smiles.

"Slow." They both laugh. She takes the file and walks out.

"Be seated, Father," Sister Mary Ann says. "Sister, you too." She points to another chair. "Father, the state is going to schedule an inspection appointment for Lucas. You must secure a two-bedroom apartment or house right away."

"Okay, I will."

"Also, they will be looking at the kitchen. It must be clean and safe enough for food prep."

Sister Clair starts taking notes. "Okay, I can do that. What else do I need?" Father asks.

"The place has to be safe from any potential accidents. No chemical cleaners were left in the open where Lucas could reach them. You should cover the outlets that are not in use. Plenty of clean clothes, that type of thing."

"Okay, I can do all that. Thank you, Sister, for helping me with this. When are they coming?"

"Soon, so get an apartment right away, like today or at least within the next few days. Lucas is scheduled for his exam next Friday at General."

"Okay." Sister Clair continues to take notes.

"Sister, what about Carla? What is her status?" Father asks.

"We did get a police report filed. So far, nothing has happened. She was returned to her uncle." Father starts to say something. Sister Mary Ann raises her hand. "I know, I didn't like the idea either. We had no choice. Do you know her cousin Dewayne Hollins?"

Father thinks a moment. "No ma'am, I don't."

"Well, he works at the house next to the school. She is more afraid of him than she is of her uncle. I managed to get social services involved, and they are reviewing the uncle, the home, and her status regarding health, welfare, and education. I believe she is another girl who just fell through the cracks. Maybe we can get her into your school this Fall."

"That would be great. I'll pencil her into a spot."

Sister Clair's phone rings. She steps out to answer it. She returns in less than a minute. "Miss Baker is looking for you.

She wants to meet you at the school, but she is willing to come here. Which do you prefer?" Father looks at her for a moment.

"Can it wait?" Sister Clair gets back on the phone, and Father looks back at Sister Mary Ann. "About Carla, where is she now? Can she come to the school today?" Clair steps back in.

"She says it's important." Exasperated, Father turns back to Sister Clair.

"Okay, the school. We'll leave in just a few moments." Sister turns back towards the door and passes the message. Father turns back to Sister Mary Ann.

"I will follow up about Carla. You concentrate on Lucas. You have to have a secure place before the state's visit," Sister Mary Ann says.

Father stands. "Yes, ma'am. Please keep me updated on Carla. You should have seen the fear in her eyes."

"I have seen that fear many times, Father."

On the trip back to the school, Sister Clair continues to take notes as Father Mark drives. "I'll start calling some real estate agents about the apartment," she says.

"Great, I appreciate that. We have to be sure that Carla has a spot at the school."

Sister Clair writes in her notebook. "Yes, Father."

"She was so scared. It was unbelievable, and she has to deal with that fear daily. I'll keep praying for her and ask you to do the same."

"Yes, Father, I will."

They continue driving, deep in thought. "I'd like to know how she ever ended up at that drug house. She told me she does not take any drugs. We need to get the full story. Hopefully, she will come visit us soon."

They pull into the schoolyard and find Baker standing outside, waiting for them. "That was fast," Father says as they unhook their seatbelts.

"Father?"

"Miss Baker, she got here fast."

"Yes, sir."

They get out as Baker walks over. "Hello, Miss Baker," Father says.

"Good afternoon, Father."

"Let's go inside," he says. They start inside after Father greets several of the workers and signs greetings to the deaf volunteers.

In the office, Father Mark first hugs Lucas and signs to him. They both laugh. Father Roberts walks in. "They are getting ready to pour new concrete. I thought Lucas would like to see that," he says. He then signs to Lucas very slowly. Lucas nods his head and smiles.

"Be careful!" Father Mark says. They walk out, and Sister Clair takes a seat. Baker walks over and sits at the table as Father Mark also takes a seat.

"Father, this dinner. It's big."

"Can I get out of it?"

"Nice try, no."

"Have you seen some of the mail that I am getting?"

"Some and it's very positive. It's great!" Baker says.

Father looks to Sister Clair. "Can you get the mail that I stacked on my desk?"

"Yes, sir." Sister walks out.

Father looks back at Baker. "Not all of it. You know we're running a risk each time we deal with the press and the public. I think we should just do what I came here to do."

Baker smiles at him. "Father, you being in front of a microphone has only helped us. We have raised a substantial amount of money; you have given the church a new face. People love you - even people that are not Catholic!"

Sister Clair walks back in. "Oh, really?" He takes a small stack of envelopes and places them on the table. He then pulls out the first letter and starts reading it. "Dear Catholics. You bunch of child molesting con artists are all going to Hell, if such a place exists! You put a handsome priest on TV, and he lies about what you're going to do with the next several million that you are asking for. How can you take money from the poor to give to homosexual men who like little boys? I hope you die today. Die, die, die!" He opens the next one. "Slick. You bastards are slick. Always the money. We all get to go to heaven as long as we give you money." He retrieves the third letter. "I am sick of the spin-"

Baker interrupts. "Okay Father, some people will never be happy or believe that we are trying to do a good thing, but for every one of those letters we get a hundred praising the work, the church, your mission!" He reaches the last letter in the stack, opens it, and begins reading. "I hope to kill you myself. I was one of the many boys that was molested in Boston. Now I'm a man with bullets-"

Baker grabs the letter. "That one I need. That's a clear threat!"

Father leans back in his chair. "We might be ahead to just do the good thing and not talk about it so much. There is a young woman who was raped across the street. We should be spending this time on that."

"Did you tell the bishop about this letter?"

"No."

"The security office?"

"No."

"I will!"

"Miss Baker, it doesn't matter. That man has a reason to be upset-"

"Not to the point of killing someone!"

"Why not? Someone wronged him, and now he wants to wrong someone else. I'm not condoning it, I'm just saying I understand his anger. He has carried this big burden throughout his life. No amount of settlement money is going to make that right." She sits motionless, looking into his eyes. He reaches across and retrieves the letter from her. "Don't turn it in. He was probably just venting. We need to pray for him."

She pulls the letter back and places it on her side of the table. She then gets up and goes to the window. She looks outside and sees the concrete truck pouring concrete. She looks across the street and sees the Thompsons putting up a bird feeder with the help of neighbors. "The community is a much better place with this school here," she says.

"Yes, the neighbors brought a cake over recently," he says.

She turns back to him and returns to her seat. "I'll stop taking so many requests, but we have to honor the ones we are committed to. You'll do great at this dinner. It has already raised twenty-four thousand dollars!" Father scratches his head.

"I'll be there, but this should have been the bishop's dinner. He is the bishop! He should get some credit. It's not all about me. Look outside at those workers- many of whom are volunteers- and what about the people who are sending their hard-earned money to us? They should be praised. Father Roberts, the staff, you, and the office people are putting in so much time and effort. They should be given credit. The press thinks I'm here doing it all myself."

"No, Father, they don't. We have mentioned those who are helping build this place in almost every press release. You are the poster child- like it or not- and most people would."

"I want to help the deaf and the people who help the deaf. I don't want to be in the paper, on television, or on the radio."

"Father, we'll go a little lighter on your schedule, but no one can replace you on this project. You're too far out there now."

CHAPTER 21
LUGGS IS MAD

Luggs watches out the window and sees the activity at the school. Jamal is stacking cash as he watches Minion and some other people play video games. "Look over there! They are getting stronger and braver every day! We are losing!" Luggs says.

"No, we're getting rich, Luggs. Look at this, take just from yesterday. Now that Brax has opened Hollywood, we should be looking for a yacht or something. A new car like the actors drive up in Beverly Hills."

"A Rolls?" Minion asks.

"Yeah, a Rolls-Royce! I think I'll buy two!" Jamal answers. Luggs exhales hard and shakes his head. He walks over to the table and sits down. Brax walks in. He tosses some cash on the table.

"Easy, don't get it mixed up!" Jamal says.

"You should have seen it! Billy Cole, Kung Fu master! Some dude gets lippy with us over a parking space and Billy - wop, chop!" Brax says as he demonstrates with his hands and feet. "Smack! Chop! That dude hit the ground and spat teeth out after he pulled a gun on Billy and me!"

That catches Lugg's attention. "He pulled a gun on you?"

"Yeah, told me to say I was sorry, but Billy - Hiya! Chop! - laid him out and took his gun away from him. It was beautiful, man."

"He took his gun away from him?" Luggs asks.

"Like it was candy for a baby. He charged him and took it away. Some rapper thought he was as tough as his songs, but Billy set him straight!"

Luggs sits in deep thought for a minute. "Maybe it's good we have him. You keep him near ya, let him help you with Hollywood. Any new contacts there?"

"Yeah, Luggs. The business is GOOD! The sky's the limit. I got a call on my way here. The cameraman at Sin City Productions wants a lot."

"Sin City?"

"Yeah, the porn company. He has a big wish list and cash! Brother, we are in good now!"

Jamal places the money in a bag. "See Luggs? I told you. We are fine! Forget that school!" he says.

"That school will be trouble for us! The neighbors are coming outside now! They put a bird feeder up! This ain't 'Mr. Roger's Neighborhood. This is our turf!" He shakes his head and stands to look out the window again.

Jamal looks to Brax. "The boss is really upset with that preacher man."

"I see he is."

Brax walks into the kitchen and comes out with a beer in hand. "Hey, that's my beer!" Minion complains.

"Then I owe you one, Minion!" Brax sits at the table across from Jamal.

"How much do you need and when do you need it?" Jamal asks.

"Tomorrow. All you can spare," Brax answers.

Luggs stands at the window with his hands in his pockets. "They paying C.O.D.?"

"Yeah, all except Trace Abbott. You know from the 'Dealing' show? I've spotted him a little. He has some big parties that help me get more business. That's where the cameraman came from." Luggs doesn't look at him. Brax takes a big sip of his beer. "Luggs, we're gonna own Hollywood by the time we are through," Brax says. Luggs continues to stare out the window, deep in thought.

"Go ahead and bring that Cole around. If he's that tough, maybe he can help us with that eyesore across the street," Luggs says.

"Sure, I can do that," Brax says.

"That problem over that is only going to get worse. I should have run him off on day one," Luggs says.

"Luggs, are you ready to go to the meeting?" Jamal asks.

"Yeah."

They walk out the front door and go to the car. They drive off and merge into the I-10 East. "You know that priest, well, something needs to happen to him! We can't afford the police getting sympathetic to him or any do-right causes," Luggs says as Jamal drives.

"Don't worry about him. We're gettin' stronger and bigger every day. We ain't just West Adams anymore."

"I know, but of all the places on earth for him to open a dumb school, it has to be in my front yard!" They arrive at the Los Angeles State Historic Park.

"I don't see him," Jamal says as he shuts the engine off. Luggs looks around for a second.

"Come on, let's get out. He's got too much money on the line not to show up."

They get out and walk into an open space. J.P. Stalker walks up. He has shed his LAPD uniform and is wearing a tank-top shirt and shorts. His muscles bulge as he flexes. He is also carrying a gym bag. "Aren't you afraid to be here without your uniform on?" Luggs asks.

"I'm afraid to be here with it on. My shield would draw a lot of attention here," Stalker says.

"Tell me, how is this better than my house? You wanted somewhere else, and here we are trading in broad daylight in gangland!"

"Your place is on the news a lot because of that school. That's all I need - to be seen walking in with dope in the background of the six o'clock news," Stalker says.

Luggs slams his fist into his palm. His face tightens up, and he grits his teeth. "HOW! How do you think this thing looks for us! The open market is closed! People have to come inside on some days! GET HIM OUT! I want that priest DEAD!"

"Calm down. My job is to deliver the goods to you. Your job is to maintain your business."

"He could put us out of business!" Luggs says.

"If he does, I'll be making deliveries to some other dealer!"

Luggs can't hide his anger. He paces in a circle, then charges back to Stalker. "My place from now on!" He drops a large envelope of cash at Stalker's feet. Stalker hands the gym bag to Jamal.

"No, it ain't happening that way. I'll pick a spot and tell you where for Friday," Stalker calmly says. He picks up the envelope and walks away. Luggs storms back to the car with Jamal in tow. Jamal throws the bag in the trunk, gets in the driver's seat, and starts the engine. Luggs stands outside and watches Stalker walk behind some trees and make his way to the street and out of sight. Luggs flops down in his seat and slams his door shut.

"Let's go!"

It takes almost thirty minutes to get back to the house, and Luggs doesn't say a word the whole way. When they arrive, Luggs gets out and marches into the house, flops down in a large recliner, and lays his head back. Jamal comes in with the dope. "Boss, you ain't talkin'! That always makes me worry," Jamal says.

Luggs closes his eyes. "Shut up, Jamal!"

The next evening, Brax and Cole are pulling into Trace Abbott's place. People are milling around. Mexican construction workers are working on the double doors at the entrance. Cole and Brax walk in through an open door. "Hello!" Brax shouts. No one responds.

"Maybe ain't nobody home. Either that or they're dead upstairs," Cole says.

"Not funny," Brax replies as he walks to the stairwell. "Hello! Anybody home?" A woman in a bikini walks in from the other living room and heads for the steps.

"Going for a swim upstairs, boys. Are you?" Brax takes a long look at her.

"Ah, no. Is Trace here?"

"Who?" she asks.

"Trace Abbott, the owner."

"I don't know him." She walks past them and starts up the steps.

"See? I'm not the only one who never heard of him," Cole says.

"How can that be? How can she be here?" Brax asks.

"This is Hollywood, buddy," Cole answers. He walks across the large foyer and looks in a room, then across the floor and looks in another. He goes to the steps. "HEY! Anybody here?" he asks.

Abbott walks in through the front door with an entourage. "Braxter, my man!" Abbott says as he holds his hands out. Brax steps up and takes both hands.

"I watched your show last night. You were awesome!" Brax says. "Was it on last night?"

"We have a delivery for you," Cole says.

"Well, look at Mr. All Business here," Abbott says.

Brax gets nervous. "He doesn't mean nothin' by it, Trace. Don't you worry," Brax says.

"I'm not worried. Not with you here, Brax honey." He looks back at one of the men with him. "Where's Johnny?" he asks. Johnny walks in the door with a golf bag full of clubs.

"Here, I'm here," he says.

"Johnny, Brax needs to talk to you," Abbott says.

"Let's go!" Johnny says as he motions to the door. Brax starts for the door with Cole a couple of yards behind. Johnny steps between them, cutting Cole off. Cole steps forward, passes both of them, and goes out the open door. They follow.

"Okay, how much you have?" Johnny asks as he places his Akoni Sonis sunglasses on his face.

"I got it here in the car," Brax says. They start walking to the car. "You guys always have a party going on, don't ya?" Brax asks.

"Always."

"Must be nice. Saw a fine, and I mean fine, woman heading for the pool," Brax says.

"You want her, Braxton?" Johnny asks.

"I'm sure Trace wants you to be happy."

"Yeah, right," Brax says as he retrieves a bag from the car.

"I mean it. Come with me and I'll be sure you have a good time with her!" Johnny says as he takes the bag and hands Brax a leather wallet. "Ain't sure how much is there. Put the rest on our account. Now come on, let's go back in."

Brax looks to Cole. "Wait here. I won't be long." Cole rolls his eyes, crosses his arms, and leans back against the car.

CHAPTER 22
THE FUNDRAISING DINNER

The Ritz-Carlton Hotel was selected as the venue for the fundraising dinner. Father Mark was nervous as he entered the plush place. A large foyer in front of the meeting room offered a spectacular view of L.A. Baker, who is right behind him, and Sister Clair is right behind her. Father Roberts walks into the foyer from the meeting room. "Good evening, all! We have a great crowd waiting in there." He walks over, shakes Father Mark's hand, and quickly hugs Sister. Baker extends her hand to him, and he gently shakes it. "Are you ready?" he asks Father Mark.

"I don't know."

"He's ready and he'll do just fine. Watch him!" Baker says as she pats him on the back.

They walk into the ballroom and see several circular tables across the floor. Each table accommodates up to four guests. Four long tables sit end to end at the front of the room. Bishop Kennedy stands talking with a man behind the tables. Many people wave to Father Mark. "Smile and wave," Baker says quietly without moving her lips. Father smiles and goes to the first table. An elderly man stands up to greet him.

"Father, my name is Russo," he says, his voice laced with a heavy Italian accent. He points to the people at his table. "My wife Sofia, my son Vincent, my little girl Maria." Vincent stands and shakes Father's hand.

"It's a pleasure to meet each of you," Father says.

"Father, I came to this country as a young boy. I go to school in the very school you have! I learn much, work hard. One day I started a business became wealthy! God has provided for me! I give to the church often and have donated to your school. I hope you can regain that precious place!"

People watch and wait as Father listens to Russo's story. Baker gently glides Father to the next table. A man stands. "Father, Congratulations on your school. My name is Richard Bransworth. This is my daughter, Minnie." Father shakes his hand and looks to Minnie. She signs hello. He signs back to her. "My wife, Gloria, and my business partner, Paul Henry." Henry stands and shakes hands, then returns to his seat. "As you can see, my beautiful daughter is deaf. I wish for her to attend your school. She has had the best of private tutors. I will spare no money on her education and well-being. However, I also want her to receive some religious education. I think you're just the man for that."

"Yes, sir, I can sure help there and would be more than happy to welcome her to the Catholic Deaf Academy," Father says.

They continue their conversation. Baker moves to her table, and Sister stays close to Father, taking notes when needed. They slowly work their way across the room. Jo Little sits in anticipation at a table closer to the front. She has on a short black dress with a low-cut top. She is stunning. Three other women sit at her table. She watches his every move. She gets nervous because he is taking so much time at each table. She checks her watch, ten till seven. She brushes her hair back. Father is deep in conversation with each person he meets. She continues to check the time.

Father moves to the next table. An elderly lady sits there with a young man. She has an oxygen tank on her wheelchair and breathes from the mask occasionally.

"Hello," Father says, extending his hand to hers.

"Good evening, Father. I am Mildred Hopkins. My husband, the late William Hopkins, and I ran the Hopkins Foundation. This is my nurse, Tony Wilson." Wilson stays seated and gives Father a quick wave.

"Nice to meet you both," Father says.

"I am happy to see the work you are doing. If something isn't done, West Adams will be as bad as all of East L.A. I am interested in making a substantial donation to your school. Can we meet next week?"

"Yes, ma'am. Do you have a card?" She looks to Wilson and takes a deep breath from the mask. He stands and retrieves a business card. Sister Clair steps over, and he hands it to her.

"Wow! Are all nuns this pretty?" he asks.

"Yes, in God's eyes all of his creation is beautiful," she says. "And as for the nuns, they are all very committed to God and God alone." He registers a look of disappointment and sits down.

Father finally makes it to the table beside Jo Little. Four men stand and shake hands with Father. They go into a long conversation. The lights flicker, and the room gets quiet. The lights dim, and a screen lowers from the ceiling. A short film starts playing. Bishop Kennedy comes on the screen with a prerecorded message. "Welcome all!"

A voice-over explains the size of the deaf population. "If you were to put every deaf person in one place, they would be the third largest nation in the world." The voice explains how employers are reluctant to hire deaf employees due to a lack of communication. Little looks back and sees Father quickly moving to the big tables in the front and taking his seat. Little's phone lights up. She looks at it and sees a text message from Abortion Alliance for America president Tag Collins. 'Any luck yet?' Little types discreetly, 'Not yet, just starting.' She then turns the phone face down on the table.

The film runs for ten minutes, featuring video and pictures of the school and its ongoing work. A voice-over announces key points. The film stops, the lights come up, and the people applaud. Bishop Kennedy moves to the small podium. "I'm Bishop Anthony Kennedy. I oversee part of the Archdiocese of Los Angeles. I am happy to stand here this evening and introduce a new priest to our diocese. Although new here, he has accomplished a great deal in such a short amount of time! We were on the verge of closing the project down, of selling the property, but the vision of this new priest was contagious. Against impossible odds, with the help of God, this new priest set out to do what God sent him to do." Father Mark squirms in his chair. "The work is not finished, as you have seen in the video presentation, but it is moving towards the finish line every day! You have helped make that dream a reality. You have provided the funds that help us take a drug and gang-infested property and reclaim it for righteousness, for the church, for the neighbors, and for God!"

The people applaud. The bishop raises his hand and says, "Children and adults will be able to attend and learn. Some will go back to their homes and start a deaf program to serve the hearing-impaired in their communities, including overseas. Another opportunity to spread the Good News of the Gospel."

The bishop continues his speech as Little's mind races to figure out how to get to Father Mark. "So please allow me to introduce you to the man with the vision, the man that has to be given credit for the great work that he is doing by following God's orders, the man that will make a great difference for deaf people around the globe, Father Mark Rossi!" The people stand and applaud. Father seems embarrassed as he makes his way to the microphone. He holds his hand up, and people slowly start sitting back down. Father clears his throat.

"Thank you. I have been given much praise from the time I entered the hotel this evening. I appreciate your kind words, but I must say that to God be the glory. I also want to thank the volunteers who have worked, in some cases, day and night. We have even had volunteers come from the East Coast. Then there are the donors, you. You have made this possible! We have another video that is going to show how the school is structured, what classes are being offered, and how we will help churches, schools, non-profit organizations, and volunteers reach out into their communities and make a difference." The lights dim, and the screen lights up again.

Father steps away into the darkness. He slips out a door, goes down the foyer, and into a restroom. He turns the water on at the sink and splashes his face. He places his hands on the counter, then splashes his face again. His hands return to the counter, and he leans on them, letting the water drip back into the sink. The door opens, and Father Roberts walks in. "You okay?"

"Yeah, Father, I'm fine. Just needed some fresh air."

"I understand. Miss Baker sent me in. I'll tell her you're fine and will be right back in."

"Thank you."

Father Roberts exits. Father Mark splashes his face again. He takes a towel and wipes his face. He sets it on the counter and looks in the mirror. He combs his hair and steps back into the foyer to go back into the dining room.

Jo Little is standing there. "Hello Father."

"Oh, hello."

"I wanted to see you. I think the work you are doing is wonderful."

"Thank you, but like I said, many people are helping."

"Yes, but I can see you carry a lot of stress. I'm a model and I know what stress can be like."

"Ah, yeah, it, ah... It can take a toll on a person, that's for sure."

"I have a place that I go to when I get too stressed out. It's a little place right off the ocean. It's in Notleys Landing, Carmel-by-the-Sea. I go there, watch the ocean splash against the beach and rocks, and just relax." She steps closer and rubs his shoulder. "You are tense. I enjoy having a bottle of wine, watching the sea, and simply pampering myself. For all the work you do and for all the people you help, you deserve a break. I can arrange a weekend for you, maybe us." Sister Clair comes out the door and into the foyer. Little drops her hands immediately and glares at her. Sister looks at her, then Father, then back to her.

"Father, we need to get back inside. They are serving the meal now." She walks over and wraps her arm around Father's arm and leads him away. Little steps up and hands a pre-written note with her name and phone number on it. She hands it to Father.

"Call me," she says. Sister reaches over and takes the note from Father. Little gives her a mean look, and they all walk back inside.

The meal is served. Father doesn't eat much as he spends time going from table to table, answering questions, posing for photos, and shaking hands. Father Mark moves back to the microphone for a question-and-answer period. Tom Bowers stands first. "Father Rossi, Tom Bowers from the LA Times."

"I remember you. How are you, Mr. Bowers?" Baker, Kennedy, and Muller all sit up at the same time.

"Fine, Father, thank you. Sir, my question is, has any of the previously raised money been found?" Kennedy stands immediately.

"Sir! We are still investigating that matter!"

"Good evening, Bishop Kennedy. Can you comment on the investigation from law enforcement?" Baker stands.

"Mr. Bowers, we have released all the information we can. There is a hotline for people to call if they have any information." Kennedy steps over to the microphone.

"I want to say it now loud and clear. Not one penny of the funds raised since Father Mark Rossi took control of the project is missing. An independent CPA firm, Farmer and Miller, has been retained to oversee the entire financial accounts every week. Father Rossi has complied with and has passed every single review."

"But what about the missing money? Over one million dollars had disappeared before Father Rossi took over. Has any of that money been found?"

"Sir, I'm going to refer you to the Los Angeles Police Department since it is an ongoing investigation!" Baker says.

"Thank you," Bowers says, then sits down.

Two hours later, the last of the guests leave. Father Mark is stretched out on a chair. Little parts her legs, then crosses them, then parts them again, then stands. She smiles at Father Mark. Sister Clair glares at her. Little positions her hand like a phone and whispers, 'call me,' then walks out. Father Muller and Bishop Kennedy come back in from the foyer. "Great night," Father Muller says.

"Except that reporter again!" Kennedy says. Father Mark rubs his eyes and stands.

"Long night," he says.

"You did well!" Baker says as she pats Father on the back.

Father Roberts can see how tired Father Mark is. He walks over to him. "Can I borrow your phone?" Father Mark asks.

"Sure," Father Roberts says as he pulls it out of his pocket and hands it to him. Sister Clair steps closer to hear who he is calling.

"I have to check on Lucas. Sister Mary Ann has him now, and I told him I would be back to get him and take him home."

"How's he doing?" Baker asks.

"Good, I should say great. He has really opened up and brings us smiles every day, hasn't he?" He looks to Father Roberts, and he picks up the conversation.

"Oh my yes. What a joy and what a complete change. He no longer fears each night, and he no longer has to scramble for food each day. He has really come into his own."

In the parking lot, little is texting Tag Collins. 'No luck yet, but the seed has been planted. I might need a beach house at Notleys Landing, Carmel-by-the-Sea.' She waits a moment, and a reply comes back, 'No problem, just say when. Can you come in tomorrow and brief us? 'Little types 'Yes' and sends it. She then puts the phone down, starts her car, and pulls out into the night traffic.

The next morning, Sister Clair enters Father Mark's office, where he is signing papers. "Good morning," he says after looking up at her, then returning to his papers.

"Morning." She sits a few files down and then opens a folder. Here is a list of homes to live in for your review. " He stops writing, looks up at her, and leans back in his chair.

"What's wrong, Sister?"

"Wrong?"

"Yes, what's wrong?"

"What do you mean, Father?"

"Well, last night you had very little to say in the latter part of the evening. This morning you're late to work. I"-

"I'm sorry, Father. There is no excuse for being late."

"That happens to all of us at one time or another, unless you are riding with Sister Maria. I'm not really concerned about that."

There is a long silence between them. She rings her hands and becomes nervous. "Father, ah....it's not my job to address a priest about....well, ah...."

"It's about last night. The model." She hesitates, then nods her head.

"Father, I do not assume the task of, well, pointing out that temptation is always...ah..."

"Sister, you are right. I was wrong. I had temptation in my heart. I am truly sorry. I have gone to confession this morning-"

"Father, you owe me no explanation."

"Oh, but I do. I was wrong. I just saw her and was so tempted. I was wrong."

"She was very beautiful. I can see how a man can be tempted. It's just so much is riding on this. So many would love to see the church get a big black eye right now."

"You are right, totally right. I need to keep my guard up. I failed last night. God sent you in at the right time." She smiles. "Please continue to keep me on the right path. Thank you, Sister. I promise to do better."

She takes a deep breath, then relaxes. "Great! Thank you, Father. I just want the best for you, the school, the church."

"I'm blessed to have you in my corner. Feel free to correct me anytime."

He reaches for the folder and looks at the homes. "Some of these are out of the question. I cannot afford them." He continues to look. "Wow, I like this one!" He holds it up and shows her.

"Nice," she says. He looks through some more.

"This is nice too. I want Lucas to go with me to see them."

"I'll make arrangements, Father. If I can get an appointment today, could you and Lucas go then?"

"Yes, ma'am." She takes them and walks toward the door.

"Sister." She turns back to him as she reaches the doorway.

"Yes, Father?"

"Thank you for being a friend."

Jo Little walks into an empty conference room at the Abortion Alliance for America and takes a seat. She sees a tray with several water bottles and glasses. She reaches to them, turns a glass over, and pours a few ounces of water into it, then takes a sip. Tag Collins and Shelly Tally walk in and sit down. "Tell me all about it," Collins says as she lights a cigar. Little scoots back from the smoke. Collins quickly extinguishes the cigar.

"He can be had. Easier than I thought. He undressed me with his eyes before I left as I gave him a great show, but he has a winch that stays by his side."

"Huh?" Tally grunts.

"A nun. Don't know her name, but she hovered all over him all night. He's probably making it with her!" Little says.

"Nah, I don't think so. Most nuns get caught up in marrying Jesus and all that crap. No, she's just protecting him. He's a little gold mine for the church. I heard he raised over a hundred grand at that silly little dinner! After you trap him, he's gonna want to give it to you to keep you quiet," Collins says.

Little takes another drink of water. "I don't know," she says as she sets the glass down.

"How do you know that he wants you? Did he say that?" Tally asks.

"No. No, he didn't, but I rubbed his shoulders and he melted. He loved it. He looked at me, starry-eyed, and saw himself in a beach house with me for a weekend. I was going to kiss him, but little Miss Righteous walked in on us. The little winch."

Collins stands, goes to a cabinet, and opens it. Several bottles of booze await. She pulls a drawer out, and it is full of glasses. "Can I get you a drink, Jo?"

"No thanks." She pours one glass and returns to her seat.

"Where did you leave it?"

"I gave him a paper with my name and phone number. That winch took it from him."

"Hmm, we'll have to find a way for you to see him again. Maybe a visit to the school."

"His little fairy godmother will be waiting there by his side," Little says.

"How about where he lives? You just bump into him in the neighborhood. He won't have his nun with him then," Tally suggests. Collins nods her head in approval.

"Could work. Where does he live?" Tally and Little look at each other.

"I don't know," Little says.

"Me neither," Tally adds. Collins takes a drink.

"We'll have to find out. Shouldn't be too hard. If you're sure he is interested, we'll up our game," Collins says.

"Oh, he is interested."

CHAPTER 23
COLE MEETS LUGGS

It is dark outside as Luggs sits in his big chair, reading the sports page by the dim light of a cheap lamp stand. He is wearing glasses, which is something he hardly ever does, at least not in view of the many people coming in and out of the house. The door opens, and Cole and Brax walk in. Cole is surprised. He expected to walk into a fortified command center, but it looks like he has entered someone's home, as the man sits reading the paper. The lights are dim, and Cole strains his eyes to see how many people are in the room and where they are seated. "Hey, Boss, this is Billy Cole, the man I have told you so much about. Billy, this is the boss, the man I have told you nothing about." Luggs stands and removes his glasses. He stares at Cole for a hard moment.

"So, it's Billy Cole, Kung Fu master, tough guy extraordinaire, a man that sets his own pace," Luggs says.

"I don't know about all that, but I do my best."

"So, what do you think of operations so far?"

"Well, I haven't seen much except a few deliveries."

"Well, what would you change?" Cole looks at Brax, then back to Luggs.

"Is this an interview?" Luggs looks at Brax and bursts out laughing. He walks over and puts his arm around Cole.

"Yeah, Brax, this is a righteous dude!" They walk over to the big table and sit down.

"Minion!" Luggs shouts. "MINION!" Minion comes out of the living room with a video controller in his hand.

"Yeah?"

"Get us a beer, us at the table, not you," Luggs orders.

"But it's my beer," Minion says.

"NOW!" Minion stomps into the kitchen and comes out with three beers. He sets them on the table, then storms back into the living room. Luggs looks to Cole. "What'd ya think of Hollywood?"

"Everyone is crazy there."

"About the operation?"

"Well, it should do well; everyone up there is high as a kite. I think the cops are high too." Luggs laughs.

"So, I understand you and Mr. Spitzer are the best of friends."

"Oh, yeah, we're good fishing buddies. I love the guy." Luggs laughs again.

"Yeah, Brax, I can see what you see in him. I like him."

Luggs quickly flips the table over on Cole, knocking him to the floor. He shoves the table off, but before Cole can even think of getting on his feet, Luggs jumps on his chest and aims a gun at his temple. "Are you sure you're Billy Cole?"

"LUGGS! What are you doin'?" Brax asks as he stands with spilt beer on his clothes. Minion and some others run into the dining room to see what is going on. Cole lies there calm and quiet.

"What's your problem?" he asks.

"I ain't gonna have no one checking up on me, arresting me, stealing from me, or killin' me!" Cole stares at him.

"If I were gonna kill you, you would be dead."

Luggs leans back and slowly lowers the hammer on his pistol. He then stands and looks down at Cole, holding a pistol in his hand. Luggs realizes that Cole could have shot him. Brax exhales hard. Luggs reaches out his hand to help Cole up. Cole rejects it and stands. "Yeah, you're fearless. Welcome to the biz." Cole holsters his pistol back on his ankle and stares at Brax, then looks to Luggs as he sets the table upright and sits down again. "Where did we leave off?" Luggs says as if nothing has happened.

The next afternoon, Brax drives with Cole sitting in the passenger seat. They are in a 1970 Chevrolet Chevelle SS that is in mint condition. "I'm sorry about last night. I had no idea he was going to do that. He never has before. He's stressin' over that school across the street. You were pretty cool through it all," Brax says.

"It wasn't funny."

"I ain't laughing."

"Neither am I," Cole says. He looks out the window for a few moments, then back to Brax. "Why are we in this car? It stands out to cops."

"Yeah, but it stands out to women, too." Cole shakes his head.

"Well, we'll have to remember that while we're sitting in prison."

"Not me. I ain't ever going back."

"Where did you get this thing?"

"Hey, this is a classic muscle car. Every man wants one, and they cost a ton of money IF you can find one for sale. I got this one from a guy who owed a lot. He gave it up in lieu of some of the dough he owed."

"Well, we got a load in the trunk, and we are in a flashy car. Seems like we're lookin' for trouble. Where are we going anyway?"

"Hollywood baby, Hollywood! That is after I get you up to Spitzer. Man, he makes you come every week. I don't have to do that routine anymore. Once every two weeks for me."

Cole thinks for a moment. "Are they paid up?"

"Yeah, everyone except Trace."

"He needs to pay up. It's gonna get too far behind for them to catch up," Cole says.

"Are you kidding? Trace makes big money. That show pays him over a mil a week, I bet. His house, I think Johnny told me the payments on that house are forty-two K a month! They ain't gonna go broke!"

"Yeah, but that doesn't mean they're gonna pay either!" Cole says.

"Ah! You worry too much. Trace is my friend. He wouldn't think of cheating us!"

"He'd run over you and your grandma."

They pull up and park in front of the P.O. office. Brax looks to Cole. "Try to be quick this time. We got lots to do today."

"Yeah." Cole reaches for the door handle as Brax pulls out a kit with some cocaine. He retrieves a mirror, then a razor, then the coke. He pours it on the mirror and starts cutting it up with the razor blade. "Oh boy. Don't get too jacked up," Cole says.

"I'll see ya when you get back," Brax says. Cole opens the door and walks into Spitzer's office.

An hour later, Brax is pounding the steering wheel to music on the radio. Cole walks out and gets in the car. Brax quickly pulls out into the traffic. "Well, that didn't take as long as usual. Under two hours, I think he is starting to like you now," Brax says.

"Yeah, he loves me, alright."

They arrive at Abbott's mansion. It's another large crowd. People mill around in the small space outside. Brax is forced to park on the narrow street. "I don't think you can park here," Cole says.

"Yeah, we can. We're important to Trace."

"Oh yeah? Well, we may not be so important to the police. You're blocking the street." Brax looks behind him, then back to Cole.

"Only a little." He gets out and starts walking for the front doors. Cole reluctantly gets out and follows him.

The two-story front doors are once again wide open. Cole sees many Mexicans working on the walk, doors, and some inside are laying a new tile floor. Cole waits at the door. Johnny sees Brax. "Brax, my man!" he says as he makes his way through the construction obstacle maze.

"Hey, Johnny. Trace around?"

"Entertaining company - if you know what I mean!" Johnny says as he elbows Brax in the side.

"Huh, oh, yeah. I got some goods for ya."

"Good, let's go outside." He looks to Cole. "You wait here."

"You don't tell me-"

"It's okay, Billy. I'll be right back," Brax says as Johnny leads him out the door.

Once outside, Johnny looks back to make sure they are alone, or at least as alone as they can be in a party mansion. "Hey, be careful. I think one of them Mexicans may be a cop," Johnny says. Brax stops in his tracks.

"What?"

Johnny takes a breath and looks over the Hollywood Hills, then back to Brax. "Ah, you see, the cop that is an advisor to the show 'Dealin' told me that a cop may be here."

Brax throws his arms in the air. "Oh, great. Is he sure?"

Johnny pulls a cigarette out of a gold case, taps it, and puts it between his lips. He puts the case back in his pocket and retrieves a Zippo lighter. "Who knows? We can't take a chance."

"Fire them," Brax says.

Johnny lights his cigarette and takes a big draw off of it. "Yeah? Fire them? All of them? The place would come to a halt. You know it's still not finished? Eight bedrooms are being added on to the back as we speak."

Brax turns and looks at the mansion. "How much room does he need?"

"More baby, always more. What ya' got for me today?"

"How much do you want?"

"Double last delivery."

"Double?"

"Yes."

Brax starts doing some mental math. "Stop worrying. I got a stack of cash for you."

"Enough to catch up?"

"Well, maybe not that much, but come on, you know he's good for it." Brax thinks a moment, then walks to the car and unlocks the trunk.

CHAPTER 24
LUGGS IS RUNNING
OUT OF PATIENCE

Sister Clair pulls into the schoolyard in the morning.

She sees Father Rossi walk out with a blueprint rolled up in his hands. "Good morning, Father," she says as she gets out of the car.

"Good morning, Sister." Lucas comes out of the school.

"Father, I have an appointment for you for an apartment, one of the ones that you liked."

"Great! When?"

"Seven this evening."

"Thank you. That will allow me to get some work done today. It seems the to-do list grows faster than I can mark it off."

Sister smiles and nods her head. "There is a lot to do when opening a school. I also have a full list of candidates for teachers," she looks down at her ever-present notebook, "and two candidates for maintenance."

"Thank you," Father says as Baker pulls in with two people. They get out, and the two men start looking around.

"Good morning, Father," she says as she approaches with the men behind her. "Father, I have a reporter and photographer here from So Cal Magazine. They would like to do a quick interview and promise it won't take but twenty minutes."

Father's face registers disappointment. "Okay," he says.

Baker looks at the men. "Give us one minute, gentlemen." She turns back and takes Father by the elbow and leads him inside. Sister Clair falls in behind them.

"I thought we were going to reduce the number of interviews," Father says as they stop in the hallway.

"I'm sorry. This one just came up, and they have a tight deadline to make this next issue," Baker says.

Father looks at her sternly. "Twenty minutes, okay?" Father asks.

"I promise."

They go back outside. "Sister, have you any news about Carla?"

"No, Father," Sister answers.

The men approach to begin the interview. "Father Rossi, allow me to introduce James Chatfield, reporter for So Cal Magazine, and Toby Minor, photographer."

"Good morning, gentlemen," Father says as he shakes their hands.

"Father, I know your time is limited, and I appreciate you taking time to allow us to talk to you. I have a few quick questions," Chatfield says.

"Shoot," Father replies.

Chatfield opens his reporter notebook. "Ah, I understand that this is your baby. You thought this all up and developed a plan."

"Well, it was my idea, but many people have been a part of it, and I want them to get the credit they deserve."

"Yes, Father, but this article is about you and your school."

"Well, not really my school. It is a place for the deaf and those who want to help the deaf. You see, it is very hard for the deaf to get jobs, not because they are lazy or stupid, but because employers don't know how to communicate with them. Loss of hearing has a bearing on everything in their lives. They can't communicate with landlords, in matters of law and courts, the church, schools, or entertainment; you name it, they are pretty much shut out. This school will help them, and it will help people who can hear to be able to talk with their deaf family members, co-workers, friends, and neighbors."

"How is the schedule and budget right now?" Chatfield asks.

"We are slightly over budget and ahead of schedule, I have been told."

"How can you be ahead in one and behind on the other?"

"Mr. Chatfield, we'll have to direct that question to the accounting firm, and I'll be happy to provide that contact information to you," Baker says.

Chatfield writes in his notebook. "Thank you. Father, are you concerned about the crime rate here?"

Father looks over and sees Luggs standing on the porch staring at him. "I pray that this school will be the first step, that others will start to reclaim their homes and businesses that used to be here and still are," Father says as he turns and points to the Thompson home and others on that street.

"That would be nothing short of a miracle!" Chatfield says.

Father looks at him, pauses, then says. "Sir, I work for a God that happens to be in the miracle business." Chatfield chuckles and nods his head.

The interview continues, then the photographer asks if he can take a picture. "Of everyone here, right?" Father asks.

"No, Father. How about just you?" Minor asks.

"But Father Roberts- he's just inside, we could-"

"No, Father, just you," Father Roberts says as he walks up behind him.

"I think at least both-"

"No, Father. It's okay," Father Roberts says with a smile.

Father Rossi brushes his cassock and stands tall. "No, Father, how about folding your arms?" Minor asks. Father crosses his arms.

"Like this? Are you sure?"

"Yes, Father, just like that." Minor lowers his body and snaps several photos with the school and sky in the background. "Thank you, Father, I got it!" Minor says.

Chatfield steps up and shakes Father's hand. "Thank you, sir. This will be in the next edition."

"Thank you, gentlemen," Father says as he turns to Sister Clair and walks into the school.

Across the street, Luggs shakes his head. "Jamal, look at that! Those fools are getting more publicity!"

Jamal is half asleep in a porch chair. "It's too early in the day to worry about them," he says.

Luggs continues to stare at the school and the neighborhood. "Look over there. They put a bird house up!"

Jamal tries to lie back down. "Maybe they like birds," he says.

"Get up! I want you to go over there and rip that birdhouse down!"

Jamal opens one eye. "What?"

"You heard me, rip it down. I say no one can have a birdhouse on my turf!"

Jamal opens both eyes. "You got somethin' against birds?"

Luggs turns and looks at him. "Not birds! People that put up birdhouses. This ain't Better Homes and Gardens! Take Minion and go bust that birdhouse up!"

"Now? In broad daylight?"

"Yeah, that's the best time!"

Jamal stands and shuffles into the house and returns with Minion. They start to walk into the small yard. "Wait!" Luggs shouts, then turns and disappears into the house.

Jamal looks to Minion. "Maybe he came to his senses," he says.

"Yeah, that was a crazy idea," Minion says.

Luggs comes back out with a crowbar. "Take this!" Minion and Jamal look at each other with disappointment. Jamal steps over and takes it.

They march along the sidewalk past the front of the school. "This is crazy. I think he's losing it." Minion says.

"Let's get this over with. Just bust it down, then we get right back here," Jamal says.

"We risking a lot for a stupid bird feeder," Minion says.

They arrive at the yard and hop over the small gate. They start pushing and hitting the pole that supports the feeder. Mr. Thompson runs out of his home. "Stop that! Stop!"

Mrs. Thompson runs out to him. "No, dear. Come back inside!" Mr. Thompson ignores her and tries to take the crowbar away from Jamal. Minion keeps pushing the pole. Jamal spins and hits Mr. Thompson several times, knocking him to the ground.

"AHH!" Mr. Thompson screams and grabs his upper left arm. Jamal spins back around and, in anger, hits the pole, which gives way and collapses. Jamal turns and raises the crowbar to hit Mr. Thomson again.

Mrs. Thompson covers her husband with her body. "No, please." Jamal lowers the crowbar. Minion grabs his shirt.

"Come on, let's get out of here!"

A crowd of workers from the school comes rushing across the street as Jamal and Minion walk back to Luggs' house. Mr. Thompson moans and holds his arm. Father Roberts kneels and lightly touches the knot that is growing. He looks up at a volunteer. "Call an ambulance. His arm is broken." He looks back at Mr. Thompson. "Hold on, Mr. Thompson, help is on the way."

Mrs. Thompson cries and holds his right hand. Mr. Thompson calms down. "Father, thank you. Do you have a word for a man in pain?" Mr. Thompson asks.

"Romans Eight, Eighteen, I consider that our present sufferings are not worth comparing with the glory that will be revealed in us. That's in the New Testament. I think it fits well as we prepare people for the glory that awaits us. We are all going through pain here as we reclaim this land, but the eternal glory is beyond human comprehension."

"Thank You, Father."

Father Mark arrives with Sister Clair. "What happened?" Mrs. Thompson explains the events that just unfolded. Father looks around. "Where's the ambulance?" No one says anything. "Maybe we need to call again," he says. The same volunteer turns toward the street and calls again. He returns after a short minute.

"They are waiting for law enforcement," he says.

"What?" Father Mark asks.

"They said the ambulance has to wait for a police escort." Father shakes his head, then looks back down at Mr. Thompson. He can see the man is in pain.

"Mr. Thompson, I'm going to drive you to the hospital." He looks at Sister Clair. "Bring me the car, please." She turns and goes back across the street. Father Mark kneels beside Father Roberts. "Mr. Thompson, can we try to get you on your feet?"

"Yes, alright." He starts to stand.

"Let us help you," Father Roberts says.

The two priests help him up as Sister pulls up with the car. They gently place Mr. Thompson in the back. Mrs. Thompson quickly joins him. Father Mark gets behind the wheel. He looks out the window at Father Roberts. "Watch Lucas, please. I'll be back."

"We'll be back," Sister Clair says as she jumps in the passenger seat.

At General Medical Center, Brandy, the R.N. who helped Carla, sees Father walking in with Mr. and Mrs. Thompson and Sister Clair. She rushes to them with a wheelchair. "Back again?" she asks as she helps Mr. Thompson into the chair.

"Again, and probably again and again," Father says as they stop at a desk and a hospital employee starts taking information from the Thompsons. Father looks to Brandy. "You need to put a clinic out there."

"West Adams? Never. It would be robbed,looted, and burned to the ground. We would be treating our employees for injuries every day. No, not West Adams."

Father wipes his hands across his face, then brushes his hair back. He paces in a small circle, then comes back to Brandy. "I can't believe this. It seems everyone has given up on West Adams."

"They have, I'm sorry to say it, but they have. The gangs and drugs, well, they have ruined many parts of this city." She walks away.

Sister Clair steps up. "Someone has to do something about Luggs," Father says.

"I told the Thompsons to call us when they need a ride," Sister says.

Father and Sister walk back out to the car and start the journey to the school. "Something has to be done about Luggs. He has such a grip on this neighborhood."

Sister opens her notebook and starts writing. "Do you want me to schedule a meeting with the police department?"

Father lightly slams the steering wheel. "Yeah, that's a great idea, but be sure to get the bishop's approval. It would be great if he could sit in on the meeting too!"

"Consider it done!" Sister says.

Jamal sits on the sofa listening to Luggs ramble on about the school and the priests that run it. "So where's Minion's cousin? Gone. Where's the open market where people could get high and leave the strains of life for a little bit? Gone. Where's the extra money we made selling dope in the school yard? Gone." He turns and faces Jamal. "You know why it's all gone? That damned priest. One priest with a..." He reaches over and grabs a newspaper. He looks at the article on Father Mark and the school and starts reading it out loud. "With a dream, with a mission, Father Mark Rossi has planted a flag in crime-ridden West Adams!" He throws the paper across the room. "We have run off real bad guys! Real gangs, Jamal! We bled for this spot and it's ours! Our hard-earned place on earth! Now he wants to take it all away! We have to do something, or we're gonna end up packin' our bags and moving! You wanna move Jamal?"

"No."

"You want to start from scratch? Fight it out with a rival gang to take their spot away and open shop again? We got LAPD selling us the best dope they seize! No gang got that. No gang got what we got, and we're about to lose everything over a stupid priest! A man who doesn't believe in violence is gonna hurt us more than Mo Mo shooting at us!"

Jamal sits in deep thought. Luggs sits his exhausted body in a chair. "Luggs, we gotta get the cops to arrest him."

"No, no way. You heard what they said. It's our problem." Both men sit and think for several moments. "We're gonna kill him. I'm gonna issue the command, and he will be standing with that God he loves so much."

Jamal sits up straight. "Luggs, they'll think it's us that did it."

Luggs stands as if a great burden has been lifted. His face relaxes. He smiles. "Let 'em. Be all the better for business." He walks out of the room.

CHAPTER 25
FATHER GETS A NEW APARTMENT

LAPD Captain Matt Conner is escorted into Bishop Kennedy's office. Father Mark, Sister Clair, Father Roberts, and Father Mueller join Bishop Kennedy in standing to welcome the

"Good morning, Captain. I am Bishop Anthony Kennedy." They shake hands. "This Father Rossi, Father Mueller, Father Roberts, Sister Clair." The captain shakes hands with each of them. "Please be seated, Captain," Kennedy says as he motions everyone to the large conference table. They all take a seat. Conner looks at each one of them, then smiles.

"What can I help you with today?"

Bishop Kennedy speaks up. "Captain, as you know, we are building a school."

"The school for the deaf," Conner says.

"Yes, sir."

"In West Adams?"

"Yes, sir. We could use some patrols out there," Kennedy says.

"We have patrols out there."

Father Rossi leans forward. "Yes, sir, but we need more."

"A lot more," Father Roberts adds.

Conner leans back in his seat. "Well, we, I mean, that is a problem. West Adams is not a good place for any school."

Father Rossi's eyebrows lower, and he cocks his head. "Maybe the school can help reclaim the neighborhood. You aren't suggesting that we abandon the school, are you?"

"Of course not. I just don't think I would have selected that place."

"Captain, there are many good, tax-paying citizens who still live there. Surely, they are entitled to protection," Father Roberts says.

"Sir, we have almost four million people who need protection. West Adams is in the Southwest Division. You have to understand, we are pushed to the max on calls. We are short-handed."

Bishop Kennedy says, "I'm sure you and your men are doing your best, and we appreciate all the good work that you do. But we need to get some type of plan together to reduce the violence there. We will have children there in the Fall."

Conner looks around the table. "I understand you have a child there now."

Father Rossi is shocked. "Yes, I mean no, that child has an apartment on Pickford Street in Mid-City. Moving in this week. But he will be attending the school this fall and is at the school daily now."

Conner nods his head. "I can try to increase the patrols there, but I make no promises. We have several undercover operations ongoing in our division, and at least one is in your general area. That is how we can help you the most. I can't go into any details, but if we could stop the flow of drugs into your area, we could clean up those streets quickly."

"Sir, you know more about police work than I, and I am not trying to tell you how to do your job, but can't you raid these drug houses and arrest the dealers that way?" Father Rossi asks.

"Need probable cause. Oh, and a warrant. Even if we had that, the DA lets 'em back out faster than we can do the paperwork."

"That means they know they have an open market to sell in," Father Rossi says. Conner frowns.

"I'm sure you know what you're doing, Captain. If you see an opportunity to increase your patrols, I'm sure you will," the bishop says as he stands to shake his hand.

Conner stands. "Yes. If I find a way, I will, of course. Just stay as safe as you can."

Everyone stands, and Conner walks out the door. Father Rossi has a puzzled look on his face. "What?... What was that all about?"

"Father, I think he was getting aggravated with your questions and statements. I felt it would be best to end this on a good note rather than a bad one. Remember, we need him more than he needs us," the bishop says.

"Yeah, uh,....yeah," Father Rossi says. Everyone starts packing up their things.

As Father drives the car back to the school, Sister has her notebook open. "You've got a four-thirty meeting with the representatives of the sanitation department. It's specifically about the school's trash removal this Fall," Sister informs Father.

"Find Carla, one. Two, I want you to get the lease from that place in Mid-City. I'll take that one. I'll send you with a check for the security deposit and rent. I like that place; Lucas likes that place. I prayed about it, so it'll do. Can you help me get enough furniture in it? Ask Sister Mary Ann about the things that Lucas needs. Me, don't worry. A single bed and a chest of drawers will be fine. Keep it cheap, don't forget the living room. Perhaps we can find something at a second-hand store or something similar. And don't forget the kitchen, a few pans, plates, and some silverware. Ask Sister Mary Ann about the food I should have for Lucas for the inspection."

Sister writes everything down. "How do you suppose the captain knew about Lucas being there?" Father asks.

"Don't know. Maybe some of the patrols saw him."

Father thinks a moment. "I don't know. They pass through there so fast. I just don't know."

"Don't worry, Father. Anything else?"

"No, I'm going to the grocery store after work. Lucas loves the fruity cereal."

"I don't think Sister Mary Ann would suggest that."

"Maybe not, but he loves it. It will be our little secret."

Father pulls into the school yard. The place is shaping up. He gets out and admires it. A deaf worker comes over with paint on his face and coveralls. Using sign language, he asks 'Paint job, good?' Father stands there smiling. He looks over the building and signs, 'very good'. The man smiles and slaps his knee, then walks away.

Lucas runs out, happy to see Father Rossi. He has paint in his hair and on his hands. Father hugs him close. Lucas smiles, then steps back and signs 'I paint'. Father says and signs "I see". They walk inside and start working.

By the end of the day, Father is covered in drywall dust again. Lucas has paint, sawdust, and dirt all over him. Father Roberts walks in as they are getting a drink of cold water from a water fountain. "I love this water fountain. We should have put it in first," Father Rossi says.

"Well, we had to have water in the school pipes first," Father Roberts says.

Sister Clair comes skipping in. "Father, let's go! The day is over, and I have a surprise for you," she says.

"What?" he asks.

"Come." She turns and goes back to the car. Lucas falls in behind them.

On the trip, Sister Clair looks into her notebook. "Doctor's appointment for Lugas tomorrow, three o'clock."

"Add it to my schedule, please," he says. She makes a note of it.

At his new apartment, Father picks up Lucas and walks to the front door. "Not yet," Sister says. She places her hands over Father's eyes. He finds the doorknob and opens the door. Sister Mary Ann is standing there. She is holding a mop. Sister Clair pulls her hands down. "SURPRISE!" both sisters say at the same time. Father opens his eyes and sees that the place is completely furnished. "What? WOW!" Father says as Lucus runs through the rooms.

Father looks around and goes into each room. "Amazing! How did you get the place and furniture delivered on the same day? What about the lease? I didn't sign anything yet." "The landlord said sign it in the morning. He said he has been following your story in the papers," Sister Clair says. "God has blessed me," Father says.

Sister Mary Ann pulls a VCR out of a box along with three videotapes. "The Mass, in animation for Lucas, Disney's Mulan, and Romero, the film about Father Romero for you...and Lucas."

"Sister, is that the VCR from the retreat?"

"Yes. We don't use it enough."

Father is deeply touched. "Thank you."

Sister Clair hands him his credit card and a stack of receipts. "I think you'll be happy with how little of your money we spent." Father takes them, smiles, then sits down on the sofa.

"What do you think, Sister Mary Ann? Will the state pass us now?"

"Get some food in the kitchen."

CHAPTER 26
FORCES START WORK AGAINST FATHER MARK

Shelly Tally opens Tag Collins' door without knocking.

Collins looks up, surprised, and sees Tally holding up a copy of So Cal Magazine. Father Mark is on the cover, his arms folded, with the school and greater LA behind him. He looks bold and fearless. The camera was shot at a low angle, making him appear even taller and stronger. "Oh my god!" Collins says as she is handed a copy. She slams it down on her desk, slips a pair of glasses on, and flips through the pages to the article. She reads the first paragraph. "Oh my god," she repeats.

"It gets worse," Tally says.

"Get Little on the phone," Collins orders.

Before Tally can leave the office, the intercom comes on. "Jo Little on line four. Do you want it?" the voice asks.

Collins jerks the receiver up and presses a button. "Collins.... yeah, I have a copy in my hands....See ya in five." She hangs up. "She's on her way. She's already seen it," Collins says without looking away from the article.

"Yeah, like everyone in L.A. has seen it by now!" Tally says.

She continues to read the article. "Oh my god."

"I'm sure people are making donations as we speak. He is getting bigger by the day. That stage that you were worried about becoming a pro-life platform just moved into the Super Bowl!" Tally says. Collins holds her hand up for silence, never removing her eyes from the article.

Tally steps out of the office. She returns in a minute with Jo Little. "Can you believe this?" Little asks. Collins looks up and scoots her chair back. Little tosses two copies of the magazine on the desk. "He's getting more covers than me! This is going to be a big problem! What are we going to do?" Little asks.

"This is bad, way bad," Tally says.

Collins raises her hand. "Just a minute. You're missing the opportunity here." The girls look at each other. Tally looks back at Collins.

"Huh?"

"What do you mean?" Little asks.

"He looks great there, doesn't he?" Collins asks.

"Like a male model," Tally says.

"Pride. He's eating this up. He wants this attention. He loves it. He's arrogant. That will make your job all the easier."

"You lost me," Little says.

"Simple, play into his pride. Tell him how great he is, how much you admire him, and then move him right into a hotel room." Collins stands and walks around her desk. "You see, he is just a man. You are a beautiful woman. He thinks he deserves a beautiful woman. It's all a scam. He'll raise a bunch of money, but instead of going to the church to sponsor anti-choice events, it will go to us."

Little walks over to a chair and flops down in it. "Every woman will be after him now. Look how good he looks!" Little complains.

Collins walks closer to her and gently touches her shoulder while standing behind her. "As if you have to worry about other women."

Jamal sits reading the So Cal magazine at the dining room table at Luggs' House. Minion walks in. "Carla says she doesn't have to come with me. She said the preacher man told her that!"

Jamal looks up. "Don't tell Luggs yet; he's got enough to deal with today." He holds the magazine up so Minion can see the cover. Minion whistles loudly.

"He's a real big shot now!" Minion says as he stares at Father's picture. Jamal lowers the magazine and resumes reading. "Has he seen it?" Minion asks. Jamal doesn't look up.

"No. I think we'll wait as long as possible." Minion starts into the living room where people are playing video games. Luggs walks into the dining room.

"Wait for what?" Luggs asks.

Jamal jumps in fright and slams the magazine shut, face down. 'Ah, nothing, nothing."

"What's going on?" Luggs asks as he looks around.

"Nothing," Jamal says.

"What are you reading?" Luggs asks.

"Ah, I was just looking for some sports scores. I wanted to see how I did with yesterday's game. I've been losing bets lately, oh boy, I have been losing," Jamal says, then delivers a weak smile.

Luggs stares at him a moment, then slowly walks over and takes the magazine and looks at the cover. He sits down, continuing to stare at the picture of Father Mark in front of the school.

Jamal swallows hard and clears his throat. "I knew this could happen," Luggs says in a whisper. He flips the magazine open and starts reading the article. "This is such bullshit! How can he say these things?" Luggs continues to read. "Father Rossi is bringing the past glory back to West Adams!" Luggs throws the magazine against the wall. "What bullshit!" A silence falls over the room that you could cut with a knife. Luggs stands and walks over to the window, looking out at the school.

Jamal wipes the sweaty palms of his pants. He clears his throat again. "Ah, a lot of people don't even read this rag," he says. Luggs stays silent and continues to stare out the window. He walks over and picks up the magazine.

He looks at the cover again, then walks to his chair in the other room. He picks up his glasses and starts reading the entire article. Jamal can see his chest heaving as he gets mad and takes short breaths. It seems to take him forever to finish the story. Luggs removes his glasses, closes the magazine, and looks at Jamal. He stares at him a moment. "I want you to find Scott Hardy."

"Ah, Scott Hardy?"

"Yeah, you know-"

"Yeah, I know who you're talking about."

"Good. Where is he?" Luggs asks.

"I don't know. I haven't seen him for a couple of years."

"Think he's doin' time?" Jamal shakes his head.

"I don't know. I can find out."

"Good, you do that. Then tell him I want him to come here and kill a priest."

Jamal looks around nervously. "Ah, boss, ah, are you sure you want that?"

Luggs smiles. He relaxes. "Yeah, I'm sure that is exactly what I want. I want that priest dead, dead, dead." He gets up and walks towards the door. "Make it happen fast."

CHAPTER 27
NEW ATTACK

Father Mark is heating a can of Spaghetti-Os as Lucas runs from room to room laughing and playing. The kitchen is small but ample enough for the two of them. The doorbell rings. Father turns the heat down and goes to answer the door. As he enters the living room, he signs to Lucas that someone is at the door. Lucas stops and watches the door closely as Father opens it to find Sister Clair, Sister Maria, and Father Roberts standing in the hall with a few housewarming gifts.

Sister Maria holds up a crucifix. "For Lucas' room. The bishop blessed it earlier today." Father Roberts holds up a toaster and some Pop-Tarts. Sister Clair holds up some children's books.

"It's like Christmas!" Father Mark says. He steps aside and lets everyone in. The nuns scoop Lucas up and start kissing him. He laughs and brushes them away, then jumps back into their laps for more.

The priests walk into the kitchen. Father Roberts sets the toaster down and puts the poptarts on the counter. "This is nice," Father Roberts says.

"It's perfect, isn't it?" Father Mark asks. He points to the refrigerator. "Can you hand me a hamburger out of there? I'll start some spaghetti for all of us."

"No, Father. We can't stay that long. We just wanted to stop in and wish you well."

Father Mark stops stirring the food and looks to Father Roberts. "Thank you. I mean it. Thank you for this and for being my good friend." Father Roberts smiles.

"Hey, I'm the one who is being blessed," he says, then signs 'Thank you'. Father Mark signs 'You're welcome'.

"And you're learning your sign language very well!"

"I have to keep up, at least a little, with you and that little man!" Father Roberts says as he nods his head to the living room, where Lucas is still laughing.

Both men walk into the living room. Lucas grabs Sister Clair's finger and pulls her. "What? Where are we going?" He reaches over with his other hand and pulls Sister Maria's finger, then guides them to his bedroom.

The three of them stand there as Lucas points to the bed, the dresser, then a couple of toys, and finally the Micky Mouse curtains. He signs, 'I live here, my home, my home.' The girls are moved to tears.

Father Mark walks in and signs to Lucas. "Eat? You eat?" Lucas shakes his head no and takes the nuns out to the living room.

He gets the Mulan VHS tape. He signs to them, 'we watch'. He walks over, puts it in the VCR, and starts it. He goes to Father Mark and signs 'popcorn' then 'please'.

Father laughs. "Popcorn. He thinks we have to eat popcorn each time we watch a movie."

Father Roberts takes a seat. "I guess we're not leaving right away."

As the movie begins, Father gives Luca a bowl of Spaghetti-Os. He signs 'Pray, eat this, then popcorn'. Lucas pauses the film. He crosses himself, then everyone bows their head, but still watches as Lucas signs a prayer. He crosses himself again, and everyone joins him.

"Father, you are teaching him well!" Sister Mria says.

Father Robert's phone rings. He stands and answers it as he steps into the other room. He quickly returns. "Father, the school has just been shot up! Not a drive-by!"

"Let's go!" Father Mark says as he steps for the door. "Sisters, can you all watch him until I return?" They both stand.

"Yes, Father," Sister Maria answers.

"Of course, but please be careful!" Sister Clair says.

Both men step out through the door. Father Mark runs back in, hugs Lucas, and signs to him. Lucas nods his head 'yes' and Father disappears.

One police car is parked at the school with lights flashing. The security team is standing beside two LAPD officers. Fathers Mark and Roberts pull in. They get out of the car and look at the school. It has been hit several hundred times. Father Mark glances over to Luggs, who is standing outside, smiling.

"Sorry, Father," one of his security men says. "They stopped in a van and several of them opened fire."

"Do we have video footage?" Father Roberts asks.

"Yeah, up until they shot the cameras off the wall."

Father Mark points to a camera. "They're behind bulletproof glass. We should have plenty of footage." One of the cops rolls his eyes.

"Look, mister, we'll take a look at that footage if you want, but I would take this as a message. Anyone who can fire that many rounds in such a short time is a gang made up of killers, most likely from South America or something. They are giving you a warning."

Father Mark is upset. "Are you advising me to pack up?" The other cop steps up. "Don't be so sensitive. You're lucky that they only shot at the building. Next time it could be you!"

"Is there any chance that you may find out who did this. I mean, it's a lot of damage, a lot of loss here. It'll cost money to repair and replace the damage done here tonight," Father Roberts says.

The first cop looks at him and says, "Slim chance of finding who did this. They may be a long way gone by now."

Luggs walks back into his house, happy and smiling. Two men walk in through the back door. They are dressed in black and have stern looks on their faces. "My, my, what a great job you guys did!" Luggs says to them.

"You got our money?" one of them asks.

Luggs walks over to the table and picks up a thick envelope full of cash. "Here ya go," Luggs says as he hands it to them, then turns to a sideboard against the wall. He picks up a large plastic Ziploc bag of crack. "And a little bonus for you and the boys!" The first man takes it. They turn and walk out the back door.

"Men of few words," Jamal says.

Luggs looks to the dark side of the room. "I didn't see you back there. Yes, those cats don't talk much. Kinda creepy, huh?" Luggs says with a grin.

Fathers Roberts and Mark walk into the apartment. Sister Maria is rocking on the sofa with Lucas in her arms, fast asleep. Mulan plays on the TV. Father Mark sits down in the chair. His stressed-out look disappears as a smile floods his face with joy. "He is something, isn't he?"

"He is a precious, precious child," Sister Maria says as she looks down on his innocent face.

Sister Clair brushes his hair back. "He has been through so much. I'm overjoyed that he is here with us right now!" she says. She then looks to Father Mark. "How bad is it?"

Father nods his head up and down. "Bad."

"What part did they shoot?"

"All of the Southside," Father answers.

"The same side as the drug house?"

"Yes."

"Did they do it?" Sister asks.

"No one knows, and the police do not seem that interested in finding out," Father Mark says.

"What are we going to do?" Sister Clair asks.

"Pray."

The next day, Captain Conner is standing with Father Mark, Baker, and the staff at the school. He looks at all the bullet holes. "Are you sure you don't want to move to another section of the city?" Baker rolls her eyes and steps up.

"You know that is not an option. We have invested a fortune here."

Conner looks back at all the damage. "What made you think you could open a school here?"

Baker stiffens. "I'll tell you what I'm going to do. We are going to call a press conference, right here, in front of the damage, and let the public know! Do you want to speak at it?" Conner is visibly upset.

"Okay, do it your way. Yeah, we'll be here. We're going to let the taxpayers know how much this school is costing them! Extra patrols, extra investigations, it's a lot."

Baker smiles and points to the other side of the school towards the Thompson property. "Good, you can let all of those taxpayers know that for the first time in a long time, they are getting some help!"

Conner storms off. "Ah, Miss Baker, uh,..." Father Roberts says.

"I know. I'm sorry. I went too far with him," she says.

"No," Father Mark says as he looks over at the damage. "We are committed to building this school and making a stand here, for us, for the neighbors, for the good of the community, for God." He looks to Baker. "Good job. No one said this would be easy. Let's go to work!"

CHAPTER 28
THE KNIGHTS of ST. JOHN PAUL II

The Knights of Saint John Paul II pull into the school yard in a bus. Several men get out. Inside a classroom, Father Mark is talking with a contractor as they assess the damage. Bullet holes are covering one wall. A chalkboard is shattered, with its pieces scattered on the floor. "Father, you're going to have to put in bulletproof glass," the contractor says.

"We can't. We simply could not afford that."

"You will have students in here soon. Can you afford not to?"

Father Roberts walks in. "Father, a whole bunch of volunteers are outside, mostly knights from the Knights of Saint John Paul. They are offering to assist the security team."

Father Mark follows Father Roberts outside. A man steps up. "Father, I am Gerald Mints, a knight from Saint Joe's. We've come to help."

"Well, thank you," Father says as he shakes his hand, then looks to Father Roberts.

"What did you have in mind?" Father Roberts asks.

"Well, we can patrol the street with our flag on display. We can demonstrate a force in the schoolyard. We can make this place a hard target, not a soft one."

Father Mark works through the group, shaking hands with everyone. They move into a classroom, and the knights take a seat on the floor. Father Mark moves to the front. "It could be dangerous. Someone could get hurt or killed. I wouldn't want that," he says.

"Father, you could get hurt or killed. Where does it say that you are to take all the risks?" Mints asks.

"Well, I mean, ah..." Father Mark stumbles for an answer.

Father Roberts stands. "Gentlemen, we need the help, but the liability of risking your lives, I mean, that is too much."

Mints stand. "Father, I was a correctional officer. I retired from that job. I saw thousands of these gang members come and go. You would not believe the stories I could tell you. These people are killers, they enjoy killing, they really do! It seems they have no respect for anyone. It seems they have no soul. That's what you're up against. Now we thought this through. You need the help, and we're here to provide that help." Several men nod their heads and sound off in agreement.

Another man stands. He is younger and dressed well. "Father, my name is Joey. I have to ask you how much time you are losing on security problems. My niece is six years old and she is deaf. My brother has prayed for a place close to home for her. God answered his prayers, and you are here. That is just one story. How many others? How many more are praying that you will finish school and open the doors to them? You need to let us take some of the burden off. You could be spending all this lost time on fundraising so kids could come for free. You could use it for school administration. There are a hundred better ways to spend your time other than dodging bullets." The men applaud and stand in agreement.

"Let me take this to the bishop. Thank you. I thank each and every one of you. May God bless you abundantly for your kind hearts," Father says.

"Let's work out a schedule and complete the proposal first, then take it to the bishop," Father Roberts says.

"You're right! Great idea," Father Mark says.

The next hour is spent with Father Roberts at a laptop, refining a proposal. He takes input from the knights. It is a productive meeting with several ideas put to paper. "If we patrol around the street with a camera and our flag flying over the car, the gangs will have to see that and be discouraged," Mints says. Father Roberts continues to type and ask questions.

After a little more than two hours, they have a complete proposal. It is fifteen pages long and very detailed. Father Roberts watches it come out of the printer. "Amazing! Look how well this looks!"

"It came together fast!" Father Mark says. The knights beam with pride and satisfaction.

Two days later, Fathers Mark and Roberts sit in a conference room down the hall from the bishop's office. The floor-to-ceiling windows offer a grand view of the city. Both men sit at the table. They fidget with their proposal, the pens, their collars, and anything else that they can to burn off the anxiety.

The door opens, and the bishop and Muller walk in. The priests stand. Bishop Kennedy shakes their hands, then Father Muller offers his. Muller then hands a folder to the bishop and takes a seat away from the table. "Please be seated," the bishop says, as the priests take their seats. The bishop remains standing. He opens the folder and removes the proposal. "Absolutely not." The priest looked at each other, then back at him. "You cannot have men on 'patrol' egging on a confrontation! What would happen if a couple of knights were killed? What about their families and loved ones? How will that look on the six o'clock news?"

"Ah, sir, they would have cameras," Father Roberts meekly says.

"You have cameras now. What has stopped them from doing?" he reaches over, and Muller hands him a sheet of paper. "Twenty-seven thousand dollars' worth of damage?" No. They fear no cameras.

They do not fear the police! Why would they fear a couple of unarmed men?" The priest looked at the other like grounded schoolboys.

"I want both of you to back it down a notch. Miss Baker, too. There will not be a press conference to embarrass the LAPD. I have already spoken to her about that, and now I'm letting you know."

Bishop Kennedy takes his seat. "Fathers, I know you have put a lot into this school. I am impressed, I admire you both. You are an inspiration to me! I mean that." There is a long pause.

Father Mark clears his throat. "Your Excellency, the damage that they do... we have students coming soon.... we need a way to secure this school. I mean.... well...."

"I know," the bishop says. "I know, but we cannot be engaging them. That's what they want. They will take it as a challenge, and they will respond in kind, and then we will have dead Catholics in the street." He picks up the proposal. "I'm sorry, but this proposal is rejected completely."

He looks at both of them. "Okay?"

They raise their heads and make eye contact with the bishop. "Yes, sir," Father Roberts says.

"Yes, sir, okay," Father Mark adds.

The bishop stands, then Muller and the priest stand. "Fathers, keep up the good work you are doing. I stand behind you," the bishop says before he exits the conference room with Father Muller right behind him.

Both the priests sit down exhausted. Father Mark pours a glass of water from a pitcher on the table. "I ah,....well..." Father Roberts says as he claps his hands together, then begins rubbing them nervously.

"Don't be discouraged," Father Mark says before taking a big drink of water.

"Says the man that is shaking," Father Roberts says as he places his right hand on Father's shaking left hand. He then gets up, walks to the window, and looks outside.

Father Mark pours a little more water into his cup, drinks it down, and then stands. "We'd better get back to the school," he says. They walk out of the room and start down the hallway. When they arrive at the reception area, they are greeted by Father Muller.

"Gentlemen, please come with me. The bishop wants to see you." They start walking to his office. "We hired a law firm, accounting firm, and a private investigator over the mess that happened before you got here, Father," Muller says as he looks to Father Mark. "The P.I. has some information for us."

They walk into Bishop Kennedy's office. Baker is standing at the table with her arms crossed. A man stands at the window with the bishop. "Father Rossi, Father Roberts, I would like you to meet Mr. Mulray." They shake hands. "He is a private investigator, and he has found some assets of our two thieves, Simms and Markley. I wanted you to hear this. There isn't really anything you can do, and this is to stay out of the press for now, but I thought you should be in the loop. Go ahead, sir, tell them what you just told me."

"Well, Markley and Simms did buy a yacht. They also left a trail, albeit a small one, which I was able to track. It seems that Simms and Markley were in a homosexual relationship with a man named Phil Ismen. Ismen threatened to make it all public unless they handed over money. So they did that, then he wanted more, then more. Finally, Markley and Simms saw there was no end in sight, so they bought a boat and took off. "Forty thousand dollars is in a bank account here. The rest, I don't know where it is or what happened to it, except for what they gave to Isman. I can find out, I think," Mulray explains.

"Where are Simms and Markley now?" Muller asks.

"South America. Living on the boat. Spreading money around for protection. It may be difficult if you want them back."

"We have to prepare a press release," Baker says.

"Not yet," the bishop says.

"Sir, the press will find out about this, and then it will look bad on us. I think we should get ahead of the ball here."

The bishop walks to the table and sets the file down. "Not yet."

As Baker and both priests exit and walk down the hall, Father Mark says, "Well, we weren't the only ones shot down today."

Baker doesn't look at them; she just continues her march to her office. "We will have hell to pay if the press finds out about this from anywhere else but us." She stops at her office, turns, and faces them. "Please not a word to anyone about this, no one, please."

"Oh, fear not about that," Father Roberts says.

CHAPTER 29
MOTIVATION

Two of the men who work for the electrical contractor are sitting at the bar in Dimpple's restaurant. Jo Little walks up and waves a bartender down. "French martini, please," she says.

"For you, the moon baby," the bartender replies.

Both the construction workers admire her shape and the tight black dress that she is wearing. She checks her watch, then looks to them. "Excuse me, I'm late to meet my girlfriend. She's a tall blonde. Have you guys seen her?"

"Does she look as good as you?" one of the men asks. Little smiles.

"No, she is really hot. She looks so much better than I!"

Both the men laugh as she sits down beside them. The bartender delivers her French martini. "Put it on my tab!" the second man says as he gets up and moves to her other side, placing her between them.

"Thank you. Oh gosh, I'm not used to this much kindness," she says.

"Well, my name is Ronnie," the first man says as he extends his hand. She shakes it and then looks to her other side.

"I'm Grant," the other man says.

"I'm Annie," Jo lies.

"Nice name," Grant says.

"Nice bod," Ronnie says as he takes a sip of his beer.

"Where are you guys working?"

"The new school. The school for the deaf - West Adams," Grant says.

"Oh yeah, I heard about that place. It's been in the paper a lot lately," Jo says.

"Yeah, and it's a dangerous job. We've been shot at twice now."

"You guys are brave men. Did the priest shoot at you?" The men laugh.

"No, gangs," Ronnie says.

"What's it like to work for that priest?" she asks.

Ronnie shoots down the rest of his beer, sets the empty glass on the bar, and holds up three fingers, telling the bartender to bring them three more drinks. "He's a good guy," Grant says.

"Goody two-shoes," Ronnie says as he takes his beer from the bartender.

"He has a little boy, right? I thought priests didn't have children," Jo says.

"He's adopting that boy or something," Ronnie says.

"And they live at the school?"

Ronnie takes a big drink and then wipes the foam from his mustache. "No, Mid-City, I think on Washington."

Jo takes a small sip of her drink. "Mid-City, Washington Boulevard. Well, that should be a little safer than West Adams. Unless he is close to West Adams," she says.

"Nah, he's near Mansfield Avenue," Ronnie says.

"No, I think Pickford," Grant says.

"Pickford runs parallel with Washington, you dummy. He's near the corner of Mansfield and Washington, somewhere right in there. I hope that kid will be okay. He's a nice boy," Ronnie says.

Jo takes another small sip and places the glass back down beside the new one. "Excuse me, boys. I'm going to try to call my friend. I'll be right back," she says. She starts walking while dialing her phone.

"Tell your friend to join us!" Ronnie says. She looks back and nods her head as she places the phone to her ear. She keeps walking, and the men return to their beers. She walks outside, gets in her car, and drives away.

Fathers Mark and Roberts return to the school. They park the pink-wheeled car and go inside. Luggs stands on the porch at his house and watches them. Brax and Cole pull up in front, get out of the car, and walk over to him. They see that he is just staring at the school. They turn around and see the many pockmarks from the hundreds of bullets that were fired. "Oh my god!" Brax says. "What happened?"

Luggs laughs, and a smile covers his face. "Those boys are in there packin' right now, I bet!"

Cole pulls his sunglasses down on his nose and stares. "There must be four hundred bullet holes in that place. It looks like a strong wind could blow it over," he says.

Luggs turns and faces them. Brax hands him an envelope of cash. Luggs slides it into his waistband. "Yep. That might be all it took. Jackson brothers, four thousand dollars, and a little bag of Coke can do a big bunch of damage. Ain't no way that they will stay now!" Luggs laughs again, turns back to the school and shouts, "I ain't gonna miss ya!" He laughs again and walks inside.

Jamal steps out and sees Cole and Brax on the porch staring at the school. "You boys missed the fireworks," he says.

"Anyone get hit?" Cole asks.

"Nope, but that ain't what this was about. It was a message sent with a big red bow on it," Jamal answers.

"I thought you were looking for Scott Hardy. Don't look like you'll need him now," Brax says.

"I think those priests are coming up with a plan to get out of town. Business may be like it was soon, and you know how good business was!" Jamal says.

"Life gets better every day," Brax says. "I need to get stocked up. I'm goin' to Hollywood."

Jamal turns for the door. "Come on in."

Inside the school, two discouraged priests sit in student chairs. Lucas draws in a coloring book. "Well, brother, we have seen harder days," Father Roberts says. Father Mark just stares ahead. "Cheer up, Father," Father Roberts says. He gets up and walks to the front of the classroom in deep thought. He spins and says, "I got it! Joshua chapter one verse nine, 'Have I not commanded you? Be strong and courageous. Do not be afraid; do not be discouraged, for the LORD your God will be with you wherever you go."

Father Mark smiles and gets up. "You're absolutely right! We are priests. We are to live a life that sets an example for others, one that points people to Christ! We will overcome this. Romans eight thirty-one, 'What, then, shall we say in response to these things? If God is for us, who can be against us?"

Both men start laughing and celebrating. Lucas looks up and watches them, then shakes his head, smiles, and goes back to his coloring book.

CHAPTER 30
THE PLAN FINALIZED

Shelly Tally and Tag Collins are in a Lincoln Continental driving around several blocks near Washington Boulevard and Mansfield Avenue. "I hope he leaves soon. I'm getting tired," Tally says.

"Shut up and stop whining," Collins barks. "Keep your eyes on all the restaurants, laundry mats, and fast food joints," she adds.

"I got 'em all written down from the first hour!" Tally says as she holds up a notebook.

"Well, we need a place where she will just bump into him. He'll go get some carry-out, or maybe do some laundry, and Little will be right there! He'll melt into her arms!"

"How could anyone believe that a top model would live in a dump like this place? He'll see right through this," Tally says.

"Ha! You're wrong. He won't see through this. If he sees anything, it will be through her tight pants and top!"

Tally's phone rings. She answers it. "Yeah....you're kidding? ...Alright, yeah," She hangs up. "Well, he'll be easy to find. He's coming in a car with pink wheels!" Collins laughs out loud. "This is going to be easier than I thought!"

The women move close to the corner of Mansfield and Washington and park. They watch the cars come and go, and after a while, a pink-wheeled car passes by. Father Mark is driving, and Lucas is in the back seat. They follow him to an apartment building. They watch as he gets out, retrieves Lucas, and goes into apartment 108.

"Can you believe this? What luck!" Collins says.

"I hope this plan works," Tally says.

"Tomorrow we bait the trap!" Collins says as she drives off.

At the school, Father Roberts is shutting down his computer when Sister Clair walks in. She hands Father a file. "Father, here are the cost estimates for the exterior wall. The contractor sent it over a little bit ago."

"Thank you, Sister. I'll file it. Have you sent a copy to the bishop's team?"

"Yes, sir."

Father gets up and files it in a filing cabinet. He looks back at Sister. "You look worried."

"Oh no, I'm okay."

"Do you need a ride?"

"No, sir, Sister Maria and a new sister are going to pick me up."

"Good. Well then, what is it?"

"I'm worried about Father Rossi." Father seems a little surprised.

"Why?"

"Well, he is the main link in this chain. He has people that want to kill him, he has people that want to see him fail, and..."

"And what?"

She takes a deep breath. "And I'm worried when the day comes that someone adopts Lucas. It's gonna break his heart, and I'm afraid it will also break the heart of a little boy."

Father thinks a moment. "It's been a concern of mine, too, especially after seeing them get closer each day. They really need each other. I was thinking that if all of this failed, at least a little boy was saved from these streets. We haven't even opened yet, and look at all the good that has come from this school!"

"You're right!" Sister says. A long silence falls on the room.

"Are you worried about your safety?" Father asks. She looks away. "You know you can put in for a transfer. I'm sure everyone would understand. This is not a safe assignment," Father says.

"No. God placed me here. I am willing to go anywhere He sends me. I want to be here. It's exciting, but also a little scary. I place my trust in God."

"That's good, Sister. We all need to do that. I'm trusting God that He will work everything out for this school and Father Rossi and little Lucas!" He walks to the table and takes a seat in a chair. "Sister, we are in a great line of work. The miracle business, you could say. You know, I often wonder how many people we can help? It seems people everywhere are searching for answers. I pray that I can help people and, by example or message, lead them to eternal life in heaven with our Lord and Savior. We are the ones who can give that hope to others. It will make a difference for us and a wonderful, eternal difference for the ones that make it to heaven because we shared the Good News, or lived a Christ-like life."

"You're right, Father. I think about it a lot. God has a plan."

Father Roberts looks down at the table and thinks for a long moment. "Sister, you are around Father Rossi all the time. The skills you bring to the project are tremendous! I believe you will have a bigger part in this mission than you know right now. Father Rossi needs someone to keep him on track, and you are doing a great job of that! You know, you mentioned many people would love to see him fail - and you're right! Imagine how much the Devil wants to see him fail! We are making a positive difference in this community, and I am sure Satan is aware of that."

"I know what you mean. This place, just weeks ago, was Satan's ground. We took that away from him, so I'm sure he's not happy."

"No, he's not. Ephesians six, ah, twelve says 'For our struggle is not with flesh and blood but with the principalities, with the powers, with the world rulers of this present darkness, with the evil spirits in the heavens.' We must stay strong and in prayer."

Trace Abbott sits at a large desk in his home. The room is a mess. Cameras and scripts litter the floor. Some expensive, framed art pieces lean against the wall. Across the desk, Johnny lights a cigarette. Carl Chester, a lawyer, sits in a chair near the desk. Troy Kurtz, an accountant, is typing on his computer. On a sofa against the wall, Milton Rey, Abbott's agent, sits reading the Hollywood Reporter.

"I want a bigger party this weekend! And get a different band, not so much rap. I want some rap, just we need to add something else to the mix," Abbott says.

"We need to pay the caterers or they won't come back," Johnny says.

Kurtz looks up from his computer. "We owe them more?"

"Yeah, a lot more," Johnny answers.

"Trace what about that film? You want me to tell them yes?" Rey asks.

"What film?"

"The movie to be shot on film and played in old-time theaters!" Rey says.

Abbott looks over at Johnny. "Can you believe this? A short film, shot by a new director, offering to pay me twice scale, is something that Milton is all excited about!"

"It's a great op for you! Short production time and publicity! Well, everyone will be talking about it!"

"How can that be? How many theaters still roll film? Besides, several films are still shot on film and then transferred to digital so the WHOLE world can see it!" Abbott says.

"That doesn't matter. It's the publicity we want! It will help you. This director is hot and will get us more P.R. than we could buy!"

Abbott looks around the room. "Twice scale. What are you going to make, Milton? A buck eighty-five?"

"Forget the money on this one--"

"Whoa!" Kurtz interrupts. "The money? Never forget the money!"

"Speaking of money, we need to pay Braxton, too," Johnny says.

"See Milton? How can I work at scale times two? I got high overhead," Abbott says.

"How much more money is he owed?" Kurtz asks.

"I'll check. At least ten grands," Johnny answers.

"WHAT?" Kurtz shouts.

"Yeah, at least."

"Trace, don't get tangled up in small details. Take this script and do it!" Rey says.

"I don't even have the script!" Abbott says. Rey looks around the room at the floor.

"Yeah, ten maybe a lot more," Johnny says again.

"How did you ever convince the dealer to spot you that far?" Kurtz asks.

Rey pulls a script off the floor and brushes it off. "Here it is!" He hands it to Abbott, who immediately sets it on the desk.

"The dealer loves Trace. He watches all of his shows. He likes the perks, too," Johnny answers.

Abbott snaps his fingers. "That's it! He likes perks? Bring him to the set! Let him see us making this show!"

"Great idea!" Johnny says.

"No, not a great idea. Trace, they don't like a big entourage on the set. They have already warned us about that," Rey says.

Abbott brushes his hand through the air and stands. "They'll deal with it. Get him here next week."

CHAPTER 31
THE PLAN UNDERWAY, SCHOOL SECURITY, COLE DODGES A COP

Father Mark packs a backpack with supplies that Lucas will need throughout the day. He rushes because he is already slightly behind schedule. He signs to Lucas, who is at the table playing with his breakfast, to hurry. Finally, he gets everything packed as Lucas slips on his shoes. They start out the door and head for the car, and see Jo Little jogging past. She stops and spins around. "Father Mark! How delightful to see you!" She steps closer.

"Uh, hello, good morning. We're just on our way to work."

"I still have that beach house waiting for us. I know you deserve a break. I'm so impressed with what you are doing at the school!"

Father thinks a moment and asks, "What are you doing out in this part of the city?"

"Oh, I went running this morning with my friend Janet, she lives up the block, but she dropped out, and I was just going to add one more mile to the run alone. Running keeps a body in fine shape." She turns and shows her figure to Father. "Don't you agree?"

Father adjusts his collar. "Uh, I really need to... go ah, to the school."

A car pulls up beside them, and a lady with a clipboard gets out. "Father Mark Rossi?"

Father turns and faces her. "Yes."

"Good morning. I am Jean Casey from the California Department of Social Services. I was hoping to catch you at home. I'm here for the inspection."

"Oh! I didn't know it was today. I'm sorry, but yeah, sure, you just caught me heading out, but we can go back in."

"We don't always advertise the times that we are coming. I'm sure you can understand."

He looks at Jo, then back at the case worker. "Ah, yes. I understand." He looks back at Jo. "It was nice seeing you today."

"We'll meet again. I still have that check for you," Little says with disappointment.

"Have a great and glorious day," he says as he turns and walks into the apartment with Casey behind him.

Her shoulders slump, and she looks up the street where Talley is sitting in a car, taking pictures. Talley pulls up to her, and she drops into the car. "What bad luck!" Talley says.

"It's always bad luck with him. Why is this so important? I have never had such a hard time picking up a man!" Little says.

"Because I would like to see every Christian knocked off their high perch! They are so judgmental! They think they are perfect, oh no, ah, how does it go?... Not perfect, just forgiven. What a load!"

"He may not be worth the effort," Little says as she watches Los Angeles pass by out of the window.

"Oh, yes! He's worth it. Don't you see? He took a little trashed, dilapidated building -- in the center of a drug zone, and is building a church -- I know it's a school, but it really will be a church where people learn to hate women and take their freedoms away. It was just him and a few others, then more, then people from out-of-state, then the press, then more press, then--"

"I get it," Little says.

"He gets off the ground there, then a big platform is --"

Little looks at Talley. "I get it! I get it. You told me all of that!" She looks back out of the window, then back at Talley. "I don't think he is worth all of this, and I know I can't be putting in this much time! You know I am a working model, which means I have to work. Maybe the guy just is in a place where he can't be got."

"Nonsense! You had him stuttering and stammering. He was on the ropes. If you hadn't been interrupted, we would be heading back right now with photos! Hang in there. We'll get him the next time, I promise!"

Inside the apartment, Father Mark introduces Lucas and shows Casey their home. Casey takes a few notes, checks the refrigerator, and looks in the cupboards. She turns to Father. "You seem to be doing well, Father. How is Lucas doing?"

"Do you want to ask him?"

Father kneels in front of Lucas and signs to him. Lucas signs back and smiles big. "He says he loves his home. He says he is not hungry and feels strong and safe." Father signs back, then Lucas signs again. Father stares at him a moment, then grabs him and hugs him close. Father leans back and signs 'I love you.' Father stands and looks at Casey.

"He says I'm a guardian angel sent by St. Michael, we're learning all about the archangel St Michael, to watch over him and protect him from gangs, and the devil." He wipes a tear from his eye."This little man has been through a lot. Every day, I try my best to make him feel safe and loved. It took a while for him to believe we were staying here - with his own room."

Casey looks at Father, then Lucas. She closes the papers on her clipboard. "Father, I think you are doing just fine with him."

Brax and Cole park on the street near Lugg's house and get out. A cop in plain clothes walks up to the front porch. Cole sees him and quickly gets back in the car. Brax looks confused and leans down to the open window on the driver's side. "What's wrong with you?

"Get in!" Cole says as he sinks into the seat and lowers his head.

"What?" Brax asks. He opens his door and gets in. "What's wrong with you?"

"That guy's a cop. Name is Stalker. He busted me a few years ago."

"Yeah, he's getting cash from Luggs. Don't worry."

"Don't worry? Those guys keep notes on everything and everybody! He'll come back and bust us again."

"No, he works for Luggs. He can't bust us. He sells the dope to us. He'd have to bust himself, too." He reaches for the doorknob. "Come on, let's go inside."

"No. Let's wait until he leaves."

Brax settles into the seat. "Well, we finally found something you're scared of."

Inside Lugg's house, Stalker stands at the table where Luggs is sitting. He opens his hand. "What're you doin' here?" Luggs asks.

Stalker rubs his thumb across his fingertips. "I got info for you about Hardy."

"Jamal!" Luggs shouts. Jamal comes in, eating a slice of pizza. "Get some cash for Mr. Greedy." Luggs looks back at Stalker. "What's ya got?"

The stalker waits until Jamal puts a hundred-dollar bill in his hand. Stalker stands there. He puts another, then another, then two more. "Hardy is in prison in New York State. He won't be back for at least twenty years."

Luggs sinks into his seat.

At school, the day passes quickly. Father forgets about Little and is so excited about the home inspection that he tells everyone at the school about it, some of them more than once. Father Roberts is working at his desk when Father Mark, Lucas, and Sister Clair walk in at lunchtime. "I have been managing many details while you were walking on cloud nine," he says with a smile.

"I'm sorry. You're right. What can I do to help?" Father Mark asks.

Father Roberts gives him a confused look. "That's a change. Usually, we are the ones asking you that question."

Sister Mary Ann walks in. Father Mark almost runs to her. "Sister, they came to the house today! I was, they...ah, they, I mean she liked the place!"

Sister raises her hand. "I know, Father. I already got the report and it is good--"

Father Mark slaps his hands together and looks to Father Roberts. "See!" he says.

Sister clears her throat. "Yes, Father, it passed. But I don't want you to get your hopes so high. Remember, it's very difficult for a single parent, especially a Catholic priest, in this current world, to adopt."

Father Mark steps closer to her and takes a seat in front of her. "No, Sister! I would not be the first priest to adopt a child!

J.R.R. Tolkien was raised by a priest after his mother died when he was twelve, and his younger brother, too! Others have done the same. I have been doing some research. A priest in Chicago--" he stands to grab the backpack.

Sister holds her hand up again. "Father, slow down. We are for you. I just want you to know that you're up against some tough odds."

Father sits back down, defeated. Sister takes a chair and sits down beside him. "Father, we are praying for you and Lucas - every day. We have to put our trust in God."

"I am Sister, I am."

She lightly taps his hand a couple of times. "Good! Now, we have to make sure we pass all the state requirements for the school so he'll have a place to go this Fall."

Father jumps up, recharged. "You're right! Honestly, we are ahead of schedule, well, except for rebuilding the bullet-ridden wall. The only thing that worries me is the security of the building. I know the state is going to have a problem with that."

Sister Clair speaks up. "You know the state does have some responsibility for the safety of citizens. That's why we have police departments and fire departments and courts and things like that."

Father Roberts stands. "She's got a point."

"We need to let the citizens know that we all want that help!" Sister Clair adds.

"Wait a minute. The bishop is not going to stand for anything that could be seen as an embarrassment to the police department," Sister Mary Ann says.

"We don't have to do it that way. The citizens pay taxes for this protection that we are not getting," Sister Clair says.

"It sounds like an attack on the police department. They are going to say they have increased patrols, hired more officers, and have spent more money on fighting crime - and they will prove it with stacks of reports," Sister Mary Ann argues.

Sister Clair looks to Father Mark, then slowly sits down. Father Mark runs his hands through his hair and looks at the floor. Sister Mary Ann gets up and pats Father Mark's back. "Fear not, Father. This will work out. God has provided so far. No need to doubt his ability now."

Father Mark doesn't look up. "God has a plan. We just need to wait until he shows us what it is."

The day's progress is good. Workers and volunteers carried out their tasks without gunfire or incident. At the end of the day, Father packs up Lucas and returns home. After getting a meal together and tucking Lucas into bed, he goes to his room and collapses on his bed and stays there until the dawn's early light.

As the sun breaks through the smog and enters his bedroom window, Father bats his eyes a few times, looks at the clock, then jerks himself out of bed. "I'm gonna be late for Mass!" He touches his clothes, trying to remember why he slept in them. He then goes into Lucas' room and checks on him, then retreats back into the hallway. Quickly, he moves into the bathroom and starts the shower.

Once he gets his shower, shaves, and puts on fresh clothes, he starts some coffee and moves back into Lucas' room. Although he is behind schedule, he pauses to see Lucas sleeping soundly. He smiles, then slowly wakes his little friend. 'Good morning!' he signs.

Lucas smiles big and signs 'Good morning! Let's go!'

Father laughs. "You are full of joy, young man," he says out loud to himself.

He signs 'Late for Mass. Breakfast after Mass.. Lucas nods his head up and down. Father pours the coffee into a thermos, and they rush out of the apartment. They make their way through the morning traffic and arrive at the chapel. They sit in the back so Father can sign to Lucas all that is being said. The priest at the altar, after reading the Gospel, begins his homily. He speaks of Nehemiah's rebuilding of the ancient city of Jerusalem's wall and how that provided security to the residents on many levels. Father stops signing for just a moment. His mouth falls open. He looks to Lucas with a big smile on his face.

After Mass, they drive back into the traffic to make it to work. Lucas notices how much faster they are driving today. Once at the school, Father gets Lucas out of the car and almost runs inside. He says hello to the workers and volunteers as he passes them, then heads into his office, where Father Roberts and Sister Clair are examining receipts spread out on a table.

"Guess what!" Father Mark says as he sits Lucas down.

"Good morning to you, too," Father Roberts says.

"I went to Mass!"

"Congratulations, Father," Sister Clair says in jest.

"Yeah! I got up late. It crossed my mind not to even go today, but I knew God would not approve of oversleeping and skipping Mass. So, I went!"

"Wonderful," Father Roberts says with a surprised look on his face.

"You know what? The homily that Father Paul gave was wonderful. He started talking about Nehemiah's rebuilding of Jerusalem's walls! Don't you get it?"

Father Roberts and Sister Clair look at each other, then back at him.

"A wall! A wall! We will build a wall! All the way around the school. Drive-by shootings will not pose a threat to us or the students again!"

Father Roberts and Sister Clair look at each other, then smile. "Yeah!" Father Roberts says.

Sister sits down and says, "Yes, a wall indeed! It will be cheaper than making repairs every week, not to mention the safety for the children and other students!"

Father Mark looks at them for a moment, then moves to a chalkboard. He grabs a piece of broken chalk and draws a birdseye view of the school and property. "Ok, we put it here, where the fence is now," he says as he starts drawing the border where the new wall will go. He draws another line parallel to the first. "The wall will be made of stone, two feet thick, six feet high, with a solid foundation eighteen inches deep."

Sister Clair comes out of a stare and starts writing notes.

"What about permits? Something like that could hold us up for months," Father Roberts says.

Sister and Father Mark both say, "God has a plan!" at the same time.

Both priests move to a table that has a blueprint on it. Sister gets up and goes to the door. "I'll go get the general contractor, be right back!"

Father Roberts looks at the blueprint. "Here on the fenchline. We would still be back from the city sidewalk. Two feet thick cuts into our yard a bit."

"Well, let's see what Bob says when she gets back with him. Maybe it won't have to be that thick, but it does have to stop bullets," Father Mark says.

CHAPTER 32
BRAX GOES TO HOLLYWOOD, THE WALL

After making several deliveries, Brax and Cole move onto the 101 highway and head to Hollywood in a red, 1982 Buick Riviera Convertible. "Where'd ya get this one?" Cole asks.

"One what?"

"This car. This car that screams for attention."

"I bought it yesterday. It's a classic. All this money we're making has to go somewhere."

"You know this is stupid. We're haulin' dope onto a studio lot in a car that everyone will remember!" Cole says.

"Relax, man. We're going to Paramount! It is the sixth-oldest film studio in the world! The second-oldest film studio in the United States. Only Universal Pictures is older. This is it, Baby, big time now. We are going in style," Brax says as he drives without a care in the world.

"Don't forget I still have to see the P.O. today," Cole says.

"Why are you still there? He dropped me! Dropped me early! You just need to be nice to him."

"Yeah, whatever. Just get me there by three."

"Well, my good friend, my close friend Trace, invited me to the set! I'm not sure how long this will take. I mean, I'm one of the insiders now. Me and my new Hollywood friends!"

"Okay, Mister Bigshot."

"Oh, come on. Don't tell me you're not a little excited about going to a movie studio!"

"No, not at all. I'd just as soon go to the city dump."

"You know you have a lot of inner anger. You need to let that go."

"Oh, brother."

"I'm serious. We are on top of the world. Nothing can stop us now, baby! Enjoy life. You know my friend, my close friend Trace, he gets me women, on the TV set of 'Dealin', invites me to his parties now, and I know he values me as a person, someone that he admires."

"Oh, brother."

They make their way to the Paramount lot. A security guard is talking to them when Johnny shows up with a studio employee in a golf cart. They pull up beside the car. The employee gets out and talks with the guard, who then waves them through. They park the car and get in the golf cart. They pass RVs and trailers that some of the stars of different shows and movies are using. Brax is star-struck. A large building to their left bears the number 24. At the end of the road is a large building with "Stage 30" and "Stage 31" written on it in large letters. The Hollywood sign can be seen from a great distance away in the background. The golf cart comes to a stop.

"Okay, Brax, here we go," Johnny says. They all get out of the cart. Johnny looks to Cole. "You wait out here." He looks to Brax. "We can only get one more VIP inside. I'm sure you understand, right, Brax?" Johnny asks.

Brax looks at him, disappointed. "Ah, yeah." He then looks to Cole. "You understand, right, Billy?"

Cole leans against the wall. "Yeah, whatever. Go on, have a good time. Don't forget about three p.m."

They start walking inside. Johnny turns around and marches back to Cole. "Three p.m.? Look, this is his day. We ain't coming out by three! You got it?" Cole just stares at him.

Johnny is frustrated. "You got it? You think you're such a big deal, counting money, dishing out the dope like some god. You're just the errand boy! Look, one day soon I'm going to forget all about you, so will the rest of the world." He starts to walk back into the studio.

"Maybe the rest of the world, but you? Naw, you'll remember me. I promise," Cole says. Johnny turns back to the studio and brushes his hand back, dismissing what Cole said.

At the school, three men are tearing down the Southwest corner of the fence. Jamal calls Luggs outside. "Look over there!"

Luggs looks towards the school and sees the fence being removed. "TOLD YA! They're moving. They lost the war against Luggs!" Luggs says with a smile. "Business will be good again soon!" he adds.

Inside the school, the situation is different. As the workers outside began to dispose of ten feet of fence on the corner of the property, the men inside were busy making plans. Father Mark, Father Roberts, Sister Clair, Jake Williams, one of the contractors, and six other volunteers gather around the table, looking at a land plot. "Father, we will build six or seven feet of wall so the permit people can see exactly what we want. They have our plans and proposal, but if we show them, maybe it will speed up the process. We won't build more because that will put us in violation of any permits and would definitely cause trouble," Williams says.

"Are you sure we can do it at the cost that you showed us?" Father Mark asks.

"Yes, unless we run into a foundation-type problem - which I do not expect. We will have to wait for all the utilities to mark their buried cables and lines, pipes, or anything else that we don't want to run into, but I think we have a good idea of what's under us," Williams answers.

"What about time, the time needed to finish the wall?" Sister asks.

"Before school starts, IF we can get the permits on a timely basis."

Father Mark leans back in his chair and looks at Father Roberts. "Something to add to our prayer requests," he says.

At the Abortion Alliance for America, Tag Collins sits in her office. She is wearing blue jeans and a sleeveless white dress shirt, which shows off the U.S.N. tattoo on her right arm. Shelly Tally opens the door. "You wanted to see us?"

"Yeah, come in."

Talley and two other women walk in. "Have a seat," Collins says. The women sit down on a sofa while Tally takes a seat near the desk. "You know Jo Little is running out of patience. She wants us to drop the entire campaign, which we have spent a lot of money on. I want each of you to speak honestly. What do you think we should do about that anti-abortion pig?"

The women look at each other. Tally looks back at Collins. "Get him. Stay on it until we bring him to his knees!" she says.

"Then take his head off!" one of the women says.

"I say we stay on this. He must be stopped because it will not only embarrass him but also the entire church. We don't get an opportunity like this every day. Let's not waste it. He is the golden boy of the church. He gets more publicity than anyone else. I know that the pope doesn't get this much publicity in this region. Taking him down would do more damage to the pro-life movement than anything else right now!"

Collins flips her notebook shut. "It's settled then. Off with his head!"

"What if Jo Little quits?" Tally asks.

Collins leans back in her chair. She rubs her face searching for an answer. "We hire another model," she says.

"Do you think she will quit?" Tally asks.

"I doubt it, but it is possible. She gets everything in life handed to her on a silver platter, so she does think she's a little princess, but I think she makes too much money from us every year, so she will go along."

"When do we try again?" Tally asks.

"In two days, when she is back."

Late the next morning, Jamal walks out onto the porch. He stretches and tries to wake up. The sun is high in the sky. He looks over and sees a backhoe, a cement truck, two pickup trucks with cinder blocks in the beds, and several workers on the corner of the school property. "Oh no," he says to himself. He slowly sits down on the steps and watches as the men start digging a new ditch.

The old fence and its footer were removed at the corner. Over the next hour, Jamal sits and watches. Brax pulls up in another car, a 1974 Trans Am Firebird. He gets up, then Cole slowly unwinds from his seat. "Look, Jamal! New wheels!" Brax says. Jamal just nods his head.

"Ain't you impressed? Green with envy?"

"Look," Jamal says as he points to the school. Cole and Brax turn around and see a dump truck unloading large stones. The dump bed rises, and rocks tumble to the ground. The men start sorting them.

Cole looks back at Jamal. "Luggs seen this yet?"

Jamal shakes his head. "Not yet, he's still asleep. He ain't gonna be happy at all over this. Tell me some good news so I can tell him before he sees this."

"We got new customers in Hollywood!" Brax says as he removes a money belt and tosses it to Jamal. "Lots of dough for you!"

Jamal feels how thick it is. "That's good, good weight. That TV guy paid up in full, huh?"

"Ah, no. Ah, I spotted him a little. What difference does it make? We're getting new people because of him! We should be giving him a commission!"

"No. It doesn't work like that, Brax. You know it."

Luggs walks out on the porch. "Like what?" he asks.

Jamal stands and tosses the money belt to Luggs. "We got even more new customers in Hollywood now!"

Luggs catches it and feels the thickness of the money. "That's good. Business there is good." He tosses the belt back to Jamal, then sees the construction at the school. He staggers over to the edge of the porch, then slowly steps down on the first step. "Oh my god!" He stands there staring. "What is going on? They ain't movin' they building!"

He looks back at Jamal, who just stands there in fear. He holds his hands up to say something, but the words don't come. Luggs looks back at the workers. "What are they building?"

"A wall, it looks like," Jamal says.

Luggs grits his teeth with anger. He starts to march over, but then turns back to Brax, who is standing closest to him. "Give me your piece!" Brax pulls out a nine-millimeter pistol and hands it to him.

Jamal jumps up and goes to Luggs. He grabs his arm. "Hold on, Luggs. Let's think this one through."

Luggs brushes him off with force. He marches over to the workers. They see a man full of anger with a pistol marching towards them. They drop their tools and quickly get out of the ditch.

Luggs points the gun at them. "Who wants to die first?" He aims it at each one of them. Jamal runs to his side.

"Hey, man, take it easy. We're just doing a job we got hired to do," the foreman says with fear. He starts to sweat.

"Oh, you! You want to die first," Luggs says.

Father Mark starts running out of the school and across the open yard. He gets to the men and steps in front of all of them. Some of the men retreat back to the school. "Good morning, Luggs," Father says calmly.

Luggs points the pistol at his face. "I hate you. I'm going to kill you!"

"No, you're not," Father says.

This just angers Luggs more. He cocks the hammer back. "You think I won't?"

"Oh, I think you could, but you can't do anything to me unless God allows it."

Luggs points the pistol to the side and fires it. The bullet hits the school, and the workers scramble for their trucks, and the rest run inside. Father closes his eyes, stretches out his arms, and takes a deep breath.

Jamal reaches out and slowly and gently pushes Lugg's hand down. "Come on. He ain't worth it. Come on, let's go before the pol pol show."

"AHHH!" Luggs screams. He throws the pistol down and turns to walk away. Jamal picks the pistol up and hands it back to Brax as he escorts Luggs back into the house with everyone following.

Luggs sits in his chair. "Scott Hardy. Get him, I don't care if he's on the moon, get him and get him quick!"

"Okay, ah, yeah, I'll, ah, I'll get him," Jamal says.

"I think killing a priest is bad medicine," Cole says.

Luggs slaps the arm of the chair. "Did I ask for your permission! Did I ask for your two cents' worth?" Luggs shouts.

"I'm just--"

"You get on my nerves, Billy. You do. I can't place it, but something ain't right with you!" Luggs says.

"Okay! Brax, you're on your way to Hollywood! Sell some more, make us more money!" Jamal says, trying to defuse the situation.

"No, I'm not. Not until tonight," Brax says.

Jamal stands and gently shoves him towards the door.

"Come on, let's go," Cole says.

Back at the school, everyone has gathered around Father Mark. The workers are packing up their tools. Williams walks over to the priests. "Sorry, but the workers won't stay. Life is too short to get gunned down for pouring concrete. You need to get those dealers locked up!"

"I'm sorry. Won't you reconsider?" Father Mark asks.

Williams looks out the window and sees some of the trucks already on the street. "No. Sorry." He walks out.

Sister Clair, for once, doesn't have her ever-present notebook. She sits near the water cooler, drinking several cups of water. Her hands shake. Lucas walks over and pats her hands. She hugs him.

Father Roberts is looking through some files. "We have volunteers who have worked for Masons. Maybe they can step up and get the wall built."

"Thank you all for your concern. Let's all get back to work," Father Mark says. The people start filing out of the office. Father Mark sits down. Sister Clair stays where she is sitting.

Father Roberts stops looking through the files and takes a seat in front of Father Rossi. "That was close. Too close. I didn't want to say anything in front of everybody, but that was way too close, Father Rossi."

"I know. I had to sit down before my knees gave way. I didn't want the workers or volunteers to see that."

"The bishop needs to be notified right away," Sister Clair says.

Both priests look down disappointed. "Yeah, he does," Father Roberts says. The room falls silent.

CHAPTER 33
THE MO-MO MEETING

The work at the school had slowed to a crawl as the priests looked for a new contractor to build the wall. Jamal walks out to the porch and takes a seat. Luggs comes out and stands looking at the school without outside workers.

"They ain't workin' Luggs. Maybe they have had enough," Jamal says.

"Nah, we've been down this road before. They ain't gonna stop until that priest is in the grave."

Minion walks up to the house. He wastes no time running up to Luggs. "Luggs, I just saw Mo-Mo. He stopped me while I was coming out of the video game store. He said for me to get over here and tell you he wants a truce meeting. No threats, no danger, just a talk. He said he'll meet you anywhere you want. He said he wants to do it today."

Luggs looks at Jamal, then back at Minion. "Mo-Mo wants to talk to me?" He looks back at Jamal, who shrugs his shoulders. Luggs looks back at Minion. Today?" he asks.

"Today. That's what he said. He said he would wait for me to return with your answer."

Luggs looks back at Jamal. "What'd ya think? A trap?" he asks.

Jamal gets up. "I don't know. I don't like it. He could lure us out of here to rob this place."

"That would take some nerve," Luggs says.

"Yeah, like driving by and shooting us up? That kind of nerve?" Jamal asks.

Luggs thinks hard for a moment. He looks back at Minion. "Today, here, in thirty minutes, unarmed. That's my terms."

"I'll tell him," Minion says as he turns and jogs away.

"Get everyone outside except two guys at the back door," Luggs orders. Jamal gets up and runs inside. After a moment, Jamal comes back out with two men. Luggs looks at one of them. "Go upstairs, that front bedroom, stay in there and watch out of the window. Don't let them see ya! If anything looks unsquared, then let us know." The man goes back into the house. Luggs looks at the other man. "You go across the street. Sit in a car, out of sight. They start shooting, kill 'em all." The man turns and starts across the street. "I mean it. Kill them all, even if they try to run." The man looks back and nods his head.

Luggs looks back at Jamal. "Get me a pistol and bring out that sawed-off shotgun. Put it behind this post. He starts trouble, we're gonna put an end to him."

The half-hour passed quickly, and Luggs sat on a chair on the porch. Jamal sits close by. Minion comes running up the street. "He's coming, he's coming now!" Luggs nods his head.

A new BMW 430i pulls up. Mo-Mo and two other men get out. Mo-Mo is dressed in a tailored suit. He is wearing an expensive fedora hat and an overcoat. Luggs stands. "That's far enough, Mo-Mo," he says. The three men stop. "They stay on the sidewalk. You come up on the porch."

"Very well," Mo-Mo says.

"Hold it there, Mo-Mo," Luggs orders. Mo-Mo stops again. "Little hot for an overcoat," Luggs says. He looks to Jamal. "Search him." Jamal walks down to Mo-Mo, who is taking off his coat and handing it to one of his men. He stretches out his arms to allow Jamal to search him.

Jamal pats him down, looks to Luggs, and nods. "Come on," Luggs says. Mo-Mo makes the walk to the porch and steps up on it. He is at least five inches taller than Luggs.

"Luggs, I thought we would have a little chat. No need for all the security. You can tell your man at the upstairs window to come on down. This is just a friendly chat," Mo-Mo says as he removes his hat.

"Have a seat," Luggs says as he sits down. Mo-Mo sits down. "What do you want?" Mo-Mo sees the shotgun propped up against the column.

"Well, I have a business proposal for you. We should be working together. I have the street, and you have some of the best dope in L.A. I buy a lot of dope. My supplier, from China, tells me I'm his biggest customer," Mo-Mo says.

"Congratulations," Luggs says while rolling his eyes. "Maybe he'll give you the customer of the month award."

"Luggs, I just can't figure out how you get such good dope but none of the suppliers have heard of ya."

"The moon. I get it on the moon."

"Or maybe you get it from the LAPD."

Mo-Mo watches Luggs squirm in his seat. "Keep guessing. Is that what this meeting is about?"

"No. I've come to say we need to merge our businesses. You're losing ground all the time. You know some of your customers, the ones that used to buy in that schoolyard, now come to me. They say you've got the press and the police here all the time. They don't like buying their high while being filmed by the cops or the press. Momma wouldn't like to see their faces on the front page of the Times. You know what I mean?"

"I'm not looking for a merger. I'm doin' fine right here."

"Is that right? I don't think so. That priest over there has brought a lot of attention down on you."

"Says the man is a tailored suit drivin' a new Beamer."

"Look, Luggs, here is a chance for you to get off the streets, retire, and still make a bunch of money."

"Is that right?"

"Yeah, just let me take over your dwindling operation, and you sit home counting the money every day. I'll give you ten recent, lower expenses for every dollar that the new business brings in. Just give me your contacts, supplier, and I'll even keep your people on the payroll."

Luggs laughs. "Oh, that's rich. Ten percent! How 'bout I just keep all my money?"

"Luggs, this business of yours ain't gonna last. You got the press, you got the cops, and ya got me squeezing you all the time. This is a great, and I might add, a one-time offer."

Luggs stands. "Thanks for coming. When you're ready to sell, let me know. I'll be fair about it."

Mo-Mo slowly gets up. He puts his hat on and looks at Luggs for a long moment. "I wish we could have worked this out. It could have saved some cash and bloodshed. Someday, you or I may die on these filthy streets. That ain't no way to go, not for businessmen like us."

Mo-Mo turns and walks to the car. He and his two associates get in and drive away.

Luggs walks inside with Jamal. "They're gonna hit us," Luggs says.

"I don't think so, at least not if he believes what he just said," Jamal answers.

"What?"

"He'll wait until we fold up, then take the business - if he believes what he said out there."

"He doesn't believe it."

"Well then, what do you want to do?"

"All heavy sales must be done with at least two people, or more."

"He ain't gonna try to knock down nickels and dimes," Jamal says.

"No, but some of our stuff ain't nickels and dimes. Hollywood is getting big for us. That's probably why he wants the biz. He doesn't have anyone in Hollywood, unless you count those stinkin' whores and street dealers hustling to move a nickel bag."

"He also wants our supplier. I think there is something else to the picture. Why now? What could he know that we don't know?"

"Maybe he just wants more. More, more, more, guys like him can't get enough," Luggs answers.

Jamal takes a seat. He looks stressed and tired. Luggs looks out the window. "Maybe we should bring it to him. A full war, take him out, make him lose it all. Strike before he strikes us."

"That's dangerous. And costly. It would put a dent in day-to-day sales. We would have to be able to settle in without the high rate of cash that we are getting now. I don't know if that's a good idea. We can't fight everyone on all sides."

"You're right. One problem at a time. Let's get this priest killed. I need to get arrested on the day that Scott Hardy gets here. Maybe a traffic ticket for speeding on the 405. That way, when everyone looks at me, I'll say, 'can't be me. I was with the California Highway Patrol!' It just needs to be airtight."

"Ya know, Mo-Mo asking for a meeting just gave me an idea. Why don't we take a meeting with that priest? Make him a cash offer. We could afford it, ya know."

Luggs sits down at the table. "Nah, he ain't gonna leave for money. If he won't leave by being shot at, he ain't leavin' for nothin'."

"Could be worth a shot," Jamal says.

"No, let's just wait for him to be dead."

The door opens, and Cole and Braxter walk in. Brax is high. Cole is tired. "We need more. We're going to Hollywood for the day," Brax says.

"You need to be careful. Keep your eyes open and STOP getting high while you're working!" Luggs says.

Brax stares at him a moment. He looks to Jamal, then back at Luggs. "What's going on? We're always careful. I got Kung Fu Billy with me."

"Look, Mo-Mo may be planning something," Jamal says. "So be careful."

Brax smiles, uses his hand to brush the thought away. "He ain't nothing!"

"Nothing?" Luggs asks as he steps closer. "Nothing? It only takes one bullet to get dead, Brax. Then there you lay, leaking blood while he walks off with my cash and dope."

"What's he wants?" Cole asks. Luggs looks at him a moment. "I mean, if he's a threat, I need to know what to look for," Cole adds.

"You look for a big gorilla with a Mac-10," Luggs answers.

Cole can feel the tension in the room. "He may try to cut into our turf," Jamal says.

Brax laughs. "He can't!" He looks to Luggs. "He can't! How would he get on the movie sets? Just drive up and say, 'Here's today's drug deliveries. ' No, we're in Luggs. In deep. Nothing can stop us now! You see why this is so beautiful? If I end up on the ground, 'leaking blood,' he still ain't getting Hollywood. It's a who-you-know business in that town, and I know everyone now. Nothing - Nothing can stop us now, Luggs!"

"Just be careful. They still may try to rob these growing loads that you keep haulin' up there. Is that TV dude paid up?" Luggs asks.

Brax shifts his weight to the other foot and puts his hands in his pockets. "Paid up? Paid in full?"

"Yeah, paid up! You know, like paid up so he can get the next delivery," Luggs says.

"Oh, ah... not paid in full."

"What? How much does he owe me? Luggs asks.

"Ah, I don't know off the top of my head. Ah, some."

"What? Some?" Luggs shouts. "Some? How do you not know the exact amount at this exact moment?"

"Well, I don't keep a ledger. I don't want the cops to ever get something like that, you know," Brax says nervously.

"Man, you got to be kiddin' me! I don't keep books either, but I can tell you where every cent is! When I was twelve years old, I had hundreds of customers! I knew everyone's address and phone number in my head!" Luggs shouts as he points to his head. "Hundreds, Braxton! You got one little actor. How hard can this be?"

"Ah, well, Luggs, he does bring us a ton of other business and every one of them is paid in full!"

"I want you to find out how much the Abbott dude owes me, and I want it all collected. You tell him you're gonna take his cars or house if he doesn't have the cash, but he will have the cash. All them Hollywood fags have cash!"

Jamal stands and steps between them. "Come on, Brax. I'll get ya some supplies." He turns Brax around and leads him out of the room. Cole walks into the kitchen and returns with two beers. He offers one to Luggs, who hesitates but then takes it. They both sit down. They sip their beers in silence.

"I killed my first man when I was fifteen. He grabbed the dope out of my hand and ran. I started to chase him, but I thought it would be easier to shoot the thieving son of bitch. So I shot him. Brood daylight, right in the park. People ran. I gathered up my dope and walked away."

They sip their beers in silence again. Finally, Luggs speaks up. "Watch over Brax. He thinks nothin' can happen. It happens all the time."

"What's the real problem with Mo-Mo?" Cole asks.

"He wants what mine. I earned this!" Luggs says in anger. He stands and pulls his shirt off in one fast motion. He turns around. Cole sees a bullet-hole scar on his shoulder. "Shot in the back! Ten years ago. I paid a supplier, got the dope, got out of the car, and he shot me. The last thing I remember was him pulling the dope out of my hands. Woke up in the hospital. They sent a preacher to me. I knew I wasn't gonna die. I had to get well and kill that back-shooting piece of shit. And I did."

He holds out his arm. Cole sees a bullet-hole scar below the elbow. "Driveway. Believe it or not, I wasn't the target. I was just walking by a house that some dudes decided to shoot up. I wasn't there to buy or sell. I was on my way to sell to someone four blocks away. I dove for cover. I still don't know how I got shot in the arm. It hurt. I couldn't hold anything with my left hand for a long time."

Cole finishes his beer. Luggs puts his shirt back on. "I earned this place. Ain't Mo-Mo or anyone else taking it from me." Luggs sits down.

"I'll get eyes in the back of my head. Don't worry about us," Cole says.

"If he wasn't selling so much, I would get out of Hollywood. That's a tough town unless you're on the A-list train, which it looks like that's where you guys are at," Luggs says. "I ain't kiddin'. I want my money from Abbott. He makes BIG money every day. Get my money."

Brax and Jamal come back into the room. Brax has a small army bag full of dope. "Brax didn't find him either," Jamal says.

"Huh?" Luggs grunts.

"Scott Hardy. We're running out of places to look," Jamal says.

"Great!" Luggs says as he flops back in his chair. "Great." He stews there a moment, then looks to Cole. "Go kill that priest for me. Help a brother out."

Cole exhales hard and snickers, 'Not me. That's bad medicine."

"Come on!" Luggs says. He looks back at Jamal. "Where could Hardy be?"

"I don't know. I talked to L.L. and he ain't seen him."

"Maybe he's in prison," Cole says.

Luggs looks at Cole and snaps his fingers. He looks back at Jamal. "Yeah! Did you guys look there?"

Jamal and Brax look at each other, then at Luggs. "No," Jamal says.

"When are we picking up again? The cops will know if Scott Hardy is in jail," Luggs says.

Jamal nods his head towards Cole while continuing his stare at Luggs. "We'll talk about that later."

"Oh, oh yeah," Luggs says.

"Why don't you guys go deliver this stuff?" Jamal asks.

"Alright. We'll be back tomorrow, late tomorrow," Brax says. He and Cole walk out.

"The next meeting is tomorrow. They haven't let me know where yet," Jamal says.

Luggs slaps his hand down on the arm of the chair. "This is so done! I ain't drivin' around L.A. takin' orders from them. They work for ME!"

"Hold on, bro. They do give us what nobody else is gettin'."

"I mean it. They are also getting tons of cash shoved their way. They need to learn. We can't show weakness. They'll really fall in line once that priest is dead!"

"Yeah, but until then, we'd better go along with 'em. They want to meet somewhere else, so be it. Besides, it'll make it harder for Mo-Mo to catch on to where we are gettin' it."

Luggs shakes his head. "Man, that priest.... who would have ever thought that he could cause us so much damage? One dumb priest has managed to make us weak in the face of our competitors, make our customers go away, and make our supplier nervous, all because he wants to run a school! He gets stronger every day! He's even got the locals putting up bird feeders!"

Jamal sits in deep thought for a moment. "Hey, here's another idea. Why don't we get the neighbors to sign a petition against him and the school?"

Luggs thinks a moment. "What would the petition say?"

"I don't know, noise maybe. It worked the last time. The cops shut that generator off."

Luggs stands. "Yeah!"

"The trick is to get them to sign. Some already really like him!"

"We will get every house to sign, or they will burn to the ground. Good idea, Jamal. I wish I had thought of it!"

"It's gonna take some time. We need to have a petition drawn up - real professional like."

"Yeah, maybe we could get a lawyer to write it up for us!" Luggs says.

"Who? What lawyer? Gibbons?" Jamal asks.

"No, no, not Gibbons. He's a criminal lawyer. I don't know, ah, someone downtown, one of them big fancy law firms."

"That's gonna cost."

"So be it. Money well spent. The lawyer can guide us on what the complaint should be about. Check 'em out. Start today. Let's get a lawyer!" Luggs says.

That afternoon, Luggs and Jamal are sitting in a plush law firm office. Downtown Los Angeles is in plain view outside the floor-to-ceiling window. Jamal gets up and looks out. Mr. Piddle, a white, overweight lawyer, looks at his notes, then back to Luggs.

"You want to start a petition against a school that is in the headlines weekly and has the full support of the rich Catholic Church. And you don't have a reason other than it interferes with your narcotic business. Am I missing anything?" Piddle asks.

"Not my narcotic business. You're a smart law man, you come up with some type of violation. They got to be doin' something wrong," Luggs says.

Piddle leans back and takes a deep breath. He looks to Jamal. "You ain't afraid of an earthquake knockin' this building over?" Piddle takes a deep breath and shakes his head. He looks back at Luggs.

"Do you have any idea how much this could cost?" Piddle asks.

"Nope, don't care - as long as it gets results. You see, Mister..." Luggs looks down at his business card. "Piddle, I am in a results kind of business, so if there is any doubt about results, then maybe we should part company now."

"You don't care what it costs?" Piddle asks as he sits upright at the desk.

"No, but if we can't--"

"Oh no, no, no. We can get results at some point in the future. A retainer would be twenty thousand dollars."

"Jamal, go get in the trunk. Bring me twenty thousand dollars."

"A check would be just fine," Piddle says as Jamal exits the room.

"Piddle, we don't deal in checks, I.O.U.s, maybe pay ya later. We deal in cash. That's how you will be paid, and you will get me some results."

"There could be additional charges," Piddle says as he breaks out in a light sweat.

"I'm sure."

"Now what are the neighbors complaining about?"

"They're not. Not yet. You tell me what you want them to complain about, and I will have them sign your paper for that exact reason."

Piddle stares at him a moment, then loosens his tie. "You mentioned noise. How about some type of pollution, trash, water draining into the street, something like that?"

"Okay."

"Which one?"

"All of them. We'll get the people to sign for all of it. How long will it take to get the petition written out?"

Jamal walks in with a large manila envelope. It is stuffed full of cash. He sets it down on Piddle's desk.

Piddle presses a button on his phone. "Kathy, can you come in here and bring a receipt book?"

"Yes, sir," she answers.

"We don't need a receipt," Luggs says. "We gonna trust you." He looks at Jamal and laughs. "We're trusting a lawyer, Jamal. They're bigger criminals than us!" Luggs and Jamal laugh as Kathy walks in.

Piddle loosens his tie more. "That's okay, Kathy."

She looks confused but exits anyway. Piddle starts to pull the money out and count it. Luggs slaps his hand down on Piddle's hands and the envelope. He looks to Jamal. "Did you count out twenty?" he asks Jamal.

"Yeah, twenty even."

"Don't waste time, Piddle. It's all there. You can count on it when we're gone. Now, how soon will that petition be ready?"

"Ah...next week?" Luggs shakes his head no. "Ah, tomorrow?"

Luggs removes his hand and stands. "That's better. We'll see you tomorrow." He and Jamal walk towards the door.

"What time?" Piddle asks.

"When we get here," Luggs says without looking back. They leave the office and shut the door. Piddle has a worried look on his face. He looks down at the money and smiles.

CHAPTER 34
THE WALL & JO LITTLE TRIES AGAIN

Tag Collins sits in a new Lincoln Aviator SUV. She is drinking coffee and eating a bag full of donuts as Jo Little joggs around Father Mark's apartment in short shorts and a tight tank top. Collins keeps a close watch on the apartment door, but Father Mark has not come out at his regular time. Little makes another pass and looks to Collins without stopping. Collins throws her hands up in the air, letting Little know she has no idea why he is late this morning. Little disappears up the street again, making the same loop she has run for over an hour.

Collins shoves another donut in her mouth. Her phone rings. She answers it with her mouth full of a donut. "Yeah," she says, spitting out crumbs. "You're kidding!... Alright, I'll see ya at the office." She hangs up the phone, takes a gulp of coffee, and drops the SUV into gear. She turns at the first intersection and pulls up beside Little. She rolls the passenger window down. Little looks over and does a double-take, then stops running.

"Get in. He's already at the school," Collins says.

Little exhales hard and drops her arms to her side. "You're kidding me! I must have run thirty miles today!"

"Get in!"

She opens the door, shoves a camera bag to the floor, then flops down in the seat. She slams the door shut. "This is ridiculous! How did he get to work when his pink-wheeled car is sitting in front of his place?"

"I don't know."

"This is ridiculous!"

"You said that. Be patient."

"I can't keep coming down here. There is some kind of magic on that man. This is ridiculous!"

"You said that. Want a donut? It'll calm your nerves."

"No." She stares out the window.

"Look, it can take time. We need to just mark our time, and he will fall right into place."

"This man can't be got. I said before, and I'll say it again. He can't be got. I have every man in this city falling over me. They all want a date, and I can't even get in the same place as this priest!"

"Relax. We'll get him. Let's go to the office, and I'll throw a little bonus to you."

"I don't want a bonus. Here's the deal. We do this one more time. I will go day or night, anywhere that you send me, but it's only one more time."

"We got a lot invested in you. We can do just one more time if we don't get him!"

"One more time, that's it. Make it count."

At the school, Fathers Roberts and Mark are looking at the ditch and a pile of rocks. Father Mark steps down into the ditch. "We could do this. Me and you and some of the volunteers," Father Mark says.
"Whoa! Father, a mason's job, well, it's skilled labor - skilled, very skilled. We can't just mix some concrete and start piling rocks on top of each other! Besides, we haven't received the permits yet."

Father Mark looks disappointed. "You're right, like always. I just hate to see us this close and not be able to finish before school starts. Look here, a pile of rocks, a ditch already dug, partway anyway, and we stand here looking at a hole." He climbs out of the ditch. Father Roberts looks all around.

"Maybe you shouldn't be standing this close to the street. I think you have a big bullseye on your back," Father Roberts says.

"Don't worry about them," Father Mark says, looking across the street at Luggs' house.

"Come on, let's get back to work inside. You still have to select the teachers who have applied. They need to know if they have the job, so the ones that don't live here can move before school starts," Father Roberts says.

Lucas comes running out. He signs to Father Mark. They carry on a short conversation. Father Roberts tries to follow along, but their speed is too great for his level of sign language knowledge. He waits.

Father Mark looks to him. "He says Sister Clair is looking for me and that she said I have a lot of work to do."

"Man, she is learning sign language faster than I am."

The three-start walking to the school. "First, the car won't start, now I'm in hot water with her!" Father Mark complains.

"Hopefully, they will be able to tow that car today. The sooner it gets in the garage, the faster it gets fixed," Father Roberts says.

As they walk towards the door, Sister Clair comes outside. "I have a stack of paper for you inside Father," she says.

"I know, and we're going to get to all of it," he replies.

"I don't know about all of it. It's a lot. You now have four applicants for every opening." She looks down at her notebook, and everyone stops. "You have twenty-six hundred more students than we can accommodate. And we have over eleven hundred students who are applying and asking for financial aid." She looks up from her notebook. Father looks at her for a moment. The sheer size of applicants surprises him.

"Eleven hundred in need of financial aid?"

"More than eleven hundred, yes, sir. We would need a school many times bigger than this one. You need to decide soon because the students who don't live locally will have to make the move here," she says.

"How many have the full tuition?" he asks.

"Oh, more than enough to fill the roster," she answers.

"Okay, let's make room for as many of the poor as we can. I mean it. They need our help, and we are in a position to help."

"We are over budget," Father Roberts says.

"God will provide. If it's God's will, He pays the bill," Father Mark says. They walk inside.

Sister Clair stays close as they all enter the office. "Speaking of over-budget, the accountant wants a meeting with you today. Miss Baker is on her way in, and the state has reviewed Lucas' medical record. Sister Mary Ann is on her way here about that," she says.

"Well, what else can we add to the day?" Father Roberts asks.

"I will start setting up employee interviews. A rep from the bishop's office should be present. Who else?" she asks.

"Father Roberts and Lucas, so we can see how well they interact with a student," Father Mark says.

Sister starts writing in her notebook. "What day?"

"Next week," Father Mark says as he starts looking through the application files.

Father Roberts steps over to the table where a mound of files is waiting. "This is near impossible," he says.

"No, not really. Let's start tacking up the short list on that board," Father Mark says as he points to a large corkboard.

Sister checks her notes. "There is also a meeting with the Knights of Saint John Paul this afternoon. Should be a short one, but they are volunteering more night hours." She looks up from her notes. "Their ranks are growing."

"I'm happy to hear that," Father Mark says. "What time?"

She looks back at her notebook. "Ah, five-thirty."

"Okay. Where is the file on the husband-wife team that are teachers? She's deaf. Have you seen that app?" Father Mark asks.

"Yes," Father Roberts says. He goes to the desk and pulls it out from under a fast-food bag. "I saw that one too. It looks like they are made for this job." He opens the file. "Yeah, she is deaf, working on her master's degree. She'd be perfect. Annie Kidman. Husband Nelson Kidman. Has a degree in child development? Worked the last eight years in New York City's Public-School system. They look good," Father says as he hands the file to Father Mark.

"Two down. See how well this is going?" Father Mark says.
Bishop Kennedy is sitting at his desk as Father Muller looks out the window with his hands clasped behind his back. They hear a

knock at the door. "Come in," the bishop says. Bridgette walks in quietly.

"Sir, there is a man in the lobby." She looks at the business card, then back at the bishop. "John Camden, permits office. He wants to make an appointment to see you, but I thought you might want to take a meeting now."

The bishop stands. "Yes, most definitely. Send him in, hold my calls and other appointments for a short time." She exits the office and returns a moment later with Camden.

"Your Excellency, Mr. John Camden," she says as he walks forward with his hand extended. The bishop takes his hand.

"Good morning, sir. How can I help you?"

"Your Excellency, I came by to make an appointment. Thank you for seeing me on such short notice. I will be brief," Camdem says.

"Please be seated," the bishop says, taking his own seat. "Oh, Mr. Camden, this is Father Muller, my secretary."

Muller walks over as Camden stands. "Good morning, sir," Camden says. They shake hands, and Camden returns to his seat.

"Uh, Your Excellency, I work in the permits department. I wanted to assure you that I will personally ensure your school permits do not get lost in the shuffle or get stuck on a desk somewhere. Now the permits will have to be correct, so make sure all the i's are dotted and the t's crossed."

"But of course," the bishop says.

"Sometimes it can take a while for permits to get approved. As long as everything is correct, I will make sure it goes quickly."

"Thank you. I appreciate that!" the bishop says. "And what do we owe this kindness to?"

"Father Roberts was the associate pastor at the Cathedral of Our Lady of the Angels a few years ago. That is still my church."

"Yes, he was."

"Well, my son, who was a good boy, fell in with the wrong crowd. They stole a car and had a fender bender with it. My son was fifteen and was arrested. Father Roberts knew my son, and he wrote a letter to the court on his behalf. He also appeared every day in court and even testified on behalf of my son. Well, the judge let my son go with probation before judgment on the condition that the boys pay all court costs and for the damage to the car, and a fine. My son got straight real quick. He worked three part-time jobs and paid off his mistake. He could have gone to Juvi-jail, which would have had bad results. Today he is at the Pontifical North American College in Rome studying to become a priest!"

Bishop Kennedy smiles. "That's wonderful!"

"Yes. I never forgot the kindness of Father Roberts. Now that he is at the school, whatever I can do to help, I will!" Camden stands, then the bishop stands. They shake hands. "Thank you, Your Excellency!"

"Thank you, sir. I will pray for your son. Perhaps he'll consider the good work to be done here in Los Angeles!"

"Maybe. God will lead him."

He turns and nods to Muller, then walks out.

CHAPTER 35
THE KIDMANS & NEW PROBLEMS

In less than three days, Mr. and Mrs. Kidman arrived in Los Angeles. Father Mark had them picked up at the airport by a volunteer so as not to risk a taxi driver refusing to take them to West Adams. They arrived at the school and disembarked from the car.

As the driver enters the hallway and approaches Father Mark, he can see two knights from the Knights of Saint John Paul talking to him. Father has his sleeves rolled up and is dusty from some of the other work going on.

"Father, we and other knights will stand with the contractor if he comes back for the wall. We will stand on the sidewalk between them and the gangs," one of the knights says.

"It could be dangerous," Father Mark replies.

"Excuse me, Father Rossi," the driver says. Father Mark turns and sees him and the Kidmans. "Father Rossi, I would like to introduce Mr. and Mrs. Kidman."

Father looks to the knights. "Excuse me, gentlemen." He turns and starts to walk to the Kidmans. He turns back to the knights. "I want to go with your plan."

They look at each other and step forward to shake Father's hand. "Thank you, Father," one of them says. They walk away. Father turns back to the Kidmans and offers his hand. Mr. Kidman steps up and shakes hands with him.

"Nelson Kidman, my wife Annie," he says. Father shakes her hand, then looks to the driver.

"Thank you for picking them up. You have done so much for us. I can always count on you. May God bless your effort and work!"

"Thank you, Father. I'll wait outside to take them to their hotel," the driver says before he walks away.

Father looks back to the Kidmans. "I trust your trip was pleasant," he says as he signs it.

"Yes, sir, long but without problems. We didn't even lose our luggage," Nelson says.

"That's great. Come on in. We have a make-shift office set up over here," Father Mark says as he leads them two doors down the hall. They enter, and Sister Clair, Father Roberts, Father Muller, and Lucas stand. "Hello, everyone. Please welcome the Kidmans to Los Angeles!"

Introductions are made, and everyone takes a moment to share who they are and their respective positions. Father signs to Annie along with Nelson. Lucas steps up last and signs to the Kidmans. Father Mark watches closely to see what they say and how they say it. He is impressed.

Over the course of the day, Lucas and the Kidmans get along fine. Sometimes Father Mark leaves Lucas to tell them about the school as he juggles multiple tasks and meetings.

Finally, the day starts to come to a close. The sun is setting, and the workers are leaving. Father Mark comes into the office with Sister Clair. Father Muller, Lucas, and the Kidmans are laughing. "Did I miss the punch line?" Father asks.

"Father Mark, I have always been impressed with your mission, but after today, I want to say it is marvelous! I have watched a little deaf boy and a deaf teacher communicate all day long! What a blessing! It is wonderful!" Father Muller says.

Father pours two cups of coffee and hands one to Sister Clair. "Anyone else need a cup of Joe?" he asks. Nelson signs the question to Annie. She shakes her head no. Everyone else also declines. Lucas raises his hand. "Not for you, little man," Father says, then sets the cup down and signs it to Lucas. Everyone laughs.

"He has enough energy," Father Mark says. Everyone laughs again as Father retrieves a box of juice and hands it to Lucus.

"Father, you really have come a long way. I cannot tell you how impressed I am. You are a miracle for this school, the deaf, the diocese, and Los Angeles!" Father Muller says.

"Father, you have been a big part of our success," Father Mark says.

"This is one special little boy, too!" Nelson says. Annie signs to him. "She says it breaks her heart to hear the story of Lucas."

"He is a tough little man," Father Mark says as he reaches out and rubs his head.

"We want to work here, Father. I hope you will accept us," Nelson says.

"Accept you? You are accepted!" Father says. Nelson signs to Annie, who stands and hugs Father Mark, then turns and hugs Lucas with tears in her eyes. Lucas looks to Father Mark, who signs to him that they will be teachers at the school. He jumps up and dances. Everyone laughs.

"We have a welcome package, some forms to sign, a handbook, some rules, and I'm sure even more paperwork! I'll try to get it all together so you can review it tonight and tomorrow," Father Mark says. Sister Clair reaches over his shoulder from behind and hands him two thick files. "Oh, well, thank you, Sister. She keeps me so organized. We'd be lost without her."

"That's the way I feel about my Annie!" Nelson says as he reaches over and puts his arm around her shoulders, pulling her close. "She keeps me on track, too."

Across the street, Luggs and Jamal stand at the door of a neighbor's house. Luggs knocks hard. He waits a moment with his clipboard in hand.

"Who is it?" an elderly lady asks from behind the locked door.

"Ah, the committee for cleaning up the neighborhood," Luggs says.

"Who?"

Luggs steps closer and shouts, "The committee for a clean neighborhood!"

"What'd ya want?"

"We need you to sign this petition," Luggs shouts.

The door opens. The elderly lady stands there, looking up at him. "What's it for?" she asks.

"Well, woman, this here petition will help clean up this neighborhood. Help cut down on the noise, and remove the eye sore," Luggs says as he tries to hand her the clipboard. She doesn't take it.

"You mean to get rid of the dope dealers?"

Luggs looks at Jamal, then back to her. "Yeah, you know, get rid of a lot of problems," he says, pushing the clipboard back to her.

"Some of the neighbors have already signed. I'm sure we'll have everyone of them signing by the time we're done."

She takes the clipboard and looks at the paper. "Let me get my glasses," she says.

"No time for that woman, just sign it!" Luggs orders. She becomes afraid and signs it, then hands it back to him, steps back inside, and closes the door behind her. Luggs looks to Jamal.

"This is gonna be easy," he says as he steps off the porch and starts toward the next house. He arrives at the next door and knocks. An elderly white man opens the door. "Yes?" he asks.

"Ah, we're here for the committee for a better neighborhood. Everyone is signing this petition to send to the city to clean this place up. We just need you to sign," Luggs says as he hands the clipboard to the man. He looks down at it.

"It says the school is a nuisance. The school's not a nuisance," he says.

"Look, that school has workers day and night, the noise from the place is nuts. Even the Po-Po, I mean the po-lice, agreed with us."

The man looks at it again and tries to hand it back to Luggs. "I will not sign this."

Luggs shoves it back hard into the man's stomach. "How 'bout I come back tonight and burn your house down while you're sleeping?"

The man's wife steps behind her husband. "Sign it," she says. He looks back at her. "Just sign it."

He signs it and then hands it to Luggs. "Now see how easy that was? You're doin' a good thing," Luggs says.

"Deaf children were going to come to that school. That's who you are hurting, little children," the man says.

Luggs grits his teeth. The man's wife steps in front of her husband. "I'm sorry," she says as she nudges her husband back and quickly closes the door. Luggs and Jamal walk to the sidewalk.

"Makes no sense. After all we do for this neighborhood!" Luggs says.

They continue to canvas the neighborhood using the same strong-arm tactics and start filling the pages with signatures. Jamal notices Luggs whistling as they walk.

Father Mark sits at his desk, signing papers. Sister Clair and Father Roberts work as clearing house agents, handing him new papers to sign and then filing them away in the appropriate places.

"Can't some of this wait until next week?" Father Mark asks.

"No. Next week, the mandatory Virtus program," Sister Clair says as she opens her notebook. "Half day for you, Father Rossi, Tuesday, nine to noon."

"Is Miss Baker still waiting out there?" Father Mark asked as he signed another form.

"Yes," Sister Clair answers without looking up.

"Maybe we should park these papers so we don't delay her," Father Mark says.

"Not yet, a few more to sign, then she is next," Sister says.

The office door opens, and Sister Mary Ann walks in. "Sorry to barge in, Father, but this is about Lucas."

Father Mark stands quickly. "What? What is it?"

Sister Mary Ann holds up several papers. Here is the report the doctors sent to the state." She starts reading it. "Patient may have developmental delays, has signs of respiratory infections, scabies, which may lead to serious complications like septicaemia, heart disease, and kidney problems. Patient conditions have contributed to injuries, homelessness, trauma, and inadequate nutrition. An aggressive treatment plan must be put in place to first arrest the spread of the problems, then, to allow the patient to heal over time with care. Recommend review and care for anxiety, depression, and withdrawal symptoms that have been detected." She looks up at Father Mark.

"Yes, sister, they have put a plan in place," Father Mark says. "We have been following it. He gets his medication, and I apply the cream to his wrist and sore spots. He has already gained eight pounds!"

"As of when?"

"As of today. He gets weighed every day so I can chart it."

Sister Mary Ann exhales hard and sits down. "Praise Mary, Joseph, and Jesus! The state wants to see him in the morning at the doctor's office!"

Father Mark smiles. "We are prepared. I have been researching this topic. Lack of access to food, trauma, and disruption in family life, all of this and more is what this poor child has suffered through."

Sister Mary Ann is relieved. "I'm sorry, Father, for barging in. I was just scared. It sounds like you have it all under control."

"With God's help," he says. "Sister, I appreciate your concern and your help. Please watch over us as we continue on this journey."

Sister Mary Ann stands. "You can count on that, Father. Where is Lucas? I would like to see him before I leave."

"He's upstairs playing with a hundred-foot tape measure, showing the Kidmans how to be a contractor," Father Roberts says.

Everyone laughs. Sister Mary Ann walks to the door, turns, and says, "Father, I'll go with you to the doctor tomorrow."

"Thank you, Sister," he says. She turns and leaves the room. Sister Clair writes it down in her notebook.

At the end of the day, Fathers Mark and Roberts, Sister Clair, and Lucas step out into the school yard, walking towards a car. Father Roberts has a stack of papers in his hands. He shuffles through them. "I don't know how we'll get all of this done in time," he says.

God has a plan," Sister and Father Mark both say at the same time. A city truck pulls up to the front, and a man gets out. He puts a hard hat on. "Father Rossi?"

"I'm Father Rossi."

"Here are your permits for the wall slash fence." He hands some papers to Father, then turns back to his truck. He removes his hard hat, spins to face Father Mark, and says, "You need to post those on the public board." He points to a sheet of plywood that has notices, permits, safety tips, and other information.

"Yes, sir!" Father says as the man drives away. Father Mark and Sister Clair look at Father Roberts.

"I know, I know, God has a plan. When will I learn?"

CHAPTER 36
CARLA GETS HELP, LUGGS CONFRONTS COLE

Luggs sits at the dining room table, counting the signatures that he has collected for the petition. Jamal sits at the other end, counting money. "We did good today! Tomorrow we go back to those cats that didn't open the door. They pretend they ain't home. Okay, we'll pretend they ain't home too and smash those doors down and rob 'em!"

"I think you have enough signatures already," Jamal says without looking up.

"What do you know? I think I want more, and I want those people to fall in line. You let one get away with something, then they all think they can do it too!"

Cole and Brax walk in. Brax is a little high. He starts dancing up to the table like a bird in flight. Luggs sits back in his chair and stares at him.

"You high Brax?" he asks.

"As the sky! High as the sky, baby!" Brax says.

"You high on my stuff? You drove like that?" Luggs asks.

"No, I drove," Cole says.

"Well, if it ain't Billyboy to the rescue," Luggs says.

Brax pulls money out of his pocket and tosses it on the table. "No man. It was a gift from my very close friend Trace!" He pulls more money out and tosses it in the air.

"STOP THAT! Jamal says as he gets up and tries to catch it. Brax pulls off a money belt. It is loaded with cash. He tosses it to the table.

"You rob a bank, Brax?" Luggs asks.

"No, baby, no. It's payday in Hollywood. Every day is payday now. There's some more in the car," Brax says.

Cole pulls a large stack of bills from his jacket. "No, I got it." He sets it on the table in front of Jamal, who has now returned to his seat.

"Payday, I'd say," Jamal says.

Luggs speaks up. "Man, you did--"

"WAIT! What time is it?" Brax asks.

Jamal looks at his watch. "Eight-ten."

"OH NO! I'm missin' Dealin'!" Brax turns and runs into the living room.

"Sit down, Billy!" Luggs says as he kicks a chair out from under the table. Cole looks at him. "Sit!" Cole pulls the chair out and sits down. "You can't let him get this messed up. One traffic stop and you're both gone."

"Tell him, not me."

"No, I'm tellin' you. Do as I say!"

"Look, I ain't a babysitter!"

Luggs slams the table so hard it scares Jamal. "You work for me. You do what I say to do!" The two men stare at each other. "You know, Billyboy, I just don't like you. I can't place it, but I didn't get where I am without eyes in the back of my head. They something, just something about you. I can't place it, but I'm smart and if I find you're doin' me wrong, well... I swear, it'll go bad for you."

Cole stands up and heads for the door. Jamal jumps up and stops him. "Billy, Billy, now don't go like that. Luggs is under a lot of pressure; you're under a lot of pressure. We need you."

"No, we don't. I don't need nobody," Luggs says.

Jamal walks to the table. "What's wrong with you tonight, boss?"

"We don't know him!" Luggs says.

"We know he is still seeing his P.O. All of us get early release, not him! Cause he's a bad, bad man. We know he can fight! We know he protects Brax, our biggest salesman."

A fight breaks out in the TV room, and Minion comes running out. "He turned off my video game for a stupid TV show! Tell him to get out. I was playing a game and winnin'!"

"MINION! Let him go. When you start making me money like Braxter, then you can do what you want here!" Luggs shouts. Minion looks hurt and runs out the front door. "Bring your cousin back here!" Luggs shouts through the door. He shakes his head and goes outside after Minion.

"We cool?" Jamal asks Cole.

"You know, I don't need this. I could just go work for someone else."

"No, no. Come on. You're doing well here." Jamal reaches across the table and pulls out a few hundred-dollars bills and shoves them into Cole's shirt pocket. "A little bonus today. We cool now?"

Cole thinks a moment. "Yeah, we cool."

Jamal sits back down and cuts a line of cocaine. "Here, for you."

"Nah, not for me," Cole says.

"You don't do Coke?" Jamal asks.

Cole points to the living room. "Are you sure you want both of us doin' Coke?"

Jamal laughs. "No, you're right - again."

"You got a beer?" Cole asks.

Jamal points to the kitchen. "Man, help yourself to all of it. Even Minion's beer!" Cole walks into the kitchen. He comes back out and sits down at the table.

"You know you've got quite the operation here," Cole says.

"Huh?"

"Yeah, those people in Hollywood love this stuff. They'd crawl to here to get it."

"Oh, yeah. It's good, ain't it? Everyone knows we have the best. It's been lab tested, you could say," Jamal says.

"You have a lab too?" Cole asks.

"No, man, you might say the police help us out."

"Huh, what are you talking about?"

Jamal pauses a moment. "Billy, just know that we are gonna keep you stocked up forevermore. You're gonna be so rich that you'll be buying one of them houses in Hollywood."

"Ha! Not me. You can keep those fruit cakes up there. I'm not impressed like Brax is. He may leave you to get a job as a P.A. on a movie set!"

"Huh? What?"

"Just kidding. But I'm not impressed with those people. As much as me and Luggs I clash, I will say I'm impressed with his business. I once sold a little, had a good supplier, but they gave me some pure junk. The problem was that I couldn't always get it. Sometimes we ran out. Now that hurts, having people trying to give you money but you ain't got nothing to sell them."

"Yeah, well, you don't have to worry here. We got the bases covered for ya. You just keep sellin' and I'll keep giving it to ya," Jamal says.

"Can you get more?" Jamal looks at him suspiciously. "I mean, if we start selling more because that's what's happening. Brax is a selling machine, Mr. Hollywood."

"We ain't runnin' out, brother. Sell on," Jamal replies.

"He loves it, and I wouldn't tell him this, but he's a natural. He fits right in with those nuts."

"Maybe he finally found his calling, 'dealer to the stars'. You watch, someday they'll make a movie about him."

Cole breaks out laughing. "Oh my God! Don't tell him that!"

Jamal laughs. "Yeah, you'll be in the movie too. Kung Fu master, sidekick. He'll always come out smelling like a rose, and you'll always end up fighting."

"Is that what your crystal ball says?"

"I see it in the stars. Yeah, you'll be famous."

"And you and Luggs?"

"Masterminds, but that will have to be a separate movie."

Terry Arquette from the California Department of Social Services walks into the school. There is a line waiting in the hallway. Some people are standing, some are sitting. "Excuse me, can someone tell me where I can find Father Rossi?"

A contractor looks her over. "Line starts here, lady." Sister Clair walks out of the office into the hallway.

"Oh, what about Sister Mary Ann?"

"Just left," Baker says.

"Maybe I should leave a card. Can someone take a card?" Arquette asks.

Baker points to Sister Clair. "She is Father Rossi's executive assistant. She can," Baker says.

Sister Clair sees Baker pointing at her. "Can what?"

"Take my card. I came down here about someone in our care at the California Department of Social Services."

Sister Clair takes Arquette's arm and leads her straight into Father Rossi's presence. "Father, the California Department of Social Services is here," Sister Clair announces. She looks to Arquette. "Is this about Lucas?"

"Lucas? Oh, no, you mean the little boy who was living here? No."

Father Rossi stands. "How can I help you?"

"Father, I came down to see Sister Mary Ann, but I understand she left. I wanted to tell her, and you know, that we have custody of Carla Washington. She said someone told her that she could attend this school."

Father slaps his hands together. "YES! Absolutely! We were just talking about her!"

"She would have to come on a scholarship, at least a partial scholarship. She was removed from her home because of sexual abuse. That means she could be a problem student. Often they lash out at--"

"No, we want here. We have scholarships available," Father says.

"She could go to the Marlton School. She is deaf, abused, has been subjected to drugs, and is far behind because she hasn't attended school for the last couple of years. She could be a hard case, Father."

"We want her. Sister Clair, can you get an application started for Carla?"

"Yes, sir. Right this way, Miss Arquette." They walk out of the room as Baker walks in.

"Father, I'm sorry, but I have to get back to the office soon. This is my second trip out here."

"Please, Miss Baker, have a seat right here. We're going to get to you right now. I'm sorry for the delay," Father Mark says.

They both sit down. "We have more interview requests," she says.

"Well, as you can see, I have nothing but time on my hands to do some interviews," Father says.

"No one said your job would be easy. You need to take a couple of them. They could be big, and they are local. TV News wants to come and report the progress. Tom Bowers with the L.A. Times is writing a story next week with or without us. He has been hard on the church since this school. Let's not lose a good thing."

"Oh boy. Miss Baker, this school is set to open in a little over a month. We haven't even got all the approvals yet." Father says.

"We need to get more people," Baker suggests.

"I have an army working here now!"

"Father, at least two of them, Bowers and the TV news."

Father Mark leans back and places his pen on the table. "Alright."

"Thank you, Father. I'll schedule both of them for here at the school," Baker says as she stands to leave.

"Miss Baker, can you set it up for the Monday after next?" he asks.

"Father, that's almost two weeks from now," she says.

"Yes, but I will set aside four hours for them!" He looks to Sister Clair. "Can I do that?" She opens her notebook.

"Yes. I can change some things. How about ten until noon, then one to three?"

Baker looks at her, then back to Father Mark. "That's almost two weeks from now!"

"Miss Baker, I would just like to have more done on the school."

"You already have a lot done on the school."

"Please, four hours, you can even add more interviews," Father pleads.

"Alright, Father."

Father stands again. They shake hands.

"Thank you, Miss Baker."

She walks out.

"The Kidmans walk in with Lucas. "Father, quick question. A realtor just called us and has a place to show. Can we take Lucas and then get some ice cream?" Nelson asks.

Father stands there. Father Roberts steps closer. "Ah, yes, ah, his car seat. Watch the traffic and the gangs, ah, maybe...Father Roberts, do you want to go with them? You know, just to show them the streets that--"

Father Roberts looks at the Kidmans. "Have a good time." He looks back at Father Mark, who is standing there with his mouth open.

"Ah, yeah, just be careful," Father Mark says. He walks over to Lucas and hugs him. They sign back and forth. Once Lucas learns he is going for ice cream, he jumps up and down with excitement. Father hugs him again, then stands. "Be careful," he says again.

The day moves on, and Father clears the hallway except for the last meeting. Father Roberts and Sister Clair notice he keeps checking his watch and, from time to time, goes to the window to look outside.

Father Roberts calls the people for the last meeting. Knights of Saint John Paul member Gerald Mints and two other knights walk in.

"Good evening, Fathers and Sister. I have some good news. We have a contractor for the wall. He's in Florida but is willing to come out. His name is Peter Rockwell. He has worked on twenty-one Catholic churches as a stone mason. A wall he could do in his sleep!"

"That's great!" Father Roberts says.

"What about the contractor we have?" Father Mark asks.

"He quit. I just haven't had a chance to tell you yet. He said he will not come back," Father Roberts says.

"Oh boy," Father Mark replies as he sits down.

"Don't be discouraged," Sister says. "These gentlemen have solved our problem."

Father Mark stands again and goes to them. "Yes, indeed, you have. Thank you. Thank you so much. You gentlemen have been a great asset to this project. Thank you."

Father Roberts looks to Mints. "Can you get him here soon?"

"I can have him here in two days," Mints says.

Suddenly, Lucas came running into the office. Father Mark's mood improved immediately. Lucas was covered in ice cream on his face and hands. Father Mark scooped him up and hugged him closely. The Kidmans came in next with ice cream for everyone.

"He is one special little boy," Nelson says.

"He is!" Father agrees.

Sister and Father Roberts look at each other. They both realize how close Father Mark and Lucas have become.

CHAPTER 37
PROBLEMS, PROBLEMS &
MORE PROBLEMS

Father Rossi sits at a table with three contractors, Father Roberts, and a city building inspector. Sister Clair sits nearby, taking notes. Father Mark looks at a short report, then sets it in front of him. "So everything is looking good?"

"Yeah, except those few minor corrections," the inspector says.

"That's great news. We can move on then?" Father Roberts asks.

"Yes, absolutely," the inspector says. He then looks to the contractors. "Make sure you have the sprinkler system complete by my next visit."

"That's not a problem," Bob says.

Father Mark smiles. "Outstanding! Another answered prayer."

They all stand, and both priests escort the inspector to the front doors. "Thank you, sir, for working with us," Father Mark says. They all shake hands, and the inspector leaves.

"Father Roberts turns to Father Mark. "Finally, we are getting a break! Now we can move ahead of schedule and get caught up on the budget!"

"This is great. I think we're gonna open a school in the Fall!" Father Mark says.

A man walks into the school as both priests are standing in the hallway. "Father Rossi? Are either of you Father Mark Rossi?" he asks.

"I am," Father Mark answers.

The man pulls some papers out of his jacket and hands them to him. "You are served!"

Father Mark takes them and unfolds them. "Served? What?"

"You must appear in court, and there is a cease and desist order in there also," the man says.

"Cease and desist...what?"

"Construction," the man shouts as he walks back outside. Both priests scramble over the papers.

In a short time, both priests sit across the desk in Michael Bergman's office. They both fidget in their seats. Father Roberts keeps adjusting his collar. "Do you think he is on the phone with the bishop?" Father Roberts asks.

"I don't know, but Bishop Kennedy will find out soon enough. We just don't need this, especially now," Father Mark says.

"Bergman is a good lawyer. He has worked for the church for years. He'll know what to do."

"Yeah, but time is of the essence. We can't afford to lose a day, or your budget is going out the window."

"Father Rossi, stop worrying. Let's see what the lawyers say."

Finally, Bergman walks back in. He takes his seat in the chair and looks at his legal pad, then back at the priests. "Okay, we will, of course, fight this," he says.

"How bad is it?" Father Mark asks.

"Father, this type of thing goes on from time to time. Usually, construction can resume quickly. The only thing that concerns me is the number of signatures on that petition. That's going to be a tough hurdle."

"I don't know of a single neighbor that is unhappy with us except the drug dealers," Father Mark says.

"Well, somehow it looks like almost all of the neighbors have signed. We'll try to force them onto the stand - if it goes that far."

"How long will all of this take?" Father Roberts asks.

Bergman looks at them for a long moment. "It could take some time."

"How much time?" Father Mark asks.

"You might be delayed in opening the school this semester, maybe even next year."

"No, no, that can't even be an option. We already have teachers here, payroll, the state, the--"

"Father, I'm going to do my best. I promise. I want to see you get this school opened, but first, we have to get this over with. They could sue the neighbors, that is. Now, this is not just a cease and desist letter; it is a cease and desist order. It was issued by a government entity, the city of Los Angeles. That means we have to stop construction until the issue is resolved. First, I'll try to take a meeting with the goal of resolving this without going to court. If that fails, we go to court. That will be expensive and take a lot of time. Let me do what I can, and I'll brief you in a couple of days."

"A couple of days? Can we at least work inside?"

"I wouldn't recommend that. Let's not anger the people that we are trying to get to help us."

"But..."

Father Roberts stands. He reaches out and places a hand under Father Rossi's arm, lifting him to his feet. "Thank you, Mr. Bergman. We know you'll do your best," Father Roberts says.

Bergman stands and shakes hands with them. The priests exit the office. "Look, maybe this will give us some time to catch up on paperwork, and give you more time with Lucas and getting him squared away," Father Roberts says.

"Yeah," Father Mark says as they both walk outside. They stop and check the traffic on the street before crossing. The traffic is heavy.

"I have Virtus training next week on Wednesday. What day are you scheduled for?" Father Roberts asks.

"Ah, I'm not...Sister Clair told me, but I can't remember," Father Mark answers.

Father Roberts laughs. "Yeah, you need a break." They cross the street and go to the parking deck.

Tag Collins sits in the conference room at the Abortion Alliance for America. Several women and two men sit around the table. Collins looks up at them. "Okay, let's get started. Where's Tally?"

"I don't know," one of the women says.

Collins exhales hard and shakes her head. "Well, let's get this meeting started. Alright, Father Mark Rossi; he's been a tough one to catch. We might lose Jo Little if we don't get something done soon."

"We could hire a private investigator," one of the men says.

"Yeah," Collins says as he nods her head. "We could do that. See how much dirt we could dig up."

"And at least know where he is and his weekly plans, hopefully," the man adds.

The door opens, and Shelly Tally comes in with an ice cream cone. "Sorry I'm late, traffic, you know," she says.

"And stopping for ice cream," one of the women says.

"I got it while the traffic was stopped!"

"Hold up. We were talking about hiring a P.I. That's all you missed," Collins says.

"Oh, good idea," Talley says as she sits down at the table.

"We would know when he is coming and going," the man says.

"Oh, I know where he is going next week," Talley says before licking her ice cream.

"Really?" Collins asks.

"Yeah. He'll be at one of those required training seminars. He has to attend, all priests do. It's something to help them identify abuse."

"Well, that's training they could all use!" one of the women says. Everyone laughs.

"How do you know?" Collins asks.

"I looked at their website. Every priest will be at the Omni, California Plaza. It's a three-day event."

"How can every priest leave their jobs for three days all at the same time?" the man asks.

"Because they don't have anything to do anyway," another woman says. Everyone laughs again.

Tally takes a bite of her ice cream cone. "It's half a day to a full day for each one. They rotate through," Tally says with a mouth full of ice cream.

"This could be our chance," Collins says. "Maybe we could get Little in the lobby or in the parking deck!"

"He'll see through that," the man says. "No man is going to believe that he just keeps bumping into L.A.'s hottest model!"

"Yeah, you're right," Collins says.

"Meet him as he comes out of the apartment again," Talley suggests.

Collins leans back and rubs her chin, deep in thought. "We could do that, but he'll probably have that rug rat with him."

"How about at the hotel? But this time, she will be on a shoot, a fake photoshoot. We'll hire a photographer, obtain the necessary permits, and shoot outside the hotel. There's a wall, a fountain, water runs over the wall right in front of the hotel," Talley says.

"What if he parks in a parking deck?" the man asks.

"No parking deck there. Only valet parking at the Omni. He has to go to the front, and they will park his car. He'll be sure to see her there at the wall. She'll call for a break and go to him. We get just one photo of him kissing her," Talley says.

Everyone thinks for a moment. "Not bad," Collins says. "What if he doesn't kiss her?"

"She kisses him. In a photo, no one will know who started the kiss," the man says.

"He won't have the kid with him then," Talley says.

"That's true," Collins says in agreement. "Can we get a photographer and all the permissions, especially from the hotel, that quickly?"

"Yes, we can," one of the women says. "We'll pay a nice location fee, keep the shoot short, and use a small crew. They'll approve that fast."

"Get Little on the phone," Collins says.

Father Mark sits in his apartment looking at the wall. Lucas is watching TV. Father Mark comes out of his daze when a knock is heard on the door. He stands and opens the door to see Father Roberts. "Come on. We're taking Lucas to the Tot Lot park," he says.

"The what?" Father Mark asks.

"The Tot Lot. It offers a variety of activities for children. Let's go." He turns and walks back to a rental car. Father Mark signs to Lucas, and they get up and go outside, then he puts Lucas in the car.

"I don't know if this is a good idea today," Father Mark says as he puts the seatbelt over Lucas.

"Come on, he'll love it, and you need to get some sunshine. All this work, well, you know the saying, 'all work and no play makes Father Rossi a dull boy.' Something like that."

Father Mark slips into the front passenger seat and fastens his seatbelt. "Have you heard any news?"

"No. I don't think we will until Mr. Bergman calls us." He drops the car in gear and they drive off. They arrive at the Tot Lot, and Lucas can't get out of the car fast enough. They all get out, and Lucas runs to the many toys and then the train. He jumps in and out of many of them.

"Told ya he would love it!" Father Roberts says. Father Mark sees Lucas laughing and running. He smiles. "A smile, looks like you like my idea too."

"I'm sorry, Father. You're right."

"Again," Father Roberts says with a smile.

"Again. I'm just so caught up in the school, and we have all the deadlines running up on us. It's getting tougher all the time."

"Well, just a breather, you need to relax and enjoy the day. 'This is a day the Lord has made and I will rejoice in it'. It could be worse."

"Yes, you are right. We have come so far, and then we get knocked down again. But you're right, I should be thankful for the progress we made."

"Now you're talking."

Father Mark looks over and sees Lucas standing back as two boys near his age laugh and talk to each other. One of the boys turns to Lucas. "You want to ride this next?" Lucas doesn't answer. He looks scared. "Well? Do ya?" Lucas just stares at him. "Are you stupid or just plain deaf?" Both boys laugh.

Father Mark marches over. "Boys, he is deaf. He can't hear you."

The mother of one of the boys walks over. She takes her son by the hand. "Say you're sorry, Josh!"

The boy looks embarrassed, then looks to Father Mark. "Sorry."

Father Mark signs it to Lucas, who breaks out in a smile. He throws his arm around the boy for a quick hug. The boy tightens up and weakly smiles at Lucas. Lucas turns and signs to Father Mark.

"He wants to know if you want to play on the train?"

The boy smiles. His smile disappears quickly when his mother grabs his hand again. "No, we're leaving!" she says. She then turns and marches off the playground with both boys in tow. Lucas looks back at Father Mark, very confused. Father Mark lowers his eyes to the ground, then looks back at Father Roberts, who is now making his way to them.

"This is what deaf people deal with so often!" Father Mark says.

Father Roberts takes Lucas by the hand. "I'll play on the train with you," he says, then quickly signs it as best as he can. Lucas forces a smile and takes his hand to lead him to the train.

The next Monday, Father pulled up to the Omni Hotel. He saw the photoshoot going on, but was more concerned about the man who came to park his rental car. He steps out and hands his keys to the man. "Mark Rossi! Hey!"

Father turns to see Jo Little running to him. She is wearing a low-cut top and a very short skirt with a split in it. Her long legs glimmer in the sunshine as she runs to him.

CHAPTER 38
THE INVESTIGATION

Father Mark is escorted into a conference room at the Diocese. He sees Michael Bergman and Father Muller sitting on the side of the long table.

"Please be seated," Father Muller says.

"Good morning, gentlemen," Father Mark says as he nervously takes a seat. He sees Bergman has a stack of files in front of him and his ever-present legal pad.

"Father, these are some serious allegations. I wanted to talk to you before we go to the police station. They said you have to be there by four. I want you to tell me the whole and complete truth," Bergman says.

"Of course!" Father Mark says.

Bergman looks at the file. "You went to the training on Monday at the Omni Hotel. You pulled in and you saw a photoshoot underway. What happened then?"

"I pulled in, a man came to my car to park it, I saw the photoshoot, but I didn't know, nor care, what it was about. I wasn't paying attention to it. I heard my name being called, and it was Jo Little, who keeps showing up in my life. She--"

"What do you mean she keeps showing up in your life?" Bergman asks.

"She was at the fundraising dinner, she was jogging in front of my apartment once, she tells me she wants to give money to the school."

"What else did she say? Think a moment, and where else did you meet her?"

"I didn't 'meet her'. She just kept showing up."

"What else did she say?"

"That day or all together?"

"Okay, let's start at the very beginning."

"She said she wanted to give money to the school. She said she wanted me to come to a beach house with her for the weekend. She--"

"Oh my!" Father Muller says as he squirms in his seat.

"No, I didn't meet with her! I didn't go to any beach house!"

"Did you kiss her?" Bergman asks.

"NO! I didn't touch her!"

"She is accusing you of molesting her. I tried to obtain video footage from the hotel, but the people on the shoot placed a large photo reflector in front of where she alleges all this took place. Now it appears to be a 'he said, she said' story. That's not good, Father. We'll lose this in the court of public opinion!" Bergman says.

Father slumps back in his chair. "I didn't kiss her. I didn't touch her. That's the honest truth!"

"Did she kiss you?" Bergman asks.

"No, sir. She put her arm around me and started talking about us spending the weekend together. I broke away and told her I couldn't do that and that I had to go to the training session inside. She said she had a room there and wanted me to come to it after my training."

"What did you say?" Bergman asks.

"I told her no. She shouted out a room number as I started walking away. She grabbed my cossack to stop me from leaving. I pulled it back and marched off."

"Where was the photo crew?" Bergman asks.

"There, they were there."

"Not good because they say you kissed her and grabbed her."

"They're lying. I just told you the truth."

"Father, you may be arrested when we go to the police station. Did you see any other priests outside?"

"No."

Anybody else?"

"There were people around. I just didn't pay close attention to who was there. It's not something that I would usually do."

"Father, they have five witnesses all saying the same thing, and what they are saying does not match up with what you are saying," Bergman says.

"I'm telling the truth."

"Well, let's go to the police station," Bergman says as he stands.

"Father, are you willing to take a lie detector test?" Father Muller asks.

"Yes, sir!"

"Doesn't really matter. It wouldn't hold up in court unless both sides agreed. Come on, let's see what the police want to do," Bergman says. Father Mark looks to both men. They don't look at him; they just get some things together for the police meeting.

Fifteen minutes into the interview at the police interrogation room, Detective Sergeant Henry Frye is getting impatient. The room is green with a couple of bare bulbs overhead. The place is dirty and depressing. Bergman sits at one end near Father Mark. Frye sits across the table from him.

"Father Rossi, let's start all over again. You would not be the first man tempted by the beauty of a top model. She is stunning. I saw a billboard ad with her in it on my way to work, and, well, let's just say if I were Catholic, I would have to go to your confessional booth! Did you go to confession over her?"

Bergman stands. "Okay, that's it. This interview is over."

"Oh, come on! He needs to come clean! Confession is good for the soul."

"Release him or charge him. Either way, the interview is over."

Frye looks at him for a long moment, then turns to Father Mark. He stands and pushes his chair in. "Alright, Mark Rossi, I am placing you under arrest for sexual assault. You have the right to remain silent."

He continues telling Father Mark his rights as Father stands and Frye handcuffs him. "Mr. Bergman, what do I do?" Father asks.

"He has to arraign you. Bail will be set. I'll be there."

Frye escorts Father out.

CHAPTER 39
THE ATTACK IS ON

The lights flicker on in Bishop Kennedy's office. The bishop walks in and goes to the window. He looks out at the city. A moment later, Miss Baker walks in, pulls a chair away from the conference table, and stands behind it.

"Good evening, Your Excellency."

He slowly turns to see her. She notices that he looks older and tired, maybe a little disappointed too. "Is it?" he asks, then quickly adds, "Good evening."

Father Muller walks in. "Hello, Miss Baker, Your Excellency," he says as he quickly moves to the conference table. They both greet him. Kennedy walks to the table. "I appreciate you both meeting with me so late in the day. Please be seated." They both sit down. He pauses, then he also sits down. "I am very concerned about the allegations against Father Rossi. Public opinion of the Catholic Church has deteriorated in the last several years. In some cases, the public has turned against us. They are more aware of the mistakes we make. They will know soon about these charges against Father Rossi."

Baker squirms in her chair. "Ah, yes, sir, Bowers from the LA Times has already called asking for a comment." She opens her notebook, retrieves a piece of paper, and then slides it to the bishop. "I have a rough draft of our response for your approval."

The bishop picks it up and reads it. He places it back on the table and sits silent for a moment. The room has a high level of tension. Father Muller looks to Baker and makes eye contact. She looks to Bishop Kennedy. "Of course, sir, we can change anything on that," she says.

The room goes silent. The bishop leans back and gazes up at the ceiling. He runs his hands through his hair, then looks back at Baker. "The Archbishop has agreed to an eight-hundred-million-dollar lawsuit settlement over the sexual predator cases. He plans to issue a press release in the morning."

Baker and Father Muller are stunned. "I thought that was at least a few weeks away," Father Muller says.

"As did I, too, but he agreed to bring closure to this mess," the bishop says. He looks down at Baker's press release. "And now this. I just can't believe these charges. But I also couldn't believe some of the names of priests on the sexual predator settlement. We have a grave sin in the church."

"Your Excellency, I believe Father Rossi is innocent," Father Muller says.

"Perhaps, but what you think and what I think are of little matter now. It's what the public thinks, and they think we're a bunch of child-molesting, sex-addicted, power-hungry nuts - especially after this settlement hits the news."

The room falls silent again. Baker sinks into her seat. Father Muller looks to Baker, then back to the bishop. "Sir, I have assigned Mr. Mulray to investigate the Rossi case."

"He's on the investigation of the missing money," the bishop says.

"Yes, sir, he is, but I moved him over to this case."

"Alright, but why? The witnesses are many, but no evidence supports Father Rossi's statement."

"That's true, but Mulray may find something."

"He's expensive."

"Yes, sir, but he does get results. He found where Simms and Markley went. He found what they did and how they did it. He may find something to support Father Rossi."

"Long shot."

"It is worth the effort. So much is on the line."

"Well, okay. It's worth rolling the dice."

At the Department of Social Services, Jack Nicks sits at his desk. Janie Milton and Terry Arquette sit across from him. "I told you! I told you this priest was bad news. I wish I had not been talked into apologizing to that nun! Get that kid out of that apartment. That sex-addicted priest will not get custody of him or any other children."

"But he hasn't gone to trial yet. We don't know if he's guilty or not," Milton says.

"We take kids out of homes all the time based on allegations of abuse. I agree with Mr. Nicks," Arquette says.

"That's right. Get that kid today!" Nick's orders.

"And put him where?" Milton asks.

"Anywhere! Anywhere would be better than being in that apartment."

"What should I tell Sister Mary Ann?" Milton asks.

"You tell that fat nun that our job is to protect children, not place them into predators' homes," Nicks says.

Father Mark sits in the chapel alone. He is just staring at the Tabernacle. Father Roberts silently opens the chapel door, steps in, and then stands there. Father Mark doesn't hear him, or if he does, he does not turn around. Father Roberts can see that his friend is in distress. He walks over, kneels, makes the sign of the cross, gets up, and then sits down beside Father Mark, who continues his stare straight ahead. Father Roberts waits several minutes, then clears his throat.

"Father, we're all here for you. I know this is hard, but a great priest once told me that God has a plan."

Father Mark stares ahead for a moment without saying a word. "They took Lucas from me."

"I know. But it is only as the investigation is underway."

"No, they took him. I haven't been found guilty of anything. They could have let me keep him, but they didn't."

Father Roberts looks to the large Crucifix behind the altar. "God will not fail you at this time of need."

"They took Lucas from me."

"Father Rossi, they took him. Not God, there is still hope." Father Mark shakes his head no, then drops his head into his hands. He places his elbows and his knees and sobs. Father Roberts places his arm around him. Both men are speechless. Finally, Father Roberts says, "You know now is the time to fall into your faith, that faith that has guided you for years. That faith that your mother gave you."

Father Mark continues to sob. He stops, then looks ahead again. "The school...well, this may be the death of the school too. I didn't do anything wrong!"

"I know you didn't. Anyone who knows you knows you didn't."

"This hurt. This is real pain. I can't figure this out."

"You know, Father, sometimes things can happen to us. Things that can rattle our trust in our fellowman, things that can shake our faith to the core. That is more so the time to lean on God, to build and replenish our faith, to give all our problems to Him. To let Him carry the ball for a while, let Him figure it out."

They sit in silence for a while. The door opens, and Sister Clair walks in, kneels, crosses herself, then stands and takes a seat behind them. She doesn't say a word, just slips onto her knees and starts praying.

"This is a hard loss. We may not recover from this," Father Mark says to Father Roberts.

"Father Roberts looks ahead. "We'll make it. With God and by God we'll make it."

CHAPTER 40
THE AFTERMATH

Joyce Kilmer has worked for the Department of Social Services for twelve years. She knows how to get things done, how to work the system that is designed for failure. She drives west on Rosecrans Avenue in Compton, then makes a right onto North Willow Avenue. A small home and driveway sit behind an iron fence and gate. It is a tiny house, but clean. She parks on the street and walks to the gate at the sidewalk. She looks around, then opens the gate, steps into the yard, closes the gate, and walks to the front door. She knocks on it after removing her sunglasses. She can hear the television blaring. She knocks again, louder this time. The TV goes off and the door opens.

Mick Swanson stands there looking at her. "Inspection?" he asks.

"No. Can I come in?"

He looks back at the living room. It's a little messy but not trashed. He opens the door wide. "Come in." She steps in and opens her notebook.

"How would you like to take another child in?"

"I don't know. Jason was a bad kid. He cost me more than I was making."

"Well, here is a way to make some additional money. This little boy will come with a bigger check," she says.

"A bigger check?"

"That's right, to the tune of twice what you are getting with Jason."

"Oh..ah, yes. I was just telling Brandy we should see you about getting another child, you know, for Jason."

"Great! This can go really quickly. I just need---"

"Wait a minute. Why does he come with a bigger check?"

"He's deaf, a good boy and -"

"Oh no! I don't speak deaf! How could I talk to him?"

"You will get a tablet to write on, and we will provide sign language classes. He's a good boy. You'll have lots of resources to draw from."

"Why don't you place him with deaf foster-parents?"

"We're a little short on those, and he came to me in a hurry. I thought of you first, Mick."

He leans back on the wall. "I don't know."

"Where is Mrs. Swanson?"

"At work. She'll be home soon."

Kilmer writes a number in her notebook. "This is what you would get each month." She turns the notebook around and shows him.

"Wow! I think Mrs. Swanson would be happy to have another youngster in our humble home," he says.

She hands him a file and then retrieves a few forms from her notebook. "Here is his information, and I need you both to sign these forms. I'll be back in less than two hours with the child."

Luggs is sitting at the dining room table, drinking a beer at his house. People come and go, but all of them avoid Luggs. Jamal walks in, counting a handful of cash. Someone yells to him, and he walks back outside. In a few moments, he comes back with even more cash. He is trying to count it as he walks to the table.

"Twenty-four, twenty-five,... how come nobody is working at the school....twenty-six, twenty-seven." Luggs jumps up and runs outside. Jamal continues counting, and he hears Luggs calling for Minion. Luggs comes back in.

"Where's Minion?"

Minion runs into the dining room from upstairs with a video game controller in his hand. "You call for me?"

"Did anybody work at the school today?

"Ah...No. I don't know. I was in the game."

"You went outside fifty times today!"

"Ah, yeah. I traded my Xbox for some new games, and I got some beer and ice cream, and I --"

"WAS ANYONE AT WORK AT THE SCHOOL?"

"No, no, Luggs, I didn't see anyone." Luggs storms out.

"Minion, look around once in a while. If ya don't, you're gonna run into a phone pole!" Jamal says as he places the cash in an envelope and goes out the door.

Luggs stands on the porch staring at the school. "They ain't working!" He walks across the street and goes to the fence, and stares. Jamal slowly joins him. "Why ain't they working today?" Luggs asks.

"I don't know, ah, maybe a religious holiday?"

"Nah, man. They split. They're gone! THEY GONE!" Luggs laughs and does a dance. They GONE, GONE, GONE! We got the neighborhood back!" Jamal walks over to the main gate. It is still locked.

"No, Luggs. The lock is still in place."

"Yeah, because that's an electric lock. They'll have to have a specialist come out and get that off. They're gone, man!"

He dances back across the street. Jamal shakes his head.

The next day, Jo Little sits in the Hall and Skylar TV studio between Shelly Skylar and Tonya Hall. A crew is busy setting up the cameras and microphones. The audience is making their way to their seats.

"Thanks for coming on the show, Miss Little. I can't comprehend the trauma that you have been through. We had that little smart-mouth jerk on the show in the past. I knew he was too squeaky clean and had to be hiding something," Skylar says.

"It hasn't been fun. I'm used to guys staring all the time, but he just grabbed me!" Little says.

"Quiet on the set!" someone shouts from the dark. The lights dim, then the stage lights come on. "And five, four, three, two...."

"Good day, America. I'm Tonya Hall."

"And I'm Shelly Skylar. Today's guest is top model Jo Little. You may not know her name, but you certainly recognize her face. She has been featured on the cover of many national and international magazines, has represented products from Fortune 500 companies, and has been the face of Paris Perfumes. Please welcome Jo Little!"

The audience applauds. Little gives them a nod and a big smile. "Thank you."

"So, I hate to take you back to that dreadful moment when you were accosted by one of the Catholic Church's molesters, but can you tell us what happened?" Skylar asks.

"Yes. It is painful, but I think the story needs to get out there. A priest, Mark Rossi, was coming into the Omni Hotel, but I don't know why. I didn't know he was going to be there. Anyway, I was in a photo shoot there in front of the great hotel when Rossi practically attacked me!"

"We had him on our show a month or so ago. He was hustling his latest scam then," Skylar said.

In Michael Bergman's office, a large TV is mounted on the wall. He, along with two other attorneys, is watching the show. "We're going to sue her into the Stone Age!" he says. They watch as she starts to tear up.

"It was awful.... He just grabbed me and....."

Skylar reaches over to her and takes her hand. "It's okay. You don't have to go on," she says.

"What are your plans now?" Hall asks.

Little wipes a tear. "My lawyers are going to sue him and the church and the school after he gets out of prison."

"And this comes just a day after the church announced a whopping eight-hundred and eighty-thousand-dollar settlement to victims of the sex-abuse scandal! When will they learn?" Skylar asks.

"The newspaper had an article today where they said the church reached a settlement to bring closure to the victims. I think it's fair to point out that Mark Rossi was not named as a pedophile in that suit," Hall says.

"Exactly! Hard to tell how many others have been missed!" Skylar says.

"That's not what I am saying. The state of California allowed an exception to the statute of limitations in this case. The church opened its files to investigators. It was a complete investigation. Father Rossi was not even in the state during those times and arrived from Baltimore this year. So I just want the audience to know that we are talking about two different things," Hall says.

"Well, it still hurts, it's still bad," Little says in a soft voice.

"That's right, sister. You tell them," Skylar says.

"It was a bad day, and it was ruined by faith in priests, the church, and even in men. This is a hard ordeal to go through, it really is."

"I'm sure it is. We hold religious leaders up on a pedestal. That's where they want to be. Then they turn against us after we place ourselves in their control. They are always taking advantage of us, trying to find out how much they can get away with. I'm glad you are standing up against them," Skylar says.

"We'll be right back after these messages," Hall says as she stares at Skylar.

"We are not going to take this. He has not been found guilty, he has not even made it to trial!" Bergman says as the others continue to write in their notebooks.

"If he is found guilty, I think that point will be moot," one of the lawyers says.

CHAPTER 41
CELEBRATIONS

The next few days, Father Rossi is questioned by Bergman and the new legal team. A full audit is conducted of the school's finances, and employees, contractors, and volunteers are all interviewed by both the Los Angeles Police Department and Bergman's team. Everyone has nothing but praise for Father Rossi. The books are in order, and all the money accounted for.

Father Rossi has been placed on administrative leave and is lost without work, and Lucas is to keep him busy. Plans are underway to reassign the employees to other missions, and the church is in talks with contractors about shutting down the school.

He hears a knock at his door and gets up to answer it. He is surprised to see Janie Milton and Joyce Kilmer standing there. "Is something wrong? Is Lucas okay?"

"Father, Lucas ran away from his foster home. He placed a large teddy bear under the sheets on the bed and, at some point, disappeared," Milton says.

"Oh no, oh no."

"We need you to inform us immediately if he shows up here," Kilmer says. "I mean it. We've got everyone out now looking for him."

"I hope and pray that he is alright!"

"I think he is. He has done this before," Milton says.

Kilmer writes a number on the back of her business card. "My cell, call me the minute he shows up."

They start to walk away. "If I'm such a bad person, why would he show up here?" The women stop and looks back at him. Kilmer rolls her eyes and starts back to the car. Milton mouths the words, 'I'm sorry.'

Father Roberts and Sister Clair walk out of the diocese headquarters with grim looks on their faces. They move along to the car without saying a word. They get in. Father starts the engine. He looks over to her as she fastens her seat belt. "They will keep me here if the school closes. I'll go back to my old job," he says.

"If? If it closes? They made it sound like it will for sure. I will await instructions from my order as to where I will be sent. They have already notified them," Sister says.

"It can't end like this! I just can't believe that we fought through all of these setbacks just to get taken out in the last few weeks before we open. God does have a plan, but I sure wish I knew what it was."

"Poor Lucas. I can't even imagine the damage that this is doing to him," Sister says.

"Yeah, and we are seeing what this is doing to Father Rossi," Father Roberts says.

"It's so unfair, so unfair."

Captain Matthews sits at a large table in a conference room at the Los Angeles Police Department. Jesse Bellini from the D.A. Office sits a few feet away. Detective Sergeant Henry Frye stands across the room. A thick file is on the table.

"Your investigation is concluded, Sergeant?" Matthews asks.

"Yes, sir. I interviewed over seventy people."

"And what have you found?" The captain asks.

"Well, sir, the photoshoot crew all tell the same story. It's pretty convincing. All the others, the volunteers at the school, the contractors, and the staff, say Rossi is a good man, hardworking, and religious."

"Well, that doesn't exactly add up."

"No, sir, Captain. But the photo shoot crew all tell the same story."

"Do you think he's guilty? You'll be the one to take the stand," Bellini asks.

"I don't know. Sometimes good people do bad things. I think that's what this case is about."

"If I were on a jury, I don't know that I would convict, but my job is not to be on a jury, but to put people in front of one. That is all, Sergeant," the captain says.

"Yes, sir," Frye says. He then turns and exits the room. Matthews thumbs the pages of the report as it sits on the table.

"Lots of statements here saying he's a good guy."

"We're going to trial. We pray to the gods of justice for a case like this. The D.A. will love it. We have a lawsuit settlement for almost a billion bucks and now this," Bellini says.

"He could be innocent."

"Who cares? The publicity is worth its weight in gold in a case like this. Pretty model, a priest, and we're riding the coattails of this settlement. This is a case that will make the news every single day!"

The house party at Luggs' house is loud. People are everywhere, drinking, smoking pot, laughing. The music is blaring. Luggs is happy as he works his way through the crowd. He is laughing and talking with everyone.

"Yeah, yeah, everyone, have a good time! We reclaimed our hood! Business is back!" His phone rings, and he hands it to Jamal without looking at it. Jamal goes outside to escape the noise and answers it. He returns in a moment and leans to Luggs.

"It's the lawyer!"

"What?"

"The lawyer. The lawyer from the petition!

Luggs laughs. "Fire him. Tell him I work faster and smarter than him!" He laughs again. Jamal goes back outside.

Near the back door, Cole and Brax stand. Brax grabs a girl and starts dancing with her. "Come on, Billy! Have some fun tonight! Always so serious!" Cole leans against the doorpost. Brax looks to the woman. She is very high. "Billy is a Kung Fu master, but he never lets his guard down for a moment!"

She laughs again and starts taking her top off. She slowly removes it and takes Brax by the hand, leading him to a bedroom. Cole looks across the room and sees J.P. Stalker walking in the front door. Cole slips out the back door.

Stalker walks over to Luggs. "Are you crazy?" he asks.

Luggs laughs. "No, man, just completely in charge of my world again. The school shut down! From now on, you bring my stuff here!"

"You called me here to tell me that?"
"No, I called you here because I need more."

"More? I just delivered two days ago!"

"That was two days ago. I need more, and I want to double our deliveries."

"What?"

"Yeah, and I want Mo-Mo arrested."

"Mo-Mo? I ain't got no beef with him."

"Yeah, you do because I do. You bust him, or I kill him."

"That's up to you."

"This is how it all works now!" Luggs laughs. "Grab a woman and have fun. We back in business in our own crib!" Stalker turns and walks out.

At the Abortion Alliance for America, Tag Collins is holding a bottle of champagne. Upbeat music plays as several women drink, dance, and laugh. Shelly Tally walks in and goes to Collins. They both smile at each other, then laugh. "We did it!" Collins says.

"You're a genius boss!" Tally says.

Jo Little walks in. The music stops and everyone applauds. Collins walks over and hugs her, then places an arm around her as she turns to face the crowd. "Right here! The man of the hour! She did it!" Everyone applauds again. Little soaks it up. Someone hands a glass up, and Collins fills it with champagne, then hands it to Little. "Great job, baby. You hit a home run this time. Got a little bonus for you on my desk. Don't leave without it."

"You made it all happen. It was a great plan," Little says.

"Yeah, it cost a little more than what we projected. The witness statements weren't cheap, but it is worth every penny. Especially watching you tear up on television. Such a great actress." She leans over and kisses Little on the cheek.

Father Rossi is walking the streets near his home aimlessly. He has his hands in his pockets and is in deep thought. He looks over and stops in his tracks. Between two buildings stands Lucas. He starts to run but stops when he sees Lucas turning away. When he stops, Lucas stops. Lucas signs 'I'm okay. You?' Father signs 'Not okay. I miss you, I love you. Lucas smiles and signs, 'I love you'. He turns and runs away. Father runs to the alley and then to the end of it, but Lucas is gone.

CHAPTER 42
REDEMPTION

Several days later, Bishop Kennedy is in his office with Father Muller. They are reviewing plans on how to shut down the school. "Do we even have a list of every donor? Even the cash ones?"

"Yes, we do. We covered a lot of bases this time. I have the list." He reaches into his briefcase and pulls out a large report. He sets it on the table. A knock is heard on the door.

"Come in!" Kennedy shouts.

Bridgette opens the door and steps partway in. "Ah, Your Excellency, ah, I just got a call from Mr. Mulray. He said 'Clear your schedule, get Mr. Bergman, and a large screen TV. He said he is on his way in, and then he hung up."

"What?" the bishop asks.

Muller slowly lowers his briefcase. "Did he say anything else?"

"No, sir."

"Alright, send Mr. Bergman up," the bishop says. He reaches for a remote and turns on a television. Bridgette walks out. "What do you think this is about?"

"I hope for good news, but it could be bad. No, it's good news," Father Muller says. A few moments later, Bergman walks in with his sleeves rolled up and a legal pad in his hands. "Your Excellency, Father Muller." He nods to them. "What's up?"

"We're not sure yet," the bishop says as he moves to a table in front of the TV. "Have a seat, gentlemen." They take their places around the table.

Bridgette knocks and then opens the door. "Your Excellency, Mr. Mulray is here."

"Send him in," the bishop says. Mulray walks in with a laptop and a tattered notebook. He starts setting up.

"I should charge more for my services. I've been following the press stories about Father Rossi." He connects the last wire, then looks at them. "It doesn't look good, according to the press. Watch this."

The TV comes to life, and a video shows Father Rossi turning away from Jo Little. She grabs his cassock as he tries to retreat away from her. He puts both hands up, motioning for her to stop, and then quickly goes into the hotel. Little turns and starts talking to the photo shoot crew. Mulray turns it off.

"Every word that Father Rossi said is true," Mulray says.

"Where did you get this?" Bergman asks.

"Taxi, a taxi was there to drop off some passengers. He happened to have parked with his dash cam facing the photo shoot. I looked at every camera the hotel had, but there was nothing to be found. They were blocked by the photo crew's equipment."

"You're a genius!" Father Muller says. The bishop stares at the screen.

"He told the truth the whole time," the bishop says.

"I'll subpoena the cab driver. We'll release this to the press. This will completely exonerate Father Rossi. The police will drop all charges!" He looks over to the bishop. "Looks like the school is back in business!"

Father Rossi is just stepping out of the Chapel when Father Roberts pulls up to the curb. He blows the horn and starts to jump out, but he forgets to remove his seatbelt. Father Rossi looks at him with a confused expression on his face. Father Roberts finally gets out of the car and rushes around it, slamming his knee into the bumper like before.

"Yeah! Yeah!" he says as he points to Father Rossi. He runs over to him. "Yeah! You were right! They found, they have, The P.I., he, Mr. Bergman --"

"Slow down, Father," Father Rossi says. "What are you trying to tell me?"

"You're right! They got footage from a taxi, a dash cam, which shows you were telling the truth!" Father Rossi sinks down to a bench.

"Praise God almighty!"

Father Roberts helps him up. "Come on, they want you at the bishop's office now!"

The bishop orders all hands-on deck. Press releases are sent out, letters to donors and the faithful are mailed, and contractors are ordered back to work. Bergman meets with the D.A., and all charges against Father Rossi are dropped.

Sister Mary Ann sits in the waiting room of Jack Nick's office. He opens his door and swallows hard. "Sister, how good to see you," he says weakly.

Luggs is asleep in his bed in the early morning when the first of the equipment, employees, and contractors start work at the school. Jamal stands outside watching the wall being built again. Minion comes out eating a bowl of cereal. "What they doin'?" he asks.

"This is not good, not good at all," Jamal says.

Cole and Braxton pull up in a 1967 Chevrolet Nova. It is a cherry red, modified low rider. Brax gets out smiling, looks to Jamal and Minion, and points to his car. "What'd ya think?" he shouts. Jamal just shakes his head and then looks back at the school. Brax and Cole walk up to the porch. "What's ya think? This is my most expensive car yet. Isn't it a beaut?"

"When did they start work on the school again?" Cole asks.

"This morning. They have been coming in since daybreak," Jamal says.

"Oh boy. Luggs know?"

"Not yet."

"Oh boy," Cole says again.

"What about my car? What do ya think?" Brax asks.

"I like your car," Minion says. "Wanna play a video game?"

They all move inside. Jamal collects money from Brax and prepares the next delivery. Cole stands at the living room window, watching the construction at the school. He has never seen so many workers there at one time. The Knights of Saint John Paul and the Knights of Columbus stand guard on the sidewalk. Two dump trucks full of stone pull in and dump the rocks along the fence line. Masons drive their pickup trucks into the yard and get ready to build the wall.

Two backhoes get into position and start digging the ditch. All of this generates a great amount of noise.

Luggs storms out of the house and onto the porch. Everyone follows him out. "WHAT? What is this? They can't do that!" He picks a chair up off the floor and throws it so hard that it lands in the street. He screams and kicks the wall. The Knights close ranks around the school workers. Luggs calms down for a moment, then grabs a small table and throws it through the living room window.

Jamal tries to restrain him, but Luggs brushes him off. "Easy, Luggs. It's alright. We're making good money now. We don't even need that school."

"AUGH!" Luggs screams as he takes a glass and throws it in the direction of the school. "They can't have it back!" Cole and Brax go to the car to escape the crazy antics. Brax tries to calm Luggs down.

"Hey, Luggs, things are good. Look at my new car!" Luggs is breathing hard. He looks at the car, then runs inside the house. Brax gets in the driver's seat as Luggs comes out with a baseball bat. He smashes the windshield. He hits it again, and it shatters. He starts beating the body of the car. Brax jumps out but then runs behind the car to dodge Luggs' wrath. Luggs works his way around the car, glass and mirrors break, and dents appear everywhere.

"STOP!" Brax shouts, but Luggs just continues on. The workers at the school stop what they are doing and watch a madman destroy a car.

"I just paid thirty g's for this car. Stop Luggs! Please!" Luggs continues to demolish it. He stops, takes a breath, and tosses the bat through a broken window. He turns and goes inside. "My car! My beautiful car! LUGGS!"

Jamal comes over to Brax. Cole stays where he is in the middle of the street. "Brax, look--"

"MY CAR! Look what he did to my car!" Brax starts across the street. Cole and Jamal stop him.

"Now's not the time," Cole says in a whisper.

"He's right. Luggs will make good for you, just give him some space today," Jamal says.

CHAPTER 43
A NEW DAY

The next morning, Father Rossi walks out of his apartment and goes to the pink-wheeled car. A newspaper is folded under the windshield wiper. He removes it, and on page A-1, under the fold, is a lead-in article about him. The headline reads 'Local Priest Exonerated Over Sexual Charges'. He looks all around to see who could have placed it there. He sees Lucas staring at him with a big smile. He is standing near some trash cans at the entrance to an alley. He gives Father Rossi a thumbs-up. Father quickly signs to him, and a conversation takes place. Father tells him this is good news, and they will most likely be able to live together again. He asks Lucas to trust him. Lucas runs to him and hugs him closely.

An hour later, Father Rossi stands stunned in Jack Nicks' office. He holds in his hand paperwork granting him full and permanent custody. "All you need now is the judge's signature. I believe, based on my years of experience, she will follow our recommendations," Nicks says.

Father Rossi is speechless. Lucas is at his side. Father kneels down, hugs him, and signs that they are back together. "When will we go before the judge?" Father asks as he stands.

"In about a month. Make sure you tell Sister Mary how hard I have worked on this for you," Nicks says.

Father looks back at the papers, then back to Nicks. "Yes, sir. I will. Thank you."

At the school, Tom Bowers from the L.A. Times waits. Over one hundred people have gathered to work and welcome Father Rossi back. Balloons float from make-shift tables where coffee and donuts wait. Bishop Kennedy and Father Muller sit inside. The rest of the people mill around inside and in the school yard. Father Roberts checks his watch. "Where can he be?"

Sister Clair holds a phone to her ear. "Voicemail again."

In the chapel, Father Rossi lies in front of the Tabernacle, face down on the floor, with his feet together and his arms extended. Lucas kneels behind a pew.

At the school, Father Roberts checks his watch again. He looks up and sees the people laughing and happy. Miss Baker is showing Bowers the classes that are finished. He takes notes and asks a few questions. Father Roberts looks up the street, then down the other way for any sign of Father Rossi. He checks his watch again. "Two hours late. Unbelievable!"

Sister Clair runs outside and heads straight to him. "He just called! He was praying in the chapel. He said he has big news for us when he gets here. He's on his way."

Across the street, Luggs stares at the festive crowd. Jamal comes out on the porch to distract him. "Hey, let's go to Rodeo Drive and buy some new clothes - and a watch. You said the other day that you wanted one of those TAG Heuer Carrera Chronograph watches. Let's go get one!"

Luggs doesn't say anything; he just continues to stare. Cole and Brax walk out on the porch. Jamal sees them and hands Brax a set of keys. "Mercedes-Benz, down there," he says as he points to a new car a few doors down. "Be careful with it."

Brax takes the keys, then looks down at them in his hand. He looks back at Jamal. "Thanks, Jamal." Cole and Brax start making their way to the car. Brax has a leather bag slung across his chest full of dope. "We'll be back in the morning, after the party at Trace's house," Brax says.

Luggs never even notices them. He is just staring at the school. He sees Father Rossi pull in. A crowd gathers around the car. He steps out, then quickly removes Lucas from his seatbelt. Everyone applauds. His face turns red, and he tries to downplay the attention.

"We knew all along that you were innocent, Father!" one of the volunteers shouts. "God has blessed you!" Father Roberts says. "Yes, He has. The school is going to open on time!" Father Rossi says as he sits Lucas down.

Everyone applauds again. He holds his hand up. "And I am getting custody of Lucas!" Everyone applauds and shouts. Luggs starts walking toward the school. Jamal starts walking to Luggs. He sees Luggs pull a revolver out of his waistband.

"NO LUGGS!"

Cole and Brax see what's going on. Cole runs towards the school to get in front of Luggs. Luggs raises the pistol as he enters the school yard. Father Rossi turns to see him.

BANG.

The shot rings out loudly. Father Rossi is hit and falls to the ground. Luggs starts to shoot Father again. Cole gets between Luggs and the fallen priest. "NO! Luggs NO!" He reaches for his own pistol and pulls a badge out from around his neck. Luggs looks at him with a puzzled look on his face. He starts to realize what is unfolding. "POLICE! Drop it, Luggs!"

Luggs smiles and raises the revolver towards Cole. In a split second, Cole fires one shot, hitting Luggs in the chest. Luggs drops his revolver and falls to the ground. Brax and Jamal stand there in shock. Cole goes to the ground and compresses Father Rossi's injury. "Call an ambulance!" Cole shouts.

Jamal reaches for Lugg's gun. Cole swings quickly and aims his pistol at Jamal. "Stop! Brax and Jamal get on the ground!" They slowly get down. Cole holds his compression on Father and the pistol on Brax and Jamal. Sister Clair drops to her knees to help. Father Roberts grabs Lucas and shields him from the scene.

"What can I do?"

"Press hard on this wound so he doesn't bleed out," Cole says. A police car, with lights flashing and siren on, pulls up to the gate, and two cops jump out, draw their service pistols, and aim at Cole. Cole grabs the necklace that holds his badge. "L.A. Sheriff's Department! I'm a deputy!"

"Drop that pistol," one of the cops says.

Cole complies while still kneeling beside Father Rossi. "Those two are under arrest," he says while pointing to Brax and Jamal. "I've been working undercover."

Both cops have the pistol aimed at Cole. "Throw me your shield," one of them says. Cole removes it from his neck and tosses it to him. He gets on his shoulder microphone and calls it in, requesting backup. The other cop moves over to Luggs and checks for a heartbeat. Luggs is dead.

Two fire trucks pull in. An ambulance pulls into the scene, and people part like the Red Sea. A paramedic steps out and runs to Father Mark. He looks at Luggs, but one of the cops shakes his head no. He kneels down and rips Father's cassock open and sees a bullet entry wound, high on his chest, near the shoulder. Father Mark is unresponsive. The other medic and two firefighters arrive with a gurney. They place Father on it and start trotting to the ambulance. Sister Clair goes with them. "Stay here, lady. We have it from here," the medic says.

"Please, I need to go," she says as she boards the ambulance.

"Lady, get..., ah, let's go!" the medic says. The doors shut, and they head for the hospital.

Father Roberts takes Lucas inside. The school yard becomes a crime scene. More police cars pull in. A raid is quickly organized, and Luggs' house is stormed by the LA County Sheriff's Department. Many arrests are made. A search warrant for the house is obtained quickly and results in cash, guns, and drugs being seized.

Across the street, some of the volunteers are crying. Bishop Kennedy comes out to them. "I want everyone to pray now for Father Mark Rossi. I stand here with you, waiting for any news that will come soon. Pray, everyone, please pray. I will take a moment to pray out loud for our brave priest."

Everyone bows their heads. Workers remove their hats. Some people cross themselves. The bishop offers a brief yet earnest prayer for Father Mark, the school, Lucas, the staff, and volunteers.

The med team is waiting at the hospital when Father Mark arrives. He is pale and unconscious. His cussock is covered in blood. Sister rushed in beside the gurney as they moved him inside. A woman from the hospital stops her right away. "You have to wait in the waiting room, ma'am." She stops, and Father Mark is quickly escorted into the O.R.

Sister walks through a set of double doors, down a hall, and arrives at the waiting room. Many people are there. Some of them were bleeding, and all looked desperate. She sits down, crosses herself, and starts praying the Rosary. As she gets to the third decade of the rosary, Father Muller and Father Roberts rush in. "Any word yet?" Father Muller asks.

"Not yet. He lost a lot of blood while that whole cowboy showdown was taking place. He looked very pale. I'm waiting for an update," she said. Father Muller walks towards the nurses' station.

Father Roberts reaches into his pocket and retrieves his Rosary. He sits beside her and begins praying it too.

After two hours, a doctor walks out. He looks tired. He walks over to the trio. They all stand. "Fathers, Sister, your friend is going to be fine. I was more worried about the blood loss. I have treated several bullet wounds in my time here, and this is one of the happy cases. No permanent damage, a fairly quick recovery time, and he'll be back at work soon.

"Can he use his hands? He's a deaf interpreter. He runs the new school for the deaf in West Adams."

"Yes, I have been hearing a lot about him lately. He will make a full recovery. Before the first semester is over, he'll be signing with both hands!"

"Thank you, doctor," Father Muller says. He then steps away and starts making phone calls. Father Roberts and Sister Clair sit down like the weight of the world has just been lifted from their shoulders. They look at each other and smile, then start laughing.

CHAPTER 44
A GRAND CELEBRATION

Father Rossi sits in the front seat of Ms. Baker's Mercedes. Lucas rides in the back as Baker drives to the school. The radio is on a news station, and they hear, "Today, several arrests were made in Hollywood."

At the Abbott mansion, Johnny runs as hard as he can down the road. Cole steps out in front of him, wearing his badge with a pistol in his hand. "Hello, Johnny. I told you you would remember me. You're under arrest." Several policemen rush him, knock him to the ground, and handcuff him.

Father Rossi and Ms. Baker continue on their drive, listening to the radio. "Trace Abbott, star of the hit TV show 'Dealin' was arrested at his mansion in the Hollywood Hills. His assistant, Johnny Drysdale, was also arrested. Bail has been denied for both men. In total, one hundred and seven people were arrested in one of the largest undercover narcotics operations in recent years. It was conducted by the Los Angeles Sheriff's Department. This follows the arrest yesterday of Jamal Washington and several members of a drug gang near the new Catholic Deaf Academy in West Adams." Father Rossi and Baker look at each other as she continues the drive.

There is a big crowd at the school on opening day. Father Mark has his left arm in a sling. The press corps is there in full force. Miss Baker goes to the podium on a makeshift stage along with Bishop Kennedy, Father Muller, and Father Roberts. Lucas goes to the center of the front row beside Carla. The Kidmans serve as deaf interpreters on the edge of the stage. Balloons are tied down everywhere. The schoolyard is packed with visitors, parents, the deaf community, nuns, and priests. Volunteers and employees line the new wall.

Miss Baker speaks into a microphone. "So, there is the short story of how one courageous priest fought against what appeared to be insurmountable odds, to rally the church, the public, the city, and all of us to reach out to our deaf brothers and sisters. Please welcome Father Mark Rossi!"

The crowd stands and applauds. Father Mark makes his way to the podium. He is embarrassed and tries to way the people down to stop the applause. They just shout and clap more. It takes a full minute for them to settle down.

"I want to say that this school stands here today because of the blessing of God Almighty, because of the workers and volunteers, because of the donors, because of my friends and staff, Bishop Kennedy, and because we did not give up. We reclaimed our piece of this earth. We laid claim to a little deaf homeless boy. We stood tall when standing tall was risky. The neighbors have drawn a line in the sand and said, 'No more.' We know that with God, all things are possible. I know that God has a plan." The people applaud.

"Today, we are given an opportunity to help the deaf community, to train people to serve that underserved group, to go out into the world and spread the Gospel. To provide hope in what sometimes seems like a hopeless case or cause. Now we must do our best. God has placed us here. Pray for me, pray for the school, pray for everyone here that we will be faithful to our commission!"

The people stand and applaud loudly. Father Mark waves to them, then steps off the stage. Lucus runs to him and signs 'My superhero!"

OTHER BOOKS BY JEFF MCCOY

Finding Anna: One Mother, One War, One Mission

A gripping story of a mother and son whose paths collide with a journalist in a war-torn land. Also available on Amazon

Finding Bobby: Uncovering the Past to Heal the Present

A compelling tale of a war hero and journalist facing trauma, redemption, and the pursuit of truth.
Also available on Amazon

Connect with the Author

Website: www.writermccoy.com